INTO THE VOID

Brian Bennett

CONTENTS

INTO THE VOID

Billy Ridge arrived in Nashville, Tennessee on a greyhound bus and all he has in the way of possessions are the clothes on his back and his beat up guitar in a battered old case. Billy walks down the main drag and all around him are the wonderful sounds of country music. As he walks along he comes to a honky tonk bar, he is struck by the song that was being played, the song which was one of his favourites #A good ole boy like me#. But when the vocalist began singing, he could not believe his ears, it was really awful and the worst version of the song that he had ever heard.

Billy entered the bar and stood watching the band as they performed his favourite song, and from where he was standing the lead singer was as drunk as a skunk. He could tell by the looks from the rest of the band members that they were not happy. Billy bought a beer and stood watching the band and he was very impressed. He waited until they took a break and approached the base player

"Can I get you a beer?" he asked. The guitarist looked Billy up and down

 "We ain't got no room for another musician, as you can see it's a vocalist that we need, you don't sing do ya?"he asked, Billy smiled

"A lot better than that prick you already have" the base player turned and looked at their vocalist as he drained his glass of neat Bourbon, he turned to Billy and put his hand out

"I'm Edd, can you hang around for a bit, maybe we could give you a go" Billy told him his name and said that he would wait.

Billy was 6ft 2, whip thin, with grey hair down to his shoulders, on top of his head he wore a proper cowboy hat. But it was his voice that set him apart, his voice was deep and sounded like he had a throat full of gravel, at the tender age of twenty nine he had a long road ahead of him. As the band played no-one seemed to listening, as he looked around the bar every table was full but everybody ignored the band, and sat in deep conversation.

When the inevitable happened and the vocalist fell from the stage, the whole room burst into laughter. Edd looked at Billy and waved him over; when he arrived at the stage Edd asked him his full name. Edd stepped down from the stage and picked up the lead singer and sat him at a table, the singer laid his head down on the table and went to sleep. Edd took up his position back on the stage and tapped the microphone, when a few people looked around; he announced that they had a guest singer in the room "all the way from Denver Colorado, I would like to introduce Billy Ridge"

Billy took his battered old guitar from his case and stepped up onto the stage, He pulled a stool over and adjusted the mike to his height, he strummed the strings on his old guitar and turned to Edd and said

"let's do Good old boys again and this how it should be sung" as soon as Billy began to sing the room fell silent as every person in the room turned to listen.

At the end of the song every single person in the bar stood and cheered as they applauded, even the other band members stood and clapped their hands together, Billy strummed his old guitar and the room fell silent again and every pair of eyes were locked onto him. Billy completed the set and when the band stopped for another break, offers of drinks came from every quarter, Edd introduced him to the other members of the band and they all agreed that they wanted Billy for their new lead singer.

Whilst Billy began to sing the next set, a fat man in a big white Stetson came into the bar and sat down at one of the tables at the back of the room, the fat man didn't have a drink and sat there for a good half an hour, just before he left the bar he walked up to the stage and passed Billy his card and made a sign for Billy to call him.

CHAPTER 2

At the end of the evening the bar was full to bursting as word of Billy's singing had spread around Nashville. Billy had his hand shaken by each member of the band and many more people in the audience. Two more people had given him cards and asked him to call them. The band sat around a table having a beer when Billy placed the cards on the table, "do you know any of these people?" he asked, Edd looked at each card in turn and said

"These are the three top promoters in the country business, you are heading for big things Billy, it's a pity that you can't stay with us, we could do really well together". Billy looked from one band members face to the next as they all stared at him "don't worry boys, where I go, you all go" a giant sigh of relief spread around the table and hands were shaken all around. It was at that point that the original lead singer came up to their table and sat down, and asked
"What's all the excitement then lads, that was a good night wasn't it?" Edd turned to the singer and said

"Get lost Phil, you have shown us up for the last time, you are finished" the singer tried to apologise, but Edd was having none of it, he gave the drunk a few rolled up bills and pushed him away.

It was decided that the best agent to call was a man named John Desota, as he had the best reputation for fairness in the business, it was decided that Billy should go and see the agent on his own. When Billy turned up at the Desota office, he was met by a tall well-dressed man with a big cigar stuck in his mouth, John Desota's hand shake was limp and weak, it was the hand shake of a man who had never done a proper days work in his life, but he smiles broadly and said that he was going to make him a star, maybe the biggest country star that ever lived. When John said that he had a band in mind to back his new look Billy put his hand up

"Now you just hold on there John, I already have a band and where I go the coral 5 go" the tall man moved his cigar from one side of his mouth to the other

"But Billy, we can do better than that bunch of hill-billy's" Billy stood up and placed his hat on his head and took out the other two business cards,

"Maybe I should call one of these gentlemen" John coughed loudly and placed his arm around Billy's shoulder "now, now Billy hold onto your horses here, I was just fooling maybe we could give your band a make-over and bring them up to date and I thought that maybe you should grow a drooping moustache and we should get you a pair of real cowboy boots" it took two hours to sort everything out and when Billy phoned Edd and asked him and the lads to come over to talk about the bands future.

John Desota had made some calls. Billy and the band were sent to a tailors and kitted out in new clothes and boots, when they arrived back at Johns office, he said that he had a surprise for them, he took them all into another room in which stood a set of new drums and a selection of new guitars, the band members looked at the new instruments not quite knowing what to do

"come on boys, help yourselves" when they had all selected their new guitars and the drummer was sat behind his new drum kit, John called in a make-up girl and a photographer, the next two hours were taken up posing and having pictures taken

"What is your biggest audience so far?" asked John, Edd shrugged "Maybe a hundred, a hundred and twenty", the tall man smiled proudly "well this Sunday you will be performing in front of maybe a thousand or more at the Old Oprey house, oh and I have a little something for you Billy" he left the room and came back in carrying a tall stool

"I think that you will look good sat on this, while you sing" Billy sat on the stool and strummed his old guitar and sang "leaving on a Jet plane" while he sang this song, the room had become totally silent.

John's mobile rang and when he answered it his face broke into a big smile, for a man of maybe sixty years old the broad smile takes ten years off him. He clapped his hands and said

"Right then, do you think that you can do a set, here and now, only I have my business partner on her way to listen to you play

"John left the room and came back with a chair; he sat it in the middle of the room and waited. A pretty well dressed woman of maybe 30 years of age entered the room, she stood and studied each man in turn before taking her seat and indicated for them to start. Billy looked at the beautiful woman in a blue two piece suit and white shoes, her hair was blonde and shoulder length with curls all around the bottom, her eyes were sparkling blue with tiny crow's feet at the edges. They began to play #Tulsa time #, when Billy sang his first few words, it was as if the woman had cum on the spot, she had closed her eyes and visibly squeezed her thighs together, she opened her eyes at the end of the song and looked at her father and nodded. She stood up and walked up to Billy,

"Do you know #when a man loves a woman # "she asked Billy, he nodded and checked with his new band, Edd nodded. The woman sat back down and nodded, as soon as Billy began to sing she stood up and stopped them, she walked up to Billy and said

"I want you to sing to me and only me, look at me, look into my eyes, show me some passion "she stood there and undid the top two buttons on her silk blouse, which showed him the top of her ample breasts, she smiled and said

"Just to help you focus, you understand".

Billy did not take his eyes from her all the way through the song, and her eyes never left his, from her body actions though very subtle he knew that she had definitely cum this time. When the song had ended she just sat there looking up at him, she only averted her eyes when her father touched her shoulder, she flinched and then stood up and took her father to a corner of the room furthest away from the band. The band sat and watched as the pair had a deep conversation; they would stop talking and look at the band then carry on talking. The woman left the room with a backward glance at Billy; John walked over and stood in front of the band

"It seems that my daughter Jane thinks that you are going to make it big, and let me tell you she has never been wrong yet. Billy can I have a word in private please?" Billy and John left the room and they heard the band begin playing behind them. John said

"It seems that you have made a good impression on my Jane, she wants you to meet her for dinner tonight, it seems that she has some ideas for you, my car will pick you up, where are you staying?", Billy shook his head,

I have not had chance to look for anywhere yet, some local hotel, somewhere cheap, I guess" John went to his desk and took out a brown envelope out and handed it to Billy

"an advance, find somewhere nice and let me know where you are and my driver will pick you up at 7 " with that John left the room while talking excitedly on his mobile phone.

CHAPTER 3

Billy was picked up prompt at 7 as promised, when he climbed into the back of the limo, Jane was sat in there already

"Hello Billy" she said, he smiled at her and said

"hi" and that was the only conversation, until they were dropped off at a very nice restaurant named No9, he held his hand in the small of her back, the blue silk dress that she was wearing was very thin, so thin he could feel her body trembling under his touch, she still trembled as they were shown to their table, Jane ordered for them both before saying "tell me about yourself Billy?" she sat there staring into his eyes, as he told her all about his sheltered life in a small town in Denver, when he had finished talking she said

"do you know Billy, you have the sexiest voice that I have ever heard, and when you sing, well let me tell you it does something naughty to a woman, I don't need to tell you what you did to me earlier, because I could see it in your eyes, you knew exactly what I went through. I should not tell you this but if you direct you voice to any woman you choose, she would fall into bed with you no problem at all". When he leaned over close to her and touched the side of her hand with the tip of his little finger and moved it back and forth, he said

"What about now, is my voice working now?" she swallowed hard

"Oh yes, it is definitely working on me now, if you do-not stop that we will definitely have to skip dinner" with that she moved her hand away from his, just as the first course arrived. Having finished the meal, they were standing waiting for the car to pick them up, Billy was standing gently rubbing the back of her hand with his thumb, as he held her hand, when the car arrived she climbed in first, as soon as she was inside she put the electronic screen up so that the driver could not see into the back of the car, as soon as Billy had closed the door she pulled his lips to hers, they kissed frantically for a few second's and when he lifted his hand to her right breast she pulled away from him and pulled the top of her dress down revealing her naked firm tits.

Billy was on them in a flash, sucking her left breast while fondling her other, Jane began moaning out loud as she tried to get her hand onto his now hard cock, she knew that he was big, but she didn't know just how big. Sensing what she was trying to do he moved slightly, as her fingers felt

12

his hardness and his size, she groaned out loud and tried to get his cock out of his dress trousers. When he put his hand on her leg she pulled away from him, she looked out of the dark window to see exactly where they were; she looked into his eyes and lifted her bum

"Quick get it out" as he undid his trousers and brought his large cock into view, meanwhile she was pulling her pants down her legs. In a flash she was sat in his lap, she had her left arm around his neck and her right hand between her legs guiding his big knob between her swollen fanny lips. Jane closed her eyes as she slid down his long length; his sheer thickness stretched her insides, more than she had ever been stretched before.

Jane now hung around his neck with both hands as she bounced up and down on his big thick cock, she picked up her speed, closed her eyes and took herself to her fierce orgasm, she sank down and ground her fanny against the base of his shaft, she sat there with all of her weight in his lap, her fanny muscles gripping his thickness, she just happened to look out of the dark window to see that they were almost at her home, she lifted herself from his hard cock and began pulling her dress down, she looked at Billy and said

"Quick, put it away we are here". Miracles he can do but the impossible, he has no chance, all that he could do was do the top of his trousers up and take his coat off and try and cover himself from view. The driver opened the door and Jane climbed over him to get out first, Billy did his best to remain covered but drivers are not silly are they. Billy followed her into a large white town house with 6 white stone pillars at the front, once inside she opened the first door on the left and pushed him into the room and closed the door; he looked around the well-stocked library and listened at the door as Jane was giving out instructions. She came into the room and looked at Billy, she reached down and moved his dress jacket to see that he was still rock hard. She listened at the door, hearing nothing she dropped to her knees and took his big knob into her mouth, she had obviously sucked a cock before because her mouth sex was perfect, he gripped the back of her head and began fucking her mouth, she lifted her mouth from his cock and said

"Don't cum yet will you, Billy?" what was that he had he said about miracles?.

A door closed somewhere close by, Jane was up in a heartbeat and taking her clothes off, she looked at Billy

"c\mon Billy, I want to see you naked", she now stood in front of him completely naked and watched him remove his last item of clothing, she grabbed his hand and took him to a deep leather chair, she sat down and lifted her legs over the arms off the chair, she pushed her bum to the edge of the chair, Billy dropped to his knees and placed his thick knob at hers lightly open entrance

"Don' stop until you cum inside me" she said, he pushed all of his thick cock into her willing body and gripped her inner thighs. Billy fucked her rigid, Jane called out each of her orgasms as they came and went. Jane sensed that he was close and she lifted her legs up high and spread them wider, she closed her eyes and waited for the feeling of his hot spunk as it flooded her insides. Billy grunted out loud and pushed his giant cock forward and held it there, she felt him explode inside her body and screamed out loud, she suddenly began bouncing her hips up and down as spurt after spurt warmed her insides.

When he finally flopped limply from her fanny, a mixture of their love juices flooded from her followed by a gigantic fanny fart, she giggled out loud

"That's a first for me", Billy sat back on his haunches and looked at her twitching fanny and at his cum as it bubbled from her and dripped onto the expensive leather chair. Jane climbed around him and took a serviette from a cupboard and pushed it into her fanny, she looked down at his shrinking cock as it lay across his thigh, she then knelt by his side and said

"kiss me Billy" as his lips touched her she folded herself around him, they kissed for a very long time, Jane was obviously ready again because she had lowered her fanny down onto his thigh, she began rubbing her fanny up and down his leg, pressing down harder all of the time, she looked into his eyes

"You don' mind do you, Billy?" she whispered, as she closed her eyes and lost herself in her own sexual efforts, Billy pulled her nipples each and every way, which he knew would only increase her pleasure. Jane took herself to another intense orgasm on his thigh; this woman was totally at ease with her body, as she looked down at her parted fanny lips, as they moved back and forth getting faster and faster as she neared another orgasm, they both watched now as her hips moved back and forth as fast as she could possibly make them.

Jane opened the door a crack and looked out, seeing no-one she grabbed her clothes and said

"come on Billy, run", he grabbed his clothes and followed her up the curving staircase, she ran into a bedroom and he followed close behind, she dropped her clothes onto the floor and jumped laughing onto the bed, Billy jumped onto the bed and lay by her side, she lifted his limp cock and looked at it

"You will be able to do it again won't you, Billy?" she asked, as her hand began to move lazily up and down his thick shaft. Billy lay down on his back as she lifted herself up on her elbow, she watched the tip of his knob as it kept coming into view as she slowly wanked his big cock, she then lowered her head and licked the tip of his cock before slipping his knob into her mouth, Jane had a lot of skill and a lot of tricks, she pushed the very tip of her tongue into his piss hole and wiggled it about, she soon began to get rewarded as his cock began to grow under her ministrations. Soon he was rock hard again, Billy thought that she was going to take him all the way but she stopped and looked at Billy,

"you have the biggest cock that I have ever seen or had inside me, I want you to fuck me from behind now" she turned around and placed herself on her hands and knees, she looked back as he approached her, she held her breath as he pushed his hard cock back into her, he gripped her hips and began to ride her hard. Billy showed his skill as he fucked her harder as she neared her beautiful orgasm and slowed down as her next orgasm gently built.

On and on Billy rode her, Jane was beginning to flag a little bit as he used his hands to pull her back and forth, seeing that Jane was close to giving up so Billy changed his thoughts to his own gratification, he began to use longer strokes and concentrated harder, she was relieved when she heard him grunt out loud, she closed her eyes and waited for that familiar feeling as he emptied his balls into her, his hot spunk flooded her inner body causing a loud squelching sound to begin coming from her fanny, Billy was still hard enough to begin ramming her again,

"Please stop "she whispered. Billy stopped and pulled his almost hard cock from her, taking control for the first time, he then pulled her around and pushed his cock at her mouth, she did not hesitate and sucked him to a third and final orgasm until the next morning.

CHAPTER 4

Billy woke in the morning with himself wrapped around his lover; his cock was almost hard as it was tucked under her ass. He then reached around and began fondling her tits; her only reaction was to begin moving her hips back and forth ever so slowly. This movement went on for a couple of minutes until she lifted her right leg and reached under herself and tried to get his cock into her fanny. In a joint effort they finally succeeded and his length slid easily inside her, the fuck was slow and deliberate as they moved together as though they had been lovers for years. They gradually picked up speed in unison until they were fucking desperately, both now thrusting flat out, he began grunting and she began calling out at the top of her voice. Finally they reached their goal as they both came almost together. They lay together with his huge cock still buried deep inside her. She could feel him twitching deep inside her body, and he could feel her fanny skin pulled tight around the base of his thick cock.

Billy was driven to John's office where all the band were waiting, a trip to the Opre house had been organised and the band had been pleased that they had seen the famous house before their gig on the following Sunday. While the band were on the stage looking out, John took Billy to the rear of the room, they stood looking at the stage

"Listen?" said John, Billy could almost hear what the band members were saying and learned a valuable lesson from that. John took Billy back to the stage and left them alone for a few minutes, he came back carrying Billy's old guitar,

"You stay here Billy and play a tune while we all go to the back of the room. Standing at the back of the room, they all stood and listened to Billy singing #good ole boys# it was at that point that they realised just how good Billy was. The band members looked from one to another absolutely astounded as they listened to the man who would fulfil their dreams.

John took them all to a studio where their equipment was all set up and waiting, John said

"You will be working with a sound team on Sunday, so I have arranged for you all to work together for the next two days. After the second day was done, Billy and the band sat down and listened to a recording of their music and they could not believe that it was them performing, Edd had tears running down his cheeks as he sat and listened because his life-long dream had finally come true. When the recording stopped no-one spoke they were all spell bound by what they had just heard, it was Edd that finally spoke and said

"John sure knows what he is doing, don't he".

Billy was sat in his room strumming on his old guitar when his phone rang,

"Hello" his deep voice said, a soft voice answered

"I have just listened to your tracks from earlier, Jesus Billy you are driving me mad, I am sat in my car outside your hotel, I have my phone in one hand and my fanny in the other, get naked lover I'm coming up."

Billy didn't feel in the mood for company, he just wanted to sit and chill on his own, but best try and keep her sweet he thought. When she tapped lightly on his door he walked over and pulled the door open, Jane walked in and closed the door behind her. She had on a large fur coat and a pair of high shiny black boots; she looked at her man standing there in his black boxers and his cowboy boots. She smiled and then looked at his old guitar that was lay on his bed

"Play for me Billy, play #wonderful tonight# slow and sultry" she whispered.

Billy sat on the bed and began to play, as he sang his first word she undid her fur coat and dropped it to the floor. She stood there swaying her naked body, her eyes were closed and she was instantly lost in the tempo of the deeply moving song, the sexually aroused woman begun humming along softly. Billy watched her move her lithe body, suddenly he became interested and began to get hard. She slowly moved closer to the bed but stayed just out of range of him. She waited until he had finished his mournful song. When he looked at her she had a single tear running down her right cheek, she opened her eyes and looked down at him

"What are you doing to me Billy, I have never acted like this before, I have very rarely shown my body to any man, but you I want you all of the time. I think that I have been wet between my legs from the first time that I ever heard you sing".

She took the guitar from his hands and laid it on the floor and sat on the edge of the bed, without looking at him she whispered

"Please make love to me Billy, make me feel like a real live woman" when he reached for her she lay back and pulled him around. She slowly opened her legs and spread them wide, now standing between her open legs Billy looked down at her slightly parted fanny lips and pushed his boxers down and spread his legs, using his right hand he placed the tip of his knob at her entrance and pushed forward. Jane arched her back slightly as he stretched her internally, as soon as he began to move inside her she began humming the song that he had just played for her. She gradually began moving her hips in time with him, as the intensity grew Jane became more and more vocal as she almost screamed out her first orgasm. Billy stood and watched his giant cock moving back and forth with her fanny stretched tight around his shaft. His lover asked him to stop, he did as he was asked and she reached out and gripped a pillow and lifting her bottom she eased it under herself, he watched her settle herself and he began moving inside her again.

Jane had cum how many time he didn't know, as he stood there fucking this beautiful woman, he thought that he would never cum, He pulled his cock from her and told her to turn over, she did not hesitate and rolled over. He looked down at her and reached for another pillow, now that she had a second pillow under her, her ass was now high in the air. As he pushed his cock back to her and gripped her hips, he began to ride her hard, which made her bury her face into the bedclothes and scream. He stood looking down at the point where their bodies were joined, he then looked at her brown hole and thought why not. So he dribbled some spit onto her crinkly hole and using her middle finger of her right hand he rubbed the spit all around, when he tried to push his finger up her ass. He could tell that she wasn't keen, so he stopped fucking her, he pushed his finger at her bum hole again and again she resisted, so he said sternly

"Let me in, if you want me to fuck you" he watched as she visibly relaxed. When he pushed this time his finger slipped easily up her bum, he began to fuck her again and fingered her bum hole at the same time. Jane suddenly became even more vocal, he could hear her calling him all sorts of rotten bastards.

Billy made a decision; he fucked her hard and took her to another earth shattering orgasm. As she began to relax he dribbled a lot of spit onto his finger that was up her bum. He then gripped his hard cock and pulled it from her. When he pushed his knob at her bum hole, she began to protest loudly, but in her position there was little that she could do about it. The tip of his knob began to disappear inside her brown hole. Jane was not happy as he pushed forward; his knob was just inside her now, then as he pushed forward she screamed into the bed clothes. The more he pushed the louder she screamed. He had maybe half of his big cock inside her, when he began fucking her ass, She protested loudly for a full minute before she became very quiet, he gripped her hips and began fucking her hard, he was now on his final journey. And when he looked down he could see some blood around the base of his cock, but it was too late to stop now. As his cock slipped ever deeper inside her virgin ass, Jane began to push back at him. She made him jump when she turned and shouted

"Fuck my ass you bastard, c\mon fuck my ass "it was the most intense feeling that he had ever had as her tight ass was gripping his thick cock. Billy shot his cum up her ass making her scream out even louder, she suddenly could not get enough of his big cock up her ass as she began thrusting violently back at him, she shouted out loud,

"I'm coming, I'm coming, don't stop". Both now spent he stood there with his cock still buried deep inside her. Jane was openly crying and when he pulled his dirty cock from her bleeding brown hole she immediately jumped up and ran crying into the bathroom.

Billy could hear the shower running which was good as it drowned out her crying. He suddenly realised that he may have gone too far, he sat back on the bed and picked up his guitar. He began strumming and broke out into song, a real old country song called #love me over again# the sound of the shower stopped, and he could just imagine her sat on the toilet seat listening to him. When he had finished the song, the bathroom door opened and she came out, and without looking at him she picked up her coat and slipped it on, she then pulled her boots on. Then without a word or a backward glance she left his room.

CHAPTER 5

Billy didn't see Jane again until he walked on stage at the Grand ole Opre. Jane was sitting on the end of the front row of seats; she could have only been 8ft from him. When he looked at her she smiled up at him. Billy kicked off with a sad old song called# I'm just country boy #. Each song was greeted with a burst of applause and when the interval arrived every- one in the audience stood and applauded. Back in his dressing room John Desota came rushing in applauding,

"Fucking brilliant, fucking brilliant", he shouted excitedly,

"They love you Billy, next week we will be in a recording studio, fucking brilliant" he said as he bustled from the dressing room. Billy was wiping the sweat from his face when a light tap came on the door, when he opened the door Jane was standing there

"Can I come in please, Billy?" she asked quietly, he stood to the side and let her enter, she leaned against his dressing table staring at him, when she finally said

"I'm sorry for running out on you Billy, but that was a first for me, I had stuff running from both places and I didn't know what to do about it, it took until the next evening before your stuff stopped coming out of me, do you forgive me Billy?". He smiled

"There is nothing to forgive Jane, it was my fault for being so selfish" a knock came on the door to tell him it was time for him to go back on. She looked back at him from the door

"sing to me Billy" she said and then she was gone, when he walked back on stage he was greeted by a wall of applause, he began the second half with a very popular country song called #Till the rivers all run dry# he sang to Jane and he could see her openly crying.

The evening ended to a standing ovation, three times they were called back on for an encore. Billy and the band were in his dressing room drinking beers, when John came rushing in with two bottles of champagne,

"Boys, boys [he shouted], fantastic, bloody fantastic, they loved you, everybody is talking about you" said John excitedly, as he rushed to the door, he was just about to leave when he stopped

"Backing singers, that's what we need, backing singers "and then he was gone. Billy and the boys went back to his hotel room and ordered food and more Champagne. When Edd began laughing everyone else joined in. When Billy woke in the morning and walked into his living room, all of the band members were asleep in chairs and on couches. Billy phoned down for breakfast, when he was asked what he would like; he smiled as he looked around the room and said

"Send enough food up for 6full grown men". He came out of the shower to a knock on the door; three men each pushed a silver trolley into the room. He gave them a large tip and picked up two of the metal lids and banged them together, all the band members jumped up in fright. Each instantly regretting the drink fuelled night before. They fell hungrily onto the food and demolished the lot. They spent the quiet day at the Opre, packing up their instruments and heading for John's office. When they walked in, he came smiling towards them with his hand outstretched

"Boys, boys, come in, come in" they all sat down and a still smiling John Desota said
"Boys, the phone has not stopped ringing, everybody wants you, you are going to be huge, there are people from all over America that want to book you. And we will definitely have to think about a tour". They all chatted excitedly for a while until John said

"Take a few days off and come back here on Friday morning, that's in three days -time, be here early at 9am, we have things to do".

At 10 am on the Friday morning sat in their manager's office, John said

"I have a surprise for you boys come with me ", they followed John down the stairs and out onto the pavement, John took out his phone and made a quick call. He had a huge smile on his face as he looked along the block, into view came a brand new coach with a huge red ribbon in the shape of a bow. When the coach stopped in front of then, they all began cheering, on the side was written in big letters, were the words

"Billy Ridge and the Ridge boys" They then all climbed onto the brand new coach, all of their equipment was packed onto the coaches front seats. There was a fully equipped bathroom, seats that folded down into beds, a fully stocked bar complete with a snack bar. He introduced their driver as Mark Foster who would also act as body guard if required. John spoke to Mark and he began driving, they stopped outside a large warehouse that was up for hire. John went and unlocked the doors and they followed him inside, Mark had begun to carry equipment into the empty warehouse, everyone joined in and helped to bring everything in, John say on a chair and said

"Set your stuff up over there, I have another surprise for you, they had set everything up and were tuning their guitars, when the door opened and three tall black women nervously walked in. John jumped up

"Ah ladies, welcome, welcome", he took the ladies up to the band and said

"Boys this is your new backing group, #The Dark Spirit# the ladies were at the Opre the other night and jumped at the chance to perform with you ", introductions were made, But the only name that Billy heard was Shirelle, she had the biggest deer like brown eyes that he had ever seen. It was love at first sight for Billy and she was full of what seemed to be admiring smiles also.

The door opened and this bloke that looked like a thin gorilla with long hair loped in, his hands were buried deep in his pockets, John turned and called out
"Ah brains, come in dear boy, come in", John dragged the white guy up to the band,

"Fellows, this is brains, your new sound man, he might not look much but trust me he is the best in his business" the new man nodded to each band member in turn and they all nodded back. Brains looked at their equipment and walked out of the warehouse, he came back in dragging large boxes on wheels, they watched as he set up whatever it was that he was setting up, he rolled out cables from his boxes to the bands speaker and back again. Then Brains went out again and came back with a stool which he placed behind his array of buttons and knobs, he looked up at John and nodded. The Dark spirits were set up to the side of the band. John looked around and nodded at Billy

"Well play something then" Billy turned around to Edd and said something quietly and then counted to 4,they began to play #Till the rivers all run dry# brains had his headphones on and was nodding his head in rhythm with the song. The backing singers were brilliant, they finished the song and brains put both of his thumbs up.

John gathered everyone behind Brains who continued pressing buttons and moving slides, all of a sudden this beautiful sound filled the warehouse. The sound that filled the warehouse was loud but smooth, as the track continued to play brains tweaked things until what they could hear was perfect. Billy had not realised that Shirelle was standing next to him, when he looked at her she had her eyes closed and was tapping her foot. When the track ended she looked at him and said

"That's really nice man" and smiled. John and brains had a short discussion, and between then decided that the warehouse was perfect for making a CD.

Billy and Shirelle have a lot of sexual tension going on between then and when he suggests that they do a duet for the CD, she jumps at the chance,

"What will we sing" she asks excitedly,

"How about #Island in the Stream# he says

"Oh yes, that would be perfect, when do we start practising?" She asks,

"How about I pick you up later tonight then we can come back here and practice?" for the first time she looked a little bit doubtful, but she said

"Can I bring the girls with me?" he looked a tiny bit surprised

"Don't you trust me, Shirelle?" she lowered her head

"It just would not be right for me to come on my own, what would people say?" Billy looked at the beautiful woman; maybe he had misjudged her, or misjudged the situation, just to add a little subtle pressure he said

"Maybe I should as one of the other two girls? The tall woman moved away from him and chatted with the other women.

The band were booked to play at a large club named Joes Bar, when they arrived at the bar, Billy knew that he would enjoy singing here because they were really close to the audience. Maybe he would see a woman that he could sing to and see if what Jane says is true. The band and Brains set up the bands equipment ready for that nights gig, they were all having a beer at the bar as the place began to slowly fill up, with half an hour to go before the start, Billy looked out to see that the room was full to bursting. Billy stood at the side of the stage looking at the tables that were placed near the stage, on one table 4 young women were seated, one of the women was a black haired beauty, with big tits and a smile to die for had caught his eye. The club compare introduced him and the band, he walked on to a round of applause, he looked directly at the dark haired woman and smiled at her, and she smiled back and gave him a little wave. The set began with # Wonderful Tonight# Billy looked directly at the woman as he sang the song; her friends were nudging her, when he finished the song

23

the club erupted in applause. Billy finished the first half with # I wouldn't want to live if you didn't love me# when he stood to leave the stage he looked directly at the woman, when she gave him a tiny wave, he blew her a kiss.

Billy ended the night with a love song, he made sure that she knew that he was singing just for her, the song was called "I believe in you# this song had the desired effect on the woman, as the room stood and applauded, Billy pointed to the side of the stage while he looked at her, the woman nodded. Billy had a word with the security; he had been sat in his changing room for literally a minute when there was a light tap on the door. He opened the door and the woman was standing there smiling

"You were great Billy" she said, as he closed the door behind her and pulled her into his arms

"Every song was just for you" he said as he kissed her hard. She knew exactly what he wanted because she kissed him back and rubbed her mound against his hardening cock. He turned her around and pushed her against the door and in a heartbeat he had her tits out of her top. But she wanted it just as much as he did, as she reached down and gripped his hardening cock, as her hand gripped him she gasped out loud. Billy reached down and locked the door, he took the woman's hand and took her into the back of his dressing room, he went to lean her back but she stopped him and reached down and released his mighty cock

"Fucking hell that is the biggest cock that I have ever seen" she said, as she gripped his thick cock and pulled the skin back to reveal his big purple knob. She then reached to her own trousers and undid the belt; she pushed her trousers down her legs and took them off. She laid them over the back of a chair; she pulled her top off and stood there in a pair of white damp pants

"You take them off Billy" she said. Billy dropped to his knees and gripped the side of her pants as he slowly pulled her damp pants down revealing a thin line of trimmed pubic hair about half an inch wide. This was in a direct line with her the top of her swollen fanny lips.

As he held her pants by her ankles he waited for her to lift her foot free, as soon as her foot was free she leaned back and opened her legs. Even before he could get up she gripped the back of his head and pulled his mouth to her fanny, she gasped out loud as he licked her from end to end. She then reached down and parted her fanny lips for him; he sought out her tiny clit and sucked it hard. By this time her hips were bouncing back and forth, he reached up and pushed two fingers deep into her fanny and began frigging her at the same time as he was sucking her tiny clit. She came noisily and pushed her fanny to his mouth, he pushed his tongue as deep as he could into her in search of her cum. He took as much of her love juice as he could before she would let him up. She then pulled his lips to hers and pushed her tongue into his mouth in search of any remaining taste of herself. Billy's giant cock was pushing against her stomach, she pulled herself away from him and turned around and leaned against the dressing room desk, she spread her legs and looked back at him

"I hope you can fuck with that thing" she said, he slowly pushed his cock into her waiting body, she grunted as it stretched her inner body. The lady then bent lower to make it better for them both, from the very first thrust to the last, she met him stroke for stroke. They fucked perfectly, she called out in her orgasms and when he finally shot his spunk deep into her body, she welcomed every single one of his little soldiers. They pushed against one-another until he began to go limp, she then eased herself off his cock and looked down. A mixture of their love juices ran freely down her legs, but she was not bothered about that. She dropped to her knees and lifted his cock to her lips; she did not hesitate as she exposed his purple knob and slipped it into her mouth.

This woman whatever her name was, she was now giving him the best mouth sex that he had ever had. As she sucked his cock she gripped his shaft and wanked him hard and fast. When Billy was rock hard again, she dropped to her knees and looked back at him

"Quick before it goes down again" she said. Billy took up his position behind her and pushed his long thick cock back into her more than willing body. He then gripped her hips and rode her hard; the unknown woman was now making all sorts of unrecognisable noises. But her voice rose even higher as she went through her orgasms. He slowed down, just a fraction but it was enough to have her thrusting back at him and encouraging him onto greater efforts. Billy was shagged and he was glad when he got the familiar feeling, as his spunk made its journey up his shaft and exploded into her young woman's body. She screamed out loud and ground her sex against him until he was done. When his cock finally slipped from her, she turned around and sat down on the carpet and looked up at him

"Fucking hell Billy, you sure can fuck" she said. She stood up and took a handful of tissues from his dressing table and pushed them against her fanny, she picked her pants up and pulled them on. When she had finished dressing, she kissed him hard on the mouth, she wrote a phone number down on a piece of card and handed it to him and said

"You can ring me any-time Billy and I will come back for some more of that big cock, and if you want I can bring a friend". She kissed him again and was gone; he didn't even know her name.

CHAPTER 6

They all met up the next day at the warehouse. The talk about the night before was pure excitement, each time he looked at Shirelle, she turned away from him. She kept away from him and totally ignored him, he tried to talk to her but she turned her back on him. Betty one of the other backing singers grabbed his arm and pulled him away, she snapped at him,

"She came to your dressing room last night, and all she could hear was some woman screaming and groaning, she came back in floods of tears" he looked at her gone out
"what did she want?" he asked Betty, she frowned at him and snapped again

"What do you think she bloody wanted you dick-head" with that she turned from him and walked over to Shirelle and folded her arm around her friends shoulder as she cried.

The next two days were very quiet as brains was doing his thing with the making of the CD, They were all due to go on a road trip in three days' time to some faraway place to do a show. The band had gone off clothes shopping and taken the backing singers with them. Bored he took the black haired woman's card from his wallet and dialled the number, the black haired woman's voice answered

"Hello?" She said

Hi, it's Billy" she went quiet for a few seconds and then said

"Hi Billy, are you ok?" he answered

"Yea I'm fine, I em wondered if you wanted to meet up?" the line went quiet again before she said

"Can I bring my best friend?" he had never had a threesome and was not sure of the rules, he said

"Yea, that will be fine, but we will need to meet up first to talk about the rules" the dark haired woman chuckled and said

"The rules are simple Billy, you fuck us both rigid and cum inside the both of us, ok?" he asked

"Fine, when and where?" she asked

"Are you thinking about today?" he smiled to himself and asked her,

"Can you do today?" she said that she would ring him back in a few minutes. He sat holding his phone thinking about a three some, when the phone vibrated in his hand he jumped slightly,

"Hello?" he said, the dark haired woman said that they would meet him at a motel on route 66, she gave him the name and said that she would ring him when they had a room. Showered and in the car, he headed to a new sexual experience, he pulled into the car-park and waited, the phone rang and her voice said,

"14" and that was that, he found the room and knocked on the door, two voices said

"Come in" he entered the room to see the two women in bed. Both with their firm tits on view, he looked at the second woman; she also looked to be in her early twenties, with curly blonde hair down to her shoulders. Her bright blue eyes were locked onto the bulge in his jeans; he pulled up a chair and sat looking at the two women

"What do I call you?" he asked, the women looked at one-another, the black haired woman then said

"Call me Jo and this can be Stella, these are not our real names, as you can see we are both married" they both held up their left hands and showed him their wedding rings. Stella spoke for the first time and asked

"Can I see your big cock please Billy "he stood up and began removing his clothes. Standing in just his boxers he looked at the two women and sat back down on his chair

"I want to see you make each other cum first" he said, the women looked at one another and began kissing; a bit of tit fondling went on before Jo moved on top of the other woman. He could see some action taking place under the bed clothes, so he reached over and pulled the bed clothes off the bed. Stella had her legs wide open and Jo was lay flat out and it was obvious that they were rubbing fannies, he sat on the bed so that he could watch the action. Stella had a hairless fanny and he could plainly see the point where their bodies were rubbing together.

Stella came first followed closely by Jo, and when they were done they both turned and looked at him. His huge cock was rock hard, he then dropped his boxers. Stella gasped out loud and said

"Fuck me Jo, you were not fucking joking" with that she pushed Jo off her lover. She then moved around the bed and placed herself on the edge of the bed, she opened her legs and reached for his mighty cock, he stepped forward and she guided him into her waiting fanny, she groaned out loud as he pushed forward

"Fuck, fuck, it's killing me" she shouted, he stopped

"Do you want me to stop?" he asked her. She shook her head vigorously and used her heels to pull him deeper into her, he gripped her thighs and began fucking her. The blonde haired woman was a bit shorter than her friend but she took all of his mighty cock. Jo must have felt slightly left out because she began kissing Stella. He could see their tongues moving in Stella's mouth, as Jo reached down and began rubbing her friend's clit. This made the blonde woman begin her second orgasm; he watched as Stella searched out to her best friend's fanny, he watched as her fingers slowly moved in and out. He was convinced now that this was not the first time that they had done this. Jo began bouncing her hips up and down as the fingers in her fanny moved quicker; both women began moaning out loud as they neared a joint orgasm. He felt a little bit left out so he pulled his cock out of the blonde woman. She instantly sat up in protest and looked at him

"You ain't cum have you?" she asked, he smiled and shook his head and said

"turn over" she turned over and knelt in front of him, he re-entered her and gripped her hips as soon as he began fucking her, Jo moved around in front of her and lay down, she moved her fanny closer so that Stella could drop her head and lower her mouth onto her friends hot wet fanny.

The only time she stopped doing whatever she was doing was when she went through another glorious orgasm. After her third orgasm she signalled for him to stop, he stopped and looked at the blonde woman,

"Fuck Jo now" she said, Jo jumped up and dropped to her knees on the red carpet, she looked back and watched as his giant cum covered cock swaying, as he neared her. She looked forward as he slid his mighty cock into her, he gripped her hips and began to ride her hard, and she loved every second of it. He was not surprised when Stella knelt down in front of her friend, Jo could just about get her mouth to her friends fanny. He already knew how Jo reacted to his ministrations and he also knew when

29

she was close. She would lift her mouth from her friend's fanny and begin moaning out loud. He would then begin ramming his cock into her harder and harder, Stella sat and fingered herself as she watched her friend being well and truly fucked. The blonde woman stared at them, as she lifted her thighs high in the air as her fingers moved faster and faster, Jo finally through her head back and screamed out her orgasm at the same time as her best friend. Billy began his own journey to his own orgasm, Jo sensing this reached out for her friends hand; they locked fingers as he grunted and shot his spunk deep into her, on and on he kept shooting, each spurt bringing another earth shattering scream from Jo. Stella suddenly lay down and crawled under Jo and began licking at the place where his cock met her friends fanny, Jo went absolutely nuts and began coming all over again, he could hear the blonde woman sucking up their love juices as they flowed from her friends fanny. The blonde woman pushed him back so that his cock slipped from her friend, she took him into her mouth and sucked any remaining spunk from him, he looked down and she had almost all of his mighty cock down her throat.

Stella finally let his cock slip from her mouth, she lay there licking her lips with her legs wide open and Jo knelt there with her mouth stuck to her best friend's fanny. Stella groaned out her orgasm and Jo sat back on the floor and licked her lips. The first person to speak was Stella

"That was one hell of a good fuck" she said. Jo went to the toilet and when she came back, she took some cold beers out of a cooler bag, she passed them both a bottle and they all sat there looking at one another until Billy asked

"So how long have you two been lovers then?" the women looked at one-another. It was Jo that said

"We used to share a room at college when we were 17 and we have never really stopped seeing each other" he then asked

"And what if you become pregnant today?" they looked at each other and both shrugged. Stella went and sat by him and began wanking his limp cock, Jo crawled over and closed her mouth over his exposed knob, the female lovers worked together to get him hard again. Jo lowered her mouth at the same time as her friend and lovers hand moved upwards. It took a few minutes but he was hard again now and Stella moved over him and straddled him, Jo used her hand to guide his massive cock into her friend. Stella began riding him as fast as she could, her friend sat by and watched and waited, the blonde woman suddenly gripped her own hair and used her knees to continue riding him, as soon as she began moaning out loud Jo sprang into action and reached forward and began rubbing her friend's clit. Between the three of them Stella had her strongest orgasm yet, she flopped forward and placing her hands either side of his chest she lifted her hips and held them still and waited for him to begin fucking her. Billy did not disappoint her as he bent his knees up and using his hips began fucking her hard. Jo moved behind her friend and gripped her friend's hips, again she bided her time and sensing that the time was right she encouraged her friend to meet Billy's upwards thrusts. Stella had already begun her next journey to her blissful orgasm, almost as soon as Stella had cum her friend was trying to lift her off his hard cock because she was desperate to get his huge cock back inside her.

Stella lifted herself reluctantly from his mighty cock and flopped down to the side, lay on her back she turned her head just in time to see Billy mounting her best friend from behind, she watched as he spread his knees and grip her hips, as he began fucking her. Stella watched his big cock as it drove in and out of her friend's fanny; she could even see her friends fanny stretched tight around his thick shaft. Stella had not realised it but her knees were bent up and she had let them flop open, she had two fingers inside her fanny and they were moving in time with Billy's thrusts. Jo began scratching at the carpet as her orgasm built, seeing this Billy began fucking her harder until she was through it, he then slowed down and watched her closely. Stella crawled around the carpet until she was lay in front of her best friend, she did not hesitate as she laid herself down just as before with her legs flopped wide open. Only now her fanny was just under Jo's head, as she began masturbating again her eyes did not once leave her friends eyes.

Billy began to grunt out loud as his own orgasm became ever closer. Jo prepared herself to receive his hot cum; she closed her eyes and held her mouth wide open. She swallowed deeply and then screamed out loud as the first hot spurt flooded her insides, he pushed his mighty cock as far into her as he could and held himself there, Jo pushed back and ground herself against him. Stella had crawled under the body of her friend and waited until his cock slipped from her friends gaping fanny, mixed love juices dripped from Jo's stretched fanny lips, Stella lay there with her mouth open and let the drips silently drop onto her tongue, she could see that his cock was shrinking and when only his knob remained inside her friend. Stella reached up and pulled his knob from her friend and closed her lips around it, as she sucked his cock, love juice dropped all over Stella's face. Billy still hung onto Jo but he began to move his hips back and forth and fuck Stella's soft silky mouth. Jo pulled herself away from Billy, she turned and took in the picture in front of her, she crawled around the floor and opened Stella's legs and lowered her mouth to the gaping

31

fanny, she pushed her tongue deep into her friend's fanny and held it stiff, and she then used her head movements to tongue fuck her best friend.

Billy was now lay on his back with a woman knelt either side of him, their lips and tongues covered his limp cock in feathery light touches, he had a stupid smile on his face and his eyes closed, he was knackered and he hoped that is cock stayed down.

Back in his car he switched his phone on and it began buzzing straight away, he had 5 texts from John, the last one said

"Need to see you A,S,A,P." so Billy headed straight to John's office, he walked in and John said

At last, the wanderer returns" Billy said

"What do you want John?" John sat there looking at him for a while until he said

"This next gig on Saturday, I have found a young country singer to open for you, her name is Emma May Harris and she is a pretty little thing. Shirelle has told me that you are looking for someone to do a duet with, I have had a look at Emma, I have also had a word with her and I think that she will be just perfect." not saying anything Billy walked out and went to his hotel and showered. He came out of the shower and wrapped in a towel, he then fell onto the bed and instantly fell asleep.

CHAPTER 7

They arrived at the venue for their next gig; they all walked in and stood at the back of the large empty ornate auditorium. As they chatted a young woman came onto the stage with a guitar, she walked up to a microphone and adjusted it for height, she coughed and began singing #stand by your man# Billy and the rest of the band just stood there mesmerised. She was fantastic and she looked good as well, she had beautiful long blonde hair, she stood not much over 5ft tall, in a pair of jeans and a denim shirt. The dark spirit arrived and stood listening to the blonde woman as she sang song after song, Billy and everyone else moved to the front and sat in the first two rows of seats, they all applauded each and every song. When she stopped and looked down at them Billy said

"You must be Emma?" she nodded and said "and you are?" he stood and said

"Me, I'm just a good ole country boy, you are very good Emma, do you know # island in the stream#," she nodded

"Yea, I know it, do you?" he smiled and waved her down from the stage

"let's get a coffee while the boys here set up" she chewed her lip as she made a decision, she stood her guitar against the side of the stage and walked down the steps and stood in front of him

"Ah, your Billy Ridge [she held her hand out] Emma May Harris "she said. In return he introduced everyone around him to her and then led her outside and down the block to a coffee house. She sat opposite him and he looked at her, as her sparkling blue eyes bored into him,

"I heard you at the Opre, you were very good Billy, I'm looking forward to working with you, when you asked me about the island song, do you want us to do a duet?" he nodded

"We can run through it when we get back, if that is ok?" he asked, now it was her turn to nod in agreement.

When they arrived back the venue the band were more or less set up, brains was doing his thing with his new team of men, who were setting up lighting and speakers. The band began to tune in their instruments and the backing singers were checking out their mikes, when brains was happy Billy took to the stage and talked into his mike, so that brains could do his thing. Billy turned to Edd and said

"let's do Amanda", Emma sat in the front row on her own and Billy sang the song to her, when he was finished she applauded enthusiastically, Billy waved at Emma to join him on stage, one of brains technical men brought her a mike, they counted themselves in and sung #island in the stream# they looked at one-another and smiled at one-another, all the way through the song. When they had finished the song everyone except Shirelle applauded. Brains said that he had some things to sort out that would take maybe an hour, so Billy took everyone out for a coffee and pastries.

John sent Billy a text inviting him around for a meal at his hotel that evening, saying that he had some papers for him to sign. Billy turned up at the appointed time to find John and Jane sat at a table waiting for him, he shook Johns hand and kissed Jane on the cheek. The meal was first class and the conversation soon turned to the papers that he wanted signing. John wanted Billy to sign a legal paper saying that he and the band would pay John 50% of everything. That also included all ticket sales, CD sales and any interview fees. Billy looked at John for a good while before he said

"I can't speak for the others John but 50% seems rather a lot to me, I will run it past the rest of them tomorrow before the show and I will let you know the outcome the day after, ok?" John smiled and said

"Tell the others that they won't get a better deal anywhere else and if it helps to persuade them, I will do you a separate deal of say 25%, how does that sound?" Billy sat there thinking when John says

"Well that's enough for me, I'm going up and I will leave you on the capable hands of Jane, Goodnight Billy" the two men shook hands and John left them to it. Jane touched his hand and said

"I have a large double room, if you want to stay?" Billy looked at his past lover and said

"So you sleeping with me tonight is that part of the deal, you are supposed to sweeten me up for the deal, is that it?" she looked hurt and said

"is that what you really think of me Billy, because all I wanted was some good sex and to feel your big cock inside me again, but if that is what you think then you had better go now" with that she stood up and left the room leaving him sat there all on his own.

Billy texted every member of the band, backing singers and even brains and his crew and said to meet at the coffee bar first thing in the morning, he was the first to arrive and placed some money with the owner of the coffee bar to pay for what-ever everyone wanted. He waited until everyone had arrived and then told them all what John had said. The room fell silent until Edd said

"Sounds a bit much to me, does 50%" almost to a man everyone else agreed. Billy said

"My thoughts exactly, so what do you want to do about it?" no-one would look at each other and no-one had a suggestion, Billy said

"Well do we look for another agent or go with the 50%?" It was Emma May who said

"maybe I could ask my old agent if he would take us all on, only John was paying me in cash until he knew if it would work out or not" they all nodded but Edd asked Billy "when does John want to know by?", Billy said

"Tomorrow morning, first thing" Edd turned to Emma

"I think that you had better make your call" with that the blond singer took her mobile out of her pocket and made her phone call. When she had finished the call she looked around the table and said

"He is on his way, he will ring me when he gets here" they all nodded. Edd then said,

"John has done us proud so far, we have plenty of gigs lined up, the Cd's and he has spent a lot of money on us", it was Billy that was the voice of reason when he said

"look around this table Edd, there are twelve of us sat around here to share 50%, if what John tells us is due to us and there is one of him and he wants 50%, it just don't seem right to me" Edd looked at Billy and said

"Put like that, I see what you mean" Emma piped up again and said

"before I became a singer, I was training to be an accountant and I reckon that I could sort out all of the finances, if Mac, my old agent would find us the gigs and take care of the recording stuff, I think that I could do the rest, it is up to you "everyone was now looking at the beautiful blond singer, after Edd began smiling at her, everyone else sat around the table began smiling at her.

Mac Johanson arrived just before the gig began, he stood at the back of the room and enjoyed what he saw, he then thought about what he would have to go through with John Desota and relished the fight. Mac went and found Emma and she took him to see Billy, they sat and discussed the problems ahead, Mac said

"I have heard about Mr Desota before and I know how he works, so leave that side of it to me, saying that, that is if you want me to act for you?. We can sort out the details in a few days but I will need your permission to spend some of your initial earnings, because John will want his money back what he has already laid out, plus he will need to show a profit" he asked them what gigs they had already done and what CD's they had made, he wrote it all down and sat making phone calls for the next hour, he then said
"Right then leave everything to me, I will call you when I have something to tell you". Billy poured them all a glass of champagne and made a toast

"To new beginnings", they all clinked glasses and smiled broadly at one-another.

Left on their-own Emma said
"We could work well together you and I, I mean we sing the island song brilliantly, don't we?" he sat and studied her, she was truly beautiful, his eyes dropped to her tits, she crossed her arms and said

"My eyes are up here, thank you" and pointed to her eyes, for the first time that he could remember he blushed in front of a woman. She stood to leave and then stopped and looked down at him

"I have heard certain things about you Billy Ridge, I heard that you make women scream out in moments of passion, maybe one day I may give you the opportunity to try and make me scream, but not tonight, good night Billy" and with that she was gone.

Mac Johanson arranged a meeting with everyone for the next day, he sat at the head of the table and opened a file, he began by saying

"I have had a meeting with Mr Desota and he was not happy, saying that you should have gone to him and he would have dropped his percentage, but when I began pointing out some of his mistakes, like he should have signed you all up before you had sung your first song, and you should have known exactly what percentage you were getting before your first gig and

CD recording, and that you wanted 75% of all the money that you have earned him so far, he almost had a seizure. But at the end of the day he is a greedy man, a bit nigh-eve maybe and when I said that you were thinking of contacting the IRS he completely changed his tune, I have here a cashiers cheque for $206 thousand and some papers to sign." they signed all of the papers, then Mac said

"if I am to take you all on, then you will do things my way, I will be fair and Emma will deal with the finances, the way I work as Emma will tell you is that the lead singers will earn more than the band members, and the backing singers and brains and his men will be on a different pay scale to be sorted out between them and myself, I will take 20% if you all agree. I will get to work on your next gig, I can't tell you how I got hold of this piece of paper but on it the list of gigs Mr Desota had provisionally set up for you, the rest should be easy" Billy looked around the table at each person, and each person smiled and nodded. Billy held his hand out to Mac and the deal was done,

"I will have all of the paperwork drawn up and ready to sign in three days, if I was you I would look for somewhere to practice and get to it".

CHAPTER 8

Emma went to Billy and said
"we need to have a chat about things, as far as I can tell every one of us is single and we are all living in hotels, why don't we spend some of our money and buy a property big enough for us all to live in but big enough to keep out of each other's way" Billy nodded his head,

"And big enough so that we have somewhere to practise in" they sat silent for a while before she said

Let's call a local real estate agent and see where that takes us" and that is what they did. The agent said he had the perfect place for them; he took them to a ranch that was up for sale, The vacant ranch consisted of a large house, two barns and lots of other smaller out buildings. The agent left them there and said he would return in two hours to collect them. Billy and Emma walked slowly around the property, Emma made notes as they moved from building to building, the farm house was huge and fully furnished, en-suite, a kitchen that you could live in. They checked out the barns and decided that the bigger one would be perfect to practice in. And the other barn could easily be converted into living quarters. With all of the other buildings taken into consideration there would be plenty of room for everyone.

"Emma said "we will need some staff, cooks cleaners and a maintenance man" Billy nodded and then asked

"Do you think that we could all live together out here, Em?" she looked up at him

"there is lots of land with the farm, why don't we set up a trailer park away from the house, that way the women if they want, can live apart from the men, if that is what they want to do?" he nodded and looked around the farm, he liked the peace and quiet. Looking out over the farms land he quite liked the feel of the wide open spaces.

Emma said
"let's go back to the house because I want to have another look around" they walked into the house and she headed for the stairs, he followed behind her, watching her tight ass as she took each and every step, she walked into the master bedroom and stood to the side and let him walk in, she closed the door and stood there leaning against the door, looking at him, he stood there looking right back at her when she said

"this is your only chance to make me scream Billy and I suggest that you take it, we have maybe half an hour before the agent returns" she reached up and began undoing her shirt, she pulled the shirt open and took it off, she then reached behind her back and undid her bra but before she removed it she looked at him

"Well, are you going to join in or what?" when he began undoing his shirt, she removed her bra to reveal a nice firm pair of tits with upturned long thin nipples. She then undid her belt and her jeans and pushed then down her legs, she stood there in a pair of pink pants, she waited until he was down to his boxers, she then placed her fingers into the side if her pants and looked at him

"Let's do it together" she said and counted to three and they both removed their last item of clothing. Emma looked at his huge cock and he looked at her hairless fanny, she walked over to the bed and lay down and watched his cock as it swayed as he went to her, he leaned over and kissed her, as he kissed her he fondled her firm tits. She was no virgin as she proved when she folded her legs around his back and pulled him to her. She reached down and began wanking his limp cock, he reached down and pushed two fingers into her hairless fanny and began finger fucking her, she began moaning as he grew hard in her small hand.

He removed his fingers and she used her hand to guide his hard cock into her wet fanny, she cried out as he stretched her beyond belief. She thought that he could be splitting her internally, but it was inside her now and by fuck it felt good. She then opened her legs as wide as she could and let him fuck her; she had to admit that he was very good; all the things that she had heard from the other girls were true. She shocked herself when she screamed out loud as he drove her through her first orgasm, she had never been fucked like this before, on and on he went, the only time that he changed speed was when she was close to her orgasm. After her third orgasm he stopped and looked down at her, he pulled his cock out of her and signalled with his finger for her to turn over; she turned over onto her hands and knees. He pushed his cock even further into her, this time she was forced to arch her back as he reached his full depth. He fucked her perfectly and when he shot his hot cum into her slight body, she screamed out at the top of her voice, he pushed forward as hard as he could, he was hurting her but she could not stop herself from squirming backwards against him. When his cock slipped from her sore fanny he pulled her round and pushed her mouth towards his cock, she had only ever done it once before and she did not really enjoy it, as the other man had tried to choke her by trying to force his cock down her throat. She opened her mouth and closed it over his huge knob; she reached up and gripped the base of his cock in a bid to stop him pushing his cock down her throat. But Billy was different and let her go at her own pace as she sucked a few drops of cum from him, and when she was able to lick his shaft clean at her own pace she really enjoyed it and knew that she would be doing this to him again and soon.

They panicked when they heard a car stop outside; they broke into laughter when they heard the agent calling out their names. Emma had to stop dressing because of the amount of love juice that was running down both of her thighs; she ran to the bathroom to sort her-self out while Billy went down stairs and found the agent. Back in the car having told the agent that they would take the ranch, they agreed that what had just happened stayed strictly between them. The next day they took everyone on the coach to the farm, where Billy outlined the plans, everyone seemed happy with the arrangement and they all agreed to muck in and get the place liveable. It took them two weeks to get the place liveable. They had a local builder in to prepare the site for the trailer park and as expected the backing singers took the trailer park. The staffs needed to run the place were all found locally. Brains and his technicians spent every spare moment in the big barn, setting up lightning and the sound systems, there seemed to be wires everywhere and what they all did and where they all went, only brains knew for sure.

Billy walked into the kitchen to be greeted by a woman of maybe 40 years of age, she had long dark hair, green eyes, a slim body and small tits, he smiled and said

"Hi, my name is Billy and you are?", she smiled back and said

"I know who you are Billy and I think you are a brilliant singer, as for me I am Ellen the cook and I need to know something, do I cook for everyone at the same time or do you want me to cook for smaller groups?" he rubbed his chin "I had not even thought about it, give me half an hour and I will let you know" with that he went looking for Emma, he found her talking to brains about lighting, he took her by the arm and eased her away, he went to speak but she stopped him and said

"If you want sex, we will have to find a discreet place, somewhere we can be alone" he smiled and explained his problem with Ellen, Emma blushed deeply

"Oh, I only thought. I think we should all eat together don't you, that way we can keep everyone up to date on what is going on" Billy nodded "good idea, and if you do want sex, maybe we could use the excuse of going to see Mac about gig dates or some other excuse, all you have to do is just say that we need to see Mac and I will know what you mean" she smiled and said

"I think we need to go and see Mac". Billy nodded and said

"I will see you out front in ten minutes".

In the car heading to town Emma had her hand resting on his leg, about an inch from his bulge, she was looking at him as she began undoing the buttons on her check shirt. She undid the shirt all the way down to the waist and held it open so that he could see her naked tits. He looked at her tits and then reached over and fondled her right breast, he twisted tho hard nipple. Hei left hand was now rubbing his growing cock, she was trying to undo his zip-per but in the position that he was sat in, it was impossible, she asked him

"fancy pulling off into the desert and doing it outside in the open air?" he looked into her sparkling eyes and took the next dirt track that they passed. About a mile from the road they came upon a flat bit of pasture land near the top of a hill, he stopped the car and climbed out. He stood and looked in every direction and could see no-one or any buildings, he opened her door and waited for her to get out. As soon as she was out of the car he pushed her back against the car and attacked her tits with his mouth, she reached down and now she could get at his zip-per and within seconds she had his huge cock out, she moved her hand back and forth along his shaft. Billy pulled away from her and undid her jeans and pushed them down to her ankles. She stepped out of her jeans and pulled him to her, she then reached down and placed his hard cock between her legs and moved her hips back and forth.

Billy moved back and stripped her naked, she stood and watched as he stripped himself naked, he opened the back door of the car and pulling her around. He then bent her over so that she was gripping the back seat, she spread her legs and he placed his exposed knob to her opening. When he pushed forward he lifted her bodily from her feet, he held her weight easily as he began to fuck her. He used all of his length on long slow strokes to slowly take her to her first orgasm, when her orgasm began he spread his legs and groaned out loud, as he continued to ram his big cock into her as fast as he could, the blonde woman screamed out into the clear blue sky as her orgasm rushed through her slim body. On and on he fucked her, and she came and came, when he suddenly stopped she looked up at him shocked. He moved away from her and picked up her shirt, he went to the back of the car and spread the shirt out over the trunk. She stood and watched what he was doing, he turned to her and picked her up, he laid her down on the shirt and opened her legs, she thought that he was going to mount her again but she was wrong. As he buried his face between her legs, he then placed his mouth to her hairless fanny, he licked her from the bottom to the top, slowly but repeating the action over and over. She gripped his head and pulled him harder against her fanny; he buried his tongue into her opening and licked back and forth. Emma was close again so he moved his lips to her clit and sucked for all he was worth. Emma screamed out in another earth shattering orgasm as her hips bounced up and down, he lifted his head and looked at her

"Please fuck me, Billy" she whispered and opened her legs wide, he entered her again, as soon as he was at full depth she lifted her legs onto his shoulders. He gripped her inner thighs and fucked her hard, this time he did not slow down; he rode her to a finish. When he shot his hot spunk into her she screamed out at the top of her voice. She could not help herself as over and over she screamed out loud into the clear blue desert skies.

Billy lowered his grip and pulled her back hard, as he pushed his hips forward just as hard, Emma was still making all sorts of funny noises as she squeezed her tits. As soon as his cock began to wilt she reached down for her clit, she had licked her fingers and now she masturbated openly, he stood there watching her, her left hand pulled her left nipple and her right hand moved from side to side just like a fiddlers hand, she let her mouth fall open and she closed her eyes as she built up to her orgasm, the scream when it came was blood curdling. Emma lay on the trunk of the car with her legs wide open, love juice ran from her open fanny and dripped onto the blue paint of the car, he watched her as her chest heaved, she opened one eye and looked up at him

"I love the fresh open air, don't you Billy?", she slid from the car and folded herself around him and placed her lips onto his lips, as they kissed she moved her mound against his limp cock, after a couple of minutes she pulled her lips from his and whispered

"Use your fingers Billy and make me cum again" being a gentleman he did his best to please her and once again she screamed out in orgasm, as she soaked his fingers with her warm cum.

In the car heading into town Emma said

"you are a very good lover Billy, do you know that you are the first man that I have had, that has made me scream out loud during my orgasm, I could fall in love with you Billy Ridge" he turned and smiled at her,

"Please don't fall in love with me Em, I will only hurt you, let's just take things as they come, ok?" she nodded and sank down in the seat and closed her eyes. They spent two hours in town walking and talking, they went into the coffee shop and had coffee; they then made their way back to the farm, on the way back he asked her

"What shall we call the farm, I mean it ought to have a name" she looked across at him

"why not the B, Ridge farm, that sounds good "she said, he nodded and said

"Yea, I like that, so that is what we will call it", when they arrived back at the farm, brains came loping over to the car,

"Hi Billy, have you got a minute" he said and led them to the barn. Once inside Billy was suitably impressed, down the one side of the barn now stood a long stage, the bands instruments were all set up on the stage, opposite the stage stood brains work station, in the roof hung lots of lights, brains moved behind his station and through the mike said

"Can you sing a song please, Billy, I need to make a few adjustments" Billy went onto the stage and picked up his guitar and sat on his stool, he plucked a few strings and that is when Em walked in, she leaned against the side of the barn and watched her lover. Brains turned a bank of lights on and turned all of the speakers on, he nodded to Billy. Billy looked at Em and sang #devil woman# which made Em smile, all of the way down to her cowboy boots.

Brains did his thing and made his notes, when he was happy he called for Billy to join him. Brains then went on to explain that the way that he had everything now set up, when they had to go and do a gig everything is just unplugged and loaded into the coach. Leaving all of the wiring in place in the barn, so that when we return all we have to do is plug everything back in. A full rehearsal was arranged for the next day, with Mac and his wife invited, half way through the rehearsals Ellen came in with a tray of sandwiches and drinks, they all stopped what they were doing and ate and drank, Ellen asked Billy if she could stay and listen to them play

"Of course you can, take a seat although you may have to pay a forfeit of

43

some kind" she smiled

"I will pay whatever forfeit you want Billy Ridge, whatever you want?" she touched his arm and then walked away and took a seat. Billy decided to sing to Ellen because he knew that he was going to fuck her, it was just a question of when. Billy sang to Ellen for the next hour, his eyes never left hers and her eyes never left his, he could tell just by looking at her that she was close to coming but he couldn't do anything about it right now, she would just have to wait.

The next day he went to find Ellen, to ask her if she could put up enough cold food to last the whole crew during a ten hour coach journey, which they would be making in two days' time. He walked into the kitchen and called her name,

"in here" a muffled voice called out, Billy opened a couple of doors before he found her, she was on her knees moving one item of food from one box to a tray, she looked up and saw who it was and her face broke into a broad smile

"I was hoping that you would come around" she said, as he looked down at her he could see down her top to her small naked tits, he did not hesitate as he slid his hand down her top and fondled her right tit. She let him carry on for a few seconds before she pulled his hand from her top and said

"it is a bit too dangerous here, we will have to meet somewhere" She then stood up and faced him, under her apron she wore a gingham skirt, he bent down slightly and put his hand up her skirt to her pants. He rubbed his fingers along her hot slit, she opened her legs for him, he slid his hand down inside her pants to her hairy fanny. He did not hesitate as he pushed two fingers into her wet fanny, she reached up and folded her arms around his neck and pushed her hips forward, as soon as he began moving his fingers inside her she began moaning out loud, in a matter of seconds she had soaked his fingers, she looked into his face, and said

"We can't do it here Billy, it's just not safe" he turned her around and lifted her skirt, he pushed her pants down, she felt him unzip his jeans. He bent her forward and pushed his hard cock at her fanny, he rubbed his knob up and down her slit, before he entered her

"Fucking hell Billy, your huge "she said, she then leaned even further forward to make it better. Billy hung onto her hips and fucked her hard; he showed no finesse as he rammed his cock into her. He heard her call out a couple of times as she had cum, he grunted and shot his cum into her, she howled out loud and pushed back at him as hard as she could, he pushed hard into her as he continued to cum deep inside her.

Billy promised that the next time he would make it better for her, when they had more time. She searched in her pocket for a tissue and pushed it against her fanny, she pulled her pants on and adjusted her skirt and said

"Stay here a minute" she left the store room for a few seconds, when she came back she looked down at his limp cock

"I want to taste you" she said, Ellen licked his cock like no other woman had ever done before, she sucked some cum from him and then took her time and licked him clean. They then stood talking in the kitchen as if nothing had happened, she said

"you know when you drive into town and you see the fuel sign on the left [he nodded] well just past that sign is a turn on the left, take that turn and a hundred yards up there is my house, I live alone and I will be there when I am not here, so if you want to call round anytime, I will be wet and waiting" he promised that he would be calling in sooner rather than later.

The final plans were made for the road trip; the first venue was named The Gold Theatre. The coach was loaded with all of their equipment. Billy suggested that they all get an early night, he was sat in his room thinking when his phone buzzed, he opened his message and was shocked when he saw it was from Jo, it read= Hi Billy, just thought that I would let you know both Stella and I have both missed a period, but don't worry it will not come back to you, but if you want to make sure, we are both willing, hope to see you soon, love Jo. Billy smiled to himself as he thought back to the two women; maybe he would give them a ring when he gets back. He turned his thoughts back to Ellen, he would love to go and see her and give her a real good fucking, but he could not tell everyone else to get an early night and not do the same himself. Could he?

He was up early, showered and dressed, he went out to the coach, most of the crew were sat on board waiting, as no-one had collected the food he walked over to the kitchen. Ellen was busy loading up freezer boxes with all sorts of different food,

"I hoped that you would have come round last night, I waited up just in case" she said disappointedly. Billy explained about everyone getting an early night and that he had to set an example. Ellen looked out of the window at the coach, she could see that almost everyone was there, she took a quick look down the hallway, she turned and grabbed him and took him into the store cupboard, she lifted her skirt and pushed her pants down her legs,

"please make me cum with your fingers before you go" he pushed his hand between her legs and pushed two fingers into her wet fanny, she hung onto him as he finger fucked her to orgasm, as soon as she had cum. She pulled his hand out from between her legs and pulled her pants up. She then helped him carry the cool boxes out to the coach.

Billy sat with his fingers under his nose smelling Ellen, he wanted to fuck her badly, he took a bottle of water and cleaned his fingers luckily just before Emma came and sat by him. Emma talked about the gig ahead and about them doing more duets, he said that he would think about it, she went to get up and turned and said

"I think we should go and see Mac when we get back" he readily agreed and said

"Just as soon as it is possible" she nodded and moved away. The road trip seemed to last for ever, when they arrived they entered the arena and were surprised by the sheer size of the place, he helped the lads carry the equipment into the arena, he found himself standing next to Shirelle who was setting the heights on the mikes. He looked at the tall woman and she looked at him he smiled at her, when she half smiled back and turned away

"Some progress "he thought to himself. The arena was completely sold out; brains had come up with an idea of selling their Cd's in the interval and after the show had ended. This turned out to be a gold mine and they decided to sell the Cd's at every show that they performed.

CHAPTER 9

The show at the Gold Theatre was brilliant and they received another standing ovation, CD sales were very good and one lady asked if we were ever going to do pictures and other memorabilia. When she was told that they had not even considered it, she passed the staff a card and suggested that she could supply everything that they would need. They all discussed it the next day at breakfast and it was decided that it was a great idea. Emma contacted the woman whose name was Diane Riscoe and as they were heading further north to their next gig in Albuquerque, it was arranged for them to call in on Diane on the return trip.

They travelled through the night always heading north, the bus was quiet as everyone slept, Billy sat staring out of the window into the darkness, his mind blank as the miles passed slowly by, all of the lights inside the bus were turned off, the only light coming from passing cars and trucks. Emma came and sat by him, she looked at him but never spoke, she had a blanket with her which she spread over both of their laps and legs, she leaned against him, her head resting on his shoulder, she lifted her mouth and nibbled his earlobe, he pulled away from her and looked around the bus, no-one was awake only the two of them. Emma reached for his hand and placed it between her legs, she had on a skirt but with her legs being wide open he could rub his fingers up and down her fanny, now she had his interest, she looked all around and hitched her skirt up, she reached to the side of her pants and eased them slowly down her legs.

She took his hand again and placed his hand onto her hairless fanny, she looked at him in the darkness and holding his hand she rubbed his fingers up and down her slit, she let go of his hand and his fingers continued their pleasant work, she reached into his lap and stroked his thickening cock through his jeans. When he tried to get his fingers inside her, she had to turn sideways on to him, when he turned sideways as well, he had better access. When she pulled at his belt he stopped what he was doing and undid his belt and the top of his jeans, he pulled the zipper down and left it at that. Her hand was inside his jeans and rubbing his now almost hard cock. Emma released his giant cock and sat there wanking it with her left hand.

She lifted her top and let him feel her naked tits; she pulled the blanked around her shoulders and knelt up on the seat. He looked all around again and happy that no-one was watching them he dropped his mouth to her tits, her hand was now moving quicker up and down his mighty cock. Billy pushed his hand back between her legs and slipped two fingers into her fanny and began to finger fuck her. She buried her face into his leather jacket to stifle her moans, she soaked his fingers with her warm cum. She then pulled his sticky fingers from her fanny and sucked the fingers clean, another look around the bus and she lowered her head into his lap and closed her mouth over his exposed cock. She took her time as she was well practised at cock sucking; he had his hand on the back of her head trying to get her to speed up. Instead she lifted her head from his cock, and whispered into his ear

"do you want me to stop?" he shook his head so she dropped her head again. Emma had a plan in her head as to what she would do when he was about to shoot his hot load. She took him there in her own time, when he was at the point of no return; she lifted her mouth and began wanking him fast. Another look around the coach, seeing no-one looking she moved into his lap and guiding his giant cock into her fanny, she sank down and using her fanny muscles. She fucked him with hardly any body movement at all, she could hear his moan begin in his throat, she then put her hand over his mouth and felt him shoot his hot seed deep into her willing body.

She used her lower body to suck his cum from him, when he was empty; she lifted herself quickly from him and covering herself with the blanket again. She used her mouth to expertly clean his sticky cock; she finally managed to suck a few drops of cum from him. Emma made herself decent before she lifted the blanket from herself and pulled it up to his chin, she tucked it all around him and was gone back into the darkness of the coach. Billy made him-self decent and finally fell into a much needed deep sleep.

CHAPTER 10

The gig in Albuquerque went very well again and they were on the way home to the farm, Emma had called Diane and because she had been informed that the coach would never get near her workshops, she would meet the bus at the start of town and then take Billy to her workshops, they could then wait for him or she could put him on a train, whichever was the easiest.

Emma directed Mark the driver and when they saw a red truck pulled onto the side of the road, she told him to pull over, they pulled up behind the truck and a man of maybe 60 years old climbed out, Bill climbed down the steps of the coach and shakes hands with the old timer, who it turned out to be Diane's father Tommy, after a quick chat Billy tells them to carry on, ho will make his own way home. Tommy drove the big truck with confidence down the narrow lanes to a fairly new building, there was no business name on the building but there were plenty of cars parked out front.

Tommy took Billy into the building which was a hive of activity, printing machines were churning out reams of paper, and lots of women were sat at tables painting pictures on mugs, all manner of work related projects were taking place. Tommy took his guest up a flight of metal steps, he opened a door and walked in, behind the large desk sat a very elegant woman of maybe 40- 42 years of age, her blonde hair was tied back in a bun, she was neither thin or fat but she looked good in her trouser suite of what looked to be white cotton, when she stood up she was a tall woman with the greenest eyes that he had ever seen, he looked her over as she looked him over, he was a little bit disappointed as she did not seem to have any tits.

But when she smiled she suddenly became exceptionally beautiful, she walked around the desk with her hand held outstretched

"Billy, how nice to meet you, you look taller close up, I have to say how much I enjoyed your show the other night" on her desk he could see one of his CD's, he bent forward and picked it up

"Would you like me to sign this for you?" she smiled and nodded, he picked up a pen and signed the disk.

Diane gave him a tour of her workshops, taking her time to point out every aspect of her business, back in the office, she sat down and went through what she could do for him business wise, mugs, calendars, key rings, stickers and pictures, she said that she could do anything within reason, She seemed to blush when she realised what she had just said, she changed tact rather suddenly and began to shuffle papers around on her desk.

"Em, If you agree Billy I would like to take you out to dinner later and if you do want your own merchandise to be produced by us, I will get a photographer in tomorrow to take some pictures and then we can take it from there" Billy asked her about margins and prices and delivery times, happy with everything that she had told him he agreed to have some of everything, it seemed that the meeting was over and he stood to leave

"Are you leaving?" she asked him, he nodded

"Yea, I will have to find a hotel for the night" she shook her head

"I thought that you would stay with us for the night, I have more than enough room" he readily agreed, she picked up her bag and said

"c\mon then, I will show you the town and buy you a coffee" they strolled around the town and had a coffee, they were walking back to her car when they passed a music store, he stopped to look in through the window, she looked at him in the reflection of the glass, he smiled to himself and turned to her and asked

"Can we go in?" she turned and opened the door, they walked in and he was automatically drawn to the guitars.

Billy was being watched by two male sales assistants, Billy picked up a real old looking Winstom guitar, he strummed the strings and looked around the shop, he saw what he wanted, he took the guitar and sat on a chair, he then looked at Diane and said

"pull up a chair [when she was sat opposite him, he strummed the strings and said] "tell me, which song you enjoyed the most at the show" she stared at him and said #good ole boys# he smiled at her and said

"Happens to be my favourite song to" as soon as he began singing he knew that he would fuck her, she had this look in her eyes that said

"I'm all yours". The sales assistants stood and listened and took a recording on their phones. Diane was lost as she listened to his deep voice as he sang just for her, she was a lesbian and had been all of her life, but she was so wet between her legs, she would have to make an excuse to go to the powder room soon and sort her-self out. And when he stared at her with those intense eyes, it was all too much and she had a gentle orgasm, but the worst part was that he knew exactly what he had done to her.

She took him back to her house for a shower before going out to dinner, she had shown him around her large home He could tell by the pictures on view, and the magazines lay around that she was gay. Diane had booked a table at The Rolo Hotel, and for the first ever time he had been recognised and asked for his autograph, they were eating when a three piece band began playing back-ground music. His conversation with Diane had gone very well, now that she had calmed down. The dining room was full with every one of the twenty tables taken, no-one seemed to be listening to the old time music and he knew just what that felt like. Thoy worc 3at chatting and drinking brandy after a fine meal.

He was contented with his lot and he had given up on any thoughts of sex with this woman. But she did strange things like lean closer to him and stares into his eyes, once she accidentally kicked him under the table, and smiled an apology. When he sat back in his chair and spread his legs, he caught her looking at the bulge in his jeans. He knew that one of them was confused sexually and he wandered if it was him?

They were interrupted by a man dressed in a suit and dickey-bow, asking for silence, when everyone was looking at him he said

"ladies and gentlemen, I would like to welcome you all to the Rolo Hotel, tonight we have a celebrity in our midst, I have it on good authority that we have with us tonight the famous country singer Billy Ridge" every-one began applauding, so he stood up and took a bow. Then the man asked if he would go up on stage and sing them a song. Diane smiled broadly and began clapping loudly, he sighed and bent over and said into her ear

"I will only sing for you" she nodded and he made his way up onto the stage. He picked up the bands only guitar and ran his fingers over the taught strings, he looked out over the diners, and said into the microphone

"Good evening, I will sing a couple of songs for my friend Diane Riscoe, I know that this is her favourite song" Billy sang for almost an hour, as word got the town that he was singing, more and 0more people entered the hotel dining room. He tried to leave the stage but every time the diners called for more, he finally left the stage and then had to sign autographs, Dane found it all most amusing and when he finally sat down she kissed him on the cheek and said

"You really are a fantastic singer Billy" he smiled and said

"I am a much better lover" she blushed down to the top of her tits; he could have kicked himself for saying such a thing. They sat in the back of a cab back to her house, when the cab stopped he said

"I can go into town if you want, I don't want to cause you any further embarrassment" she shook her head, and said "don't be silly, I can trust you", he paid the cabbie and they entered the house, she poured them both a brandy, they sat on a couch and watched the fake log fire, he tried to apologise for what he had said, but she had waved a hand and told him to forget it, she then looked at him

"Did you really sing all of those wonderful songs just for me?" she asked him, he smiled

"yep, just for you and only you", they sat and stared at one another for a few seconds, when he went to lean closer, she moved away and stood up

"I think that I had better go on up, you know where everything is don't you?" she asked, he looked at her with his best look

"Everything except where your room is" she smiled and said

"I know that you know that I am gay, so shall we leave it at that" she turned and headed for the door

"you know where my room is if you change your mind" she hesitated but carried on walking.

He walked around the room and looked at the books, pictures and the row of CD's, he found his first CD and put it into the player, he turned the volume up and sat back down on the couch, he sang along quietly, then he sensed that she was stood behind the door listening to him singing, he looked at the bottom of the door and could see her shadow, He listened to a couple of more tracks then turned the player off, he watched her shadow under the door, she seemed to hesitate again before her shadow disappeared.

Billy turned all of the lights of and went up the stairs to his room, he stripped off naked and got into bed, he lay there thinking of nothing, sleep yet again escaping him, he heard a slight noise and looked at the door, he thought that he could see a shadow under the door again, but he dismissed it, he lay there a little bit longer before he got up and slipped his boxers on, he made his way quietly down the stairs, when he entered the main room where they had been sat earlier, he saw Diane standing swaying with the headphones on, she had on a silk dressing gown in a royal blue, he turned to go back upstairs without her seeing him but she must have seen his reflection on something because she turned around and looked at him

"I couldn't sleep so I thought that some soothing music may help" he walked over to her and took the headphones from her head, he knew what she was listening to before he even listened, he put one of the pads to his ear and heard himself singing.

He lay the headphones down and pulled her to him, she resisted for maybe a second, when he kissed her she just melted into his arms, she flung her arms around his neck and kissed him back, when he pushed his tongue at her lips she opened up for him and sucked his tongue into her mouth, when he touched her breast she flinched at first but when he slid his hand inside her dressing gown to her naked breast, she was finally lost, she instantly pushed her mound at him and began rubbing against his growing hardness. He took a step back and pulled her dressing gown open, she was naked underneath and her fanny was just as naked, he pushed the dressing gown off her shoulders and let it fall to the carpet, he pulled her nakedness into his arms, she looked into his eyes

"I never have with a man, I don't know what to expect, take me to my bed "he took her upstairs, she pointed to her room, he bent down and picked her up and carried her into the room and to the bed, she went to get into bed but he stopped her

"I want to look at your beautiful body" he bent forward and lowered his lips to her hard nipple, He sucked on the hardness and then rolled the nipple between his teeth making her moan out loud, he kissed her all the way down to the top of her mound, he opened her legs wide and placed his mouth against her swollen wet fanny, he lapped at her like a cat would lap at a saucer of milk, he pushed his tongue between her swollen fanny lips and moved ever so slowly upwards until she gasped out loud, now that he had located her clit he sucked and flicked the tiny button, when he closed his lips around it she pushed her hips higher and grabbed the back of his head and pulled him harder against her. Diane came very vocally as she screamed out her first ever orgasm with a man.

Billy stood up and let his boxers slip to the floor; she looked at his massive cock and gasped out loud "please don't hurt me Billy", he lifted her legs and opened them wide when he let go of her right leg to guide his cock Into her she kept her leg high, he pushed his hard cock into her, she arched her back and groaned at the top of her voice as he stretched her, he gripped the insides if her thighs and began fucking her, he took his time and used all of his skills to give her the maximum of pleasure. Diane came and came, she had tears rolling down the side of her face, he watched as her tits rocked back and forth, he slowed down and stopped she looked up at him

"Did you cum?" she asked he smiled and shook his head

"I want you to turn over" she turned over and took up a position on her hands and knees, he parted her legs and pushed his cock back Into her, again she arched her back and moaned out loud, now when he began fucking her she really began to join in, the extra depth did something to her because she was almost crying out loud, he gripped her hips but he knew that if he let go of her hips, she would continue to push back on her own, he used every bit if skill that he had learned over the last few years, he rode her hard and even harder through her orgasms, he didn't know how many times that she had cum but it was many, now it was his turn, when he grunted she shouted out loud

"oh no, oh no, oh no" and when the first spurt hit her deep inside she screamed out loud and began shaking, each spurt brought another desperate heart wrenching scream from her.

When he finally stopped spurting he just held her, her arms gave way and her front end flopped onto the bed, he could hear her crying out loud and he could feel her whole body trembling, when he began to pull his cock from her she moaned even louder, when his cock left her body she rolled onto her side and curled into a ball, and cried. Billy sat down by her side and rubbed her back

"Are you ok, Diane?" she nodded and tried to speak, but she had to swallow first,

"I never thought that it could be like that with a man, I have thought about it often but I would not have believed that I would have enjoyed it so much and when you came, that feeling inside, I will never forget that as long as I live" she closed her eyes and he thought that she was going to sleep, but she said

"Please hold me Billy" he folded himself around her and still she trembled,. After a while she lifted her head and looked at him "can I have a look at your thing please, only I have never seen one before" Billy turned onto his back and lay there for her, she sat up and looked down at his limp cock, he lifted her free hand and placed it onto his cock, she just rested her hand on his cock, he look down at her hand "take hold of it and lift it up " she lifted his limp cock and looked at it, he reached out and gripped her hand and pulled the fore skin down exposing his purple knob, she turned it this way and that way when a single drop of his seed appeared on the tip of his knob she looked at it closely, he saw where she was looking and said

"Why don't you taste it?" she wrinkled her nose up

"Go on, I tasted yours and very nice you tasted to" he said, she looked at it again and lowered her mouth she poked her tongue out and took the single drop of cum, she took it into her mouth and smiled at him

"Not as bad as I thought, not as nice as fanny, but not bad" he smiled at her

"Why don't you take into your mouth, surely you have done it to a false cock why not try the real thing?".

Diane did not hesitate as she slid her mouth over his knob, she had obviously practised a lot with rubber cocks from the way she sucked his cock, when he began to get hard again she became quite excited. He lifted her hand and folded it around his shaft, he covered her hand with his own and began moving it up and down, matching her mouth movements, when he lifted his hand he was pleased to see her hand continue on its journey. When he was hard again she lifted her mouth from his hard cock, she was pleased with herself, now that he was hard she examined his cock from top to bottom, she pulled the skin back and looked at his swollen knob, she looked into his face and asked

"Did you put all of this inside me?" he smiled

"Every little bit" she smiled and said

"I have never had anything that big before". Billy climbed from the bed and pulled her up, he pulled her playfully around the room looking for something different, the naked woman laughed playfully when she saw his thick long cock swaying from side to side. He opened the bedroom door and pulled her along behind him, they ran naked down the stairs and he pulled her into the main room, he sat her down in a large brown leather chair and lifted her legs over the arms of the chair, he reached under her and pulled her bum to the edge of the chair, she looked down and watched as he pushed his cock into her fanny, she let out a long "oooooohhhhhhh" and flopped back into the chair, she gripped the arms and closed her eyes and hung on. Billy rode her hard, he held onto her inner thighs as he plundered her lesbian body.

Billy slowed down and stopped, Diane looked up at him as if waiting for her instructions, he pulled his cock out and pulled her up to standing, she went to kiss him but instead he spun her around, he eased her forward into the chair, she looked back to see what level his cock was at, she knelt in the chair and clung onto the back, she waited for him to mount her, he rubbed his knob up and down her slit making her moan out loud, when he held his knob at her entrance she pushed back in her desperation to get his cock back into her body. Diane moaned out loud again as his cock stretched her yet again, when he began riding her this time, she found that if she bent forward more it felt a lot better, and if she pushed back in time with him, it was the best sex that she had ever had, she came again and knew that he must be getting close again and she relished the feeling of his hot cum flooding her insides again.

She thought about pregnancy and babies but if it happened then it would happen, she would tell her long term partner Jill that she had had IVF treatment as a surprise for her, then again if this man with his big cock wanted to stay around she would not hesitate in moving him in and fucking him at every opportunity, she had a life time of man sex to catch up on. His grunt brought her thoughts back to the present, she readied herself for the feeling of his seed flooding her body "aaaarrrgggggg "he shouted as he again erupted inside her, she felt the warmth spread through her body, she knew that at that precise moment that she had just become pregnant, more and more of his beautiful seed exploded into her woman loving body.

Another first for her was when she stood up and the results of their love making ran down both of her legs, she spread her legs and stood there and watched the fluid make its slow journey southwards. Billy passed her a tissue box, she grabbed a handful and pushed it against her fanny and disappeared into the bathroom, when she came out he was lay on top of her bed, his cock resembled a giant banana, she had put on a pair of pants, she sat on the bed and smiled down at him,

"You have changed me, Billy Ridge" she said, he smiled and looked down at his bent cock, she looked to where he was looking and said

"I'm not sucking it again, I'm much to sore to go through all that again" she stood up and went back into the bathroom again, she came out with a wet flannel and a towel; she washed his cock and dried it. Diane pulled his boxers up his legs and got into bed, when he went to get into her bed she smiled and said

"I have never slept with a man before" with that she pulled the bed clothes back and welcomed him into her bed.

They woke when the alarm went off, Billy had one idea and Diane had another, after breakfast they headed to her premises and a day of photo shoots, they worked all morning none stop, at lunch time she announced that they were going into town for lunch, which they did only on the way back she took a different turn off, they stopped outside a warehouse, she got out of the car and waved for him to follow, she unlocked a door and went inside, when he followed her she locked the door behind them, she said

"this is where I store all of my stock and supplies, I thought that I should show you everything" she led the way up a flight of metal steps, she unlocked a door and walked in, he followed her into a plush office with a large oak desk, in one corner stood a computer, a phone and a pad and pens, on the walls were pictures of past customer successes, she stood leaning back against the desk, she had a smirk on her face as she began undoing the buttons on her white silk blouse, she undid every button and took it off and laid it over a chair, she reached behind her back and undid her bra, that was placed on top of her blouse, she reached for the button on the side of her skirt and looked at him,

"Are you going to join in Billy, or shall I just carry on on my own?" she asked with a smile, he reached for the top button of his shirt. She sat naked on the edge of her oak desk watching him pull his cowboy boots off, she opened her legs and began rubbing her fingers up and down her fanny lips, she moved back slightly and lifted her feet onto the desk, she let them flop open and continued to rub her fanny lips, he stopped at his boxers and watched her

"let me watch you do it to yourself" she shook her head, and said

"I don't know you well enough for that", he pulled up a chair and sat in front of her. Diane took her body weight on her left hand and rubbed her fanny lips with her middle fingers, her eyes watching him, she made up her mind and climbed from the desk, she picked up her key ring, she went to a cupboard and unlocked it, she reached inside and took out a white box, she placed the box on the table and opened the lid, she looked back at him and smiled, reaching inside she pulled out a silver coloured vibrator, he had never seen anything like it before, the whole thing was a good foot long, it had a handle, then a rim with a rubber bit sticking out of the base of the rim, the shaft was 8inches long with tiny nobles all over it, she held it in front of him and when she turned it on, it vibrated and buzzed as the shaft spun around.

She held the silver beast against his cheek; he had to admit it felt erotically thrilling; she licked the silver cock as far down the shaft as she could and rubbed it up and down her slit, paying most attention around the clit area. When she entered the silver beast into her fanny she instantly began to moan out loud, as she began to fuck herself with it.

He could now see what the rubber bit was for, every time she pushed it into herself, the rubber bit rubbed against her tiny clit. After less than a minute she could have been on her own, her eyes were glazed over, her mouth was a funny shape as her hand movements became quicker, she lifted her head and stared at him but he could tell that her mind was somewhere else, he could see her cum building up around the base of the implement, she let her head fall back and she howled out loud, he watched her hand and she was fucking herself as fast as she possibly could. She pulled her knees closer together and moved her hips up and down, he was stood there now with his giant cock in his hand, she pulled the silver thing from her fanny and moved herself closer to the edge, he moved forward and pushed his cock into her, she growled out loud and lay back and then she reached down by her side and gripped the edge of the desk and let him fuck her rigid.

Billy was like a man possessed, he had got it into his head that he had to be better than that silver thing, on and on he fucked her, he watched her tits as they moved back and forth, he made her cum twice before he stopped when she looked upon at him he pulled her from the table, he turned her around and told her to grip the edge of the desk,. Billy entered her again and gripped her hips; he spread his feet and gave her the fuck of her life.

Diane was so sore but she knew that this may well be the last time that she ever had a real cock inside of her body, and she was determined to have it inside her for as long as possible, she came every two or three minutes until she heard that familiar grunt which told her that he was about to fill her body with his seed again. Knowing that they were in their own she called out at the top of her voice, urging him on, wanting him to cum inside her, when she felt the first spurt hit her insides she screamed out at the top of her voice, every hot spurt brought a blood curdling scream, this was the feeling that she never felt with a woman, and it was that feeling that would tempt her, to allow another man inside her. Finally spent Diane lay back on her big desk, sexual fluids oozed from her open fanny that twitched and throbbed, her chest rising and falling as if she had been in a race. Billy sat in his chair also breathing hard, his limp cock hung down between his legs, twitching.

They worked all afternoon and every time he looked at Diane she had a stupid grin on her face, he could swear that she was walking slightly bow legged. She had spent a fair bit of time on the phone talking to who he did not know. At the end of the day she asked him what his plans were, she needed to know if he was staying another night, because her full time lover was pestering her as she had not seen her this week,

"So do you want me to stay ?" he asked her, she leaned in close to him and said

"what you really mean is, do I want you to fuck me again, well the answer to that is yes, I want you to fuck me as often as you like" he smiled and said

"One more night then, I will leave in the morning" she nodded and said
"Only if, if you are passing this way in the future you will contact me and stay over" he nodded his agreement. They began the evening's sexual marathon in the bath, she hung onto the taps and he fucked her from behind, as the water splashed over the sides she screamed out in ecstasy.

Billy fucked her until she surrendered, he was still hard when she gave in, so he made her suck him to a finish, this was another first for her, one that she will also never forget as long as she lived.

CHAPTER 11

Billy arrived back at the farm to an air of excitement, Mac came to meet him holding his hand out, Billy shook his hand, "great news Billy we are going onto the Carson show, all of America will hear you sing, we will have more bookings than you can shake a stick at " Mac said excitedly. Billy took himself off and walked across the farms land to think, he came to the rim of some sort of quarry that had water lay in its base. All sorts of different coloured birds were using the water, Billy was lost in the tranquillity of the sight in front of him, he was taken out of thoughts when Emma turned up besides him and slipped her hand into his.

"What you thinking about lover?" she asked; he did not look at her when he said

"Do you think I could build a log cabin just here, a place where I can come to be on my own and write songs" he could feel her looking at him when she said

"You can have whatever you want Billy, if you want, I will get on it today" he nodded

"I would like that Em" she reached up and kissed him on the cheek and walked away from him, leaving him standing all alone with his thoughts.

True to her word Emma was on it straight away, within 4 days power cables were being laid to the site, a local builder was laying foundations for the Canadian log cabin, one of his men was sat on a digger, digging a long trench from the farm down to the new site for water and sewage. It took 7 days for all of the amenities to be put in place, Emma and Billy were waiting for the cabin to be delivered, when a huge lorry came into view Emma gripped his arm

"Here it comes Billy" they stood and began walking across the land to the site, the builder was directing the lorry, Emma looked around and every one of the band and crew were walking behind them. It took most of the day to get the cabin into place, the lorry driver left with a hefty tip, the builder was busy connecting the amenities, the band and crew were all looking down into the quarry pointing out this and that, all slightly shocked that they didn't even know that the quarry was there.

The builder came over and said that everything was working. Billy was chuffed with his new cabin as he stood in the doorway staring into space, he looked at all of his friends, and even Shirelle was standing looking at him. Billy and Emma went shopping for furniture and everything that he would need for the cabin, he went to turn off and head for the clearing that they had used before but she said that it was not a good time for her, getting her meaning he drove into town.

Billy let Emma sort everything out, she had even bought him a dirt bike to save him walking to the cabin, when he finally walked into the cabin he was a happy man, she had even bought him a rocking chair which he sat in now just staring and thinking, he picked up a new guitar that Emma had bought for him, he played and sang sad songs, this was his place now, his sanctuary. He had been there for most of the day when a familiar voice called out his name, he sat and waited for her to come into view, she looked round the side of the cabin and said

"Ah, there you are, I thought that you may be hungry?" she held a basket in her hand covered in a check cloth,

"Hi Ellen, how are you?" she sat down by his cowboy boots and passed him a beer, and she took one herself and looked out over the quarry

"Wow, this is perfect" she said as she passed him a plate, full with different filled sandwiches, he took the plate and began eating, she past him a bag of chips, which he also began eating. They had been sat there for a while when she asked him

"Why haven't you been around to see me Billy?" he did not even look at her when he said

"It is not that I do not want to Ellen, with all that is going on at the moment, I need some time on my own sometimes to think, and I really need to be writing songs". Ellen sat there staring into space for another hour without a word being spoken, she stood up and took his plate and put it back in the basket and walked away without saying another word.

CHAPTER 12

Billy had spent a few days on his own in the cabin, but the time had come for them to hit the road again, he rode his bike back to the farm and was full of smiles for everyone, the bus was being loaded with equipment, he went to the kitchen for the cool boxes, Ellen did not seem to be happy with him, she stood there looking at him when a single tear ran down her cheek, he pulled her into his arms and held her tightly, she folded herself into him, he could feel her gently sobbing, he lifted her face and kissed her on the lips, and said

"I promise that I will come around and see you when we get back" she nodded and pulled away from him

"See ya later then "she said and turned away from him.

For the first time Billy took his guitar onto the bus and when they were well under way, he began playing a new song that he had written called #country blues# the backing singers moved to the seats around him and listened, after a few seconds they joined in, he sang three songs that he had written and they were liked by everyone on board the bus. They were on the road for three days, doing two shows Billy had chosen the back seat this time for the trip through the night, as usual the bus was in total darkness and everyone seemed to be asleep, but he knew that one person would be wide awake and waiting for the right moment to go to him, he saw her stand up and look all around the bus, seeing that the coast was clear she made her way to him, she carried her blanket again.

As soon as she sat down she reached under her skirt and removed her pants, she leaned into him and offered him her lips, the lovers kissed long and passionately, when he touched her breast through her top, she glanced around and pulled her top up, giving him access to her lovely firm tits. While he played with her left breast his left hand was between her legs, and he began finger fucking her, she was undoing his belt and trousers, she finally got his hard cock out into the open, she began wanking his cock as fast as she could, she was close to her orgasm, she took a quick look around and lifted her knee over his lap, she reached under herself and guided his giant cock into her hot wet fanny, she sank down his length and used her hips to take her to her orgasm, when she smiled at him he gripped her buttocks and began fucking her, it must have been the quietest fuck ever.

Emma had cum four times and now it was his turn, he shot his spunk deep

62

into her body, she had to force herself not to scream out as she came again, she sat there grinding herself against him while he pushed his hips firmly upwards.

Back in her seat she was pushing some tissues between her legs when Edd turned and smiled at her, she put her finger to her lips, telling him to be quiet. Emma covered herself with the blanket and turned to the window, her fanny was tingling and throbbing, she loved his big cock but she wished that they could do it in a bed or somewhere where she can let herself go, no-one could see her or what she was doing so she pushed her hand down insides her pants and began rubbing her clit, as her finger began to speed up, she closed her eyes and took herself to another beautiful silent orgasm.

Back home at the farm, Billy left them all to unload the bus, while he jumped onto his bike and headed for his cabin; he sat in his rocking chair with the sun on his face and fell into a light sleep. He could sense someone watching him so he opened one eye and looked around to see Emma stood by the side of the cabin watching him, when she saw him look at her she moved forward and stood in front of him,

"We were seen doing it on the bus, but don't worry it was only Edd and he won't say anything because when I tell him that I know about him and Peter the drummer, his lips will be sealed. But I had to warn you Billy, just in case he did say something" she said all this standing there with her fanny wetter than it had ever been before, she went to walk away but turned back and said

"Please take me inside the cabin and fuck me "he looked at the beautiful woman standing in front of him, he did love her in his own way, he dragged himself out of the rocking chair and took her hand and led her inside his cabin, he took her into his bedroom, she stood there and let him strip her naked, he pulled his shirt off and undid his jeans and pushed them down and then kicked them off. Billy turned her around and bent her forward, she spread her legs wide and groaned when he entered her, once fully embedded inside her, he pulled her up to standing, she reached up and held him around the neck, he then reached around in front of her and fondled both firm breasts.

Emma had never done it like this before and she had to admit that she liked the closeness a lot, they moved easily with each other but she felt a bit strange with her body exposed the way it was, by pushing her hips backwards they fucked nice and slow and very very deep. Emma got her wish and screamed out each orgasm as they travelled through her body, when he grunted he bent her forward and gripped her hips and fucked her hard until he shot his spunk into her slender body.

When Emma left the cabin she saw someone walking back to the farm, it looked from where she was that that person had been to the cabin and was walking slowly back, she could not tell who it was but no doubt she would soon find out. Back at the farm she went to her trailer and took a shower and sorted herself out. Mac called Emma and informed her about further bookings, but he had had one strange request for a booking, a private party in California, all they required was Billy and his guitar, they had everything else taken care of, and the money that they were offering, well it would be difficult for him to refuse, and could she ask Billy if he would do the gig only the party wanted to confirm the booking asap. Billy said that he would do it and for that amount of money he would do it naked if they wanted him to.

Billy was on the train heading for California, he had a small overnight bag and his guitar, hour after long hour he spent looking at nothing, he slept for a while and when a refreshment trolley came along he bought a couple of beers and some food. He arrived at his station and when he went to leave the station there was a man in uniform holding a card with his name emblazoned on it, he went to the man and presented himself, he was taken to a white limousine and the man held the door open for him. Billy sat in the back of the long car, the driver told him to help himself to champagne. The driver took 40 minutes before they stopped in front of a large pair of black iron gates, the gates moved slowly sideways as if by magic, they rode along a long winding drive up to a large mansion style house that would not have looked out of place in the British countryside, when they stopped outside a large man in a blue suit walked down a flight of stone steps to meet him, he was maybe just past 60 years of age, his hair looked blue-grey and that colour matched his eyes, he was a slim man that spoke perfect English

"Ah, you must be Billy, welcome to my humble home, I am Sir Walter Himes, come in, come in. Jenson will take your things up to your room, while I show you to the ballroom" as they walked through a hallway of white marble, large paintings of long dead family members hung on every wall, some of past generals, some of old fully rigged sailing ships, when they entered the ballroom a small stage had been erected, in front of which stood maybe 60 to 80 chairs. On the stage was a stool exactly the same as the one that he used himself, a single microphone stood on the stage and in front of the stage were two speakers.

Billy stood on the stage and Jenson came in carrying his guitar case, he placed the guitar on the stage and left. Walter said

"You will be playing for my daughter Isobel and her friends, it is her twenty first birthday and you were what she wanted, and it is you that we have and I would like to thank you for accepting our humble offer, now I will leave you to do whatever it is that you have to do and when you have finished Jenson here will show you to your room, if you want to eat just tell Jenson and he will sort everything out for you. Oh, one last thing, we would like you to be on stage at 10 pm and finish whenever you feel you have given good value, a disco man will be in later to set himself up, he will play before and after you, I think that is everything, em, if you want to explore feel free to wander wherever you want, right, ok I will see you later then" and he was gone, as Billy looked around the room it took him back to his solo days around the clubs and bars.

Billy had set up the speakers and stowed his stuff in his room, he was walking through the house towards the garden when he saw a fine looking young woman lay on a sun lounger by the pool, she was stunningly beautiful with long blond hair, and she wore a tiny yellow two piece swim suit, she had a nice hand full of tit with a slim body, when she moved he felt his cock jump in his jeans, he suddenly realised that he was staring and slightly embarrassed he walked quickly past her out into the gardens.

He was strolling along a grass path towards a large pool with benches placed at its edge, a golf buggy came into view heading his way, a woman was driving the buggy, she had on a thin flowered dress and a floppy hat tied under her chin, the smiling woman stopped in front of him, when she pushed her hat back, he was shocked she was maybe 30 years old with a smile to die for, she had green eyes and skin a 16 year old teenage girl would be jealous of

"You must be Billy, I am so pleased that you could make it" she stepped from the cart and kissed him on the cheek, he did not know what her perfume was but he almost shot his load when he filled his nose with the sweet scent

"My name is Patsy Himes, hop in and I will give you a tour of the grounds" they sat side by side, their thighs touching occasionally, she pointed out all manner of things as she drove around the huge estate, she stopped at a single track and set the break

"Come and meet my special friends" she led the way along the track, they came to a five barred wooden gate, she stood leaning on the gate her tits squashed flat against the lucky wooden bar of the gate, she whistled into the open field and out from a small copse a small herd of llamas came running, some white some brown, there were maybe twenty of them, she caught him looking at her squashed tits, when the animals were all stood around the gate she said

"Just reach out and touch them" he was not sure what she meant but he had a good idea and to confirm what he thought, she bent over and lifting a lid she scooped a hand full of feed pellets, but she made sure that he had a good look at her braless tits, she stood up and smiled, she looked away and gave a slight shrug. Maybe he should grab her and give her a good fucking, but not before he had done the show, Patsy made him jump when she said

"I come out here three times a day, morning, noon and night to check on them, you can come again if you want to, say tomorrow morning, my husband will be going to the office at 7. 30 I usually come then" she had a wicked smile and he knew that he would be up in the morning, bright and early.

Billy sat listening to the disco man waiting to go on, Walter stuck his big head around the door and stuck his thumb up, Billy nodded and entered the room to a round of enthusiastic applause, what he saw shocked him, every person in the room had taken the trouble to dress in country clothing and in the front row right in front of him sat the young woman from the poolside, he looked her in the eyes and in his deepest voice he said

"Happy birthday Isobel, every one of these songs I am about to sing, is just for you" Billy sang for an hour, each song drew a round of applause, there were dancers dancing in the isle and at the back of the room, all the time he sang, Isobel's eyes never left his, he said that he was taking a short break and would be back soon for the second half. He left the ball room and went to his room to change, he was walking around in his boxers when a knock came on the door, he grabbed a towel and wrapped it around his waist and opened the door, a smiling Isobel was standing there in her hand she held a Billy Ridge CD, she walked in and closed the door behind her

"Oh Billy, you have made my birthday perfect" she stood in front of him looking at his hard chest, she was swaying from the hips, he held his hand out and said

"Do you want me to sign that Isobel?" she placed the CD into his hand and said

"Will you give me a birthday kiss please Billy" he looked at the beautiful woman, how could he refuse, he took her in his arms and kissed her hard, when he pushed his tongue at her lips she opened her mouth and sucked his tongue into her own mouth, Billy placed his hand on her ass and pulled her harder against him, she moaned out loud. Billy pulled the towel out from between them, now she could feel his growing cock, the next move was up to her, she pulled away from him and looked at his hard cock standing up inside his boxers, she turned and locked the door she then turned back and undid the belt around her dress and lifted the dress over her head, she stood there in a yellow thong, she grabbed his hand and pulled him into the bedroom. She stopped in front of the bed and reached up she placed her arms around his neck giving herself to him totally.

Billy pushed her thong down her legs and managed to get a finger into her fanny from behind her back, he felt her knees move outwards allowing him better access, he fingered her fanny for about a minute, he then moved away from her and lowered her down onto the bed, she looked at him when he dropped his boxers and gasped out loud

"Wow, that is the biggest cock that I have ever seen or heard of,"

She lifted her legs and opened them wide he looked down at the neatly trimmed fanny and put his big knob to her entrance and pushed forward, Isobel was no virgin, she arched her back and by gripping the edge of the bed, she waited for him to fuck her, he took the weight of her legs on his arms and began fucking her, she used her hips and met each of his deep thrusts with an upward thrust of her own hips, she came quietly but her body reacted differently she held her body stiff and held her breath as soon as her orgasm was over she built quickly to the next, he fucked her hard and when he grunted she knew what was coming and lifted her hips up high and received his hot spunk with relish.

They pushed and ground against each other for a couple of minutes until she pushed him out of her, she looked down at his wet still hard cock, she dropped to her knees and did not hesitate as she took almost half of his cock deep into her throat, she gripped his cock with her lips and sucked all the way up to the tip of his knob, she bounced her head up and down a few times and lifted her mouth from his cock she stood up and said

"That will have to do for now Billy, I will try and come to you later" she said, and with that she quickly dressed and was gone.

He walked back into the ballroom and Isobel was sat in her seat, only now she had her legs slightly parted and a stupid smile on her face, Billy sang to her for the rest of his time on stage, he left to a standing ovation. He did not get far before the birthday girl grabbed his hand and dragged him back into the ballroom

"Come and meet my friends "she said. As Billy was dragged around like dog on a lead and people touched him and asked for his autograph, they told him how much they had enjoyed his songs.

He finally escaped to his room, he showered and lay on top of his bed and waited for the birthday girl, he fell asleep and woke early in the morning, he didn't know what had happened to his date, he made himself presentable and walked down stairs to the dining room to find that both father and daughter had left the estate. Walter for the office and Isobel for a hard days sailing, Patsy was sat at a long dining table eating breakfast

"Morning Billy did you sleep well?" she smiled, he answered

"Like a log thank you" he helped himself to eggs, bacon, sausages and fries, he sat and devoured the food, when he had finished Patsy poured them both a cup of coffee, she stood up with hers and waited for him to do the same, he followed her out of the door that led to the pool she stood looking out over her estate, without looking at him she said

"I caught Isobel heading for your door late last night, I sent her back to bed, I hope that you are not to disappointed Billy" he did not answer her, I mean what could he say, she asked him what time he was leaving, when he explained that he had no immediate plans, she turned to him and said

"Good, you can spend the morning with me then, meet me out front in half an hour" she then turned and walked away. Billy was sat waiting on the stone steps at the front of the house when Patsy came into view in her golf buggy, she stopped in front of him and waited for him to get in, she had changed into white shorts and a white tee shirt, perched on top of her head was her floppy hat, she drove off along the grass track, she drove with confidence to the area where the llamas were.

She drove past the entrance to the lane that they had been down yesterday to a gateway, she stopped and looked at him, he climbed down and opened the gate, she drove through and waited for him, he closed the gate and climbed back into the cart, Patsy drove across the bumpy field, he could not help but notice her braless tits bouncing around, she parked in a group of trees and switched the buggy off, she passed him a basket and she picked up a blanket. She led the way through the trees, they came upon an opening in the trees, the area was maybe twenty yards square, the grass was green and lush, the only sounds were the birds singing in the tree tops, the early morning sun filled the clearing with warmth, she spread the blanket out and sat down on it, she looked at Billy and said

"Tell me about yourself Billy" he lay back in the sun and told her a story of rags to riches, she was lay down by his side in the sunshine

"Why didn't you take the hint's that I dropped yesterday Billy?" he lifted himself onto his elbow and looked down at her

"I saw the hints but I was not 100% so I played safe and did nothing" she said

"I would not say fucking my step daughter, nothing would you?" he was speechless.

"Don't you want to know how I know?" she asked, he still looked down at her,

"Go on then "he said, she opened her eyes and looked up at him

"I know because I was heading for your room myself and I could hear you fucking her through the door, I stood there listening to you, I have to tell you I was as jealous as hell" still looking at him she said

"Are you going to fuck me now or not?" he moved to her side and looked down at her, she sat up and said

"Look Billy, we are both consenting adults, I know that we both want the same thing, so let's not waste any more time" with that she removed her tee shirt revealing a perfect pair of firm tits, she undid her shorts and pushed them down her slim legs, she did the same with her pants, her fanny was as hairless as an egg, she watched him strip himself naked, when she saw the size if his cock she smiled and said,

"I knew that you had a big cock, but that is something special" she reached out and gripped his thick cock and began wanking it, he reached out and fondled her breasts, she let go of his cock and swivelled round on her back and presented her fanny to him, she reached forward and pulled his head down between her legs, she held his head in place while he gave her the pleasure that her husband would not give her, when he did want her, his pencil thin cock did little to pleasure her.

Billy puckered his lips around her clit, she screamed out her first orgasm

69

with a man for years, he lifted his head and when he had spread her legs, he pushed them forwards, now her fanny was at his mercy, she pushed his tongue deep inside her and searched out her warm salty cum, Patsy began moaning again so he licked as deep as he could inside her sex cavern, he then held his tongue stiff and fucked her with his hard tongue. Patsy began the pound her hips up and down as her second orgasm in years, racked her trembling body.

Billy decided that it was his turn for some pleasure, he moved around her and held his hard dick to her mouth, she looked at his huge knob and licked her lips she opened her mouth wide and slipped her mouth over his knob, she began to bounce her head up and down on his cock, he reached down and pushed two fingers into her fanny, she opened her legs wider and took her weight on her feet as she lifted her hips high, he straightened his arm and finger fucked her in a straight line, when she was close again he bent his fingers upwards to behind her mound and searched out her secret ridged place. Billy stroked the special place, Patsy spat his cock out and gripped hands full of grass and growled deep inside of herself, her eyes were screwed tight, this time her orgasm exploded from her in the shape of a howl, the more that he rubbed the secret spot, the more that she bounced her hips and howled, Patsy came and came, her fanny juices were running from her, in the end she could take no more and snatched his fingers from her fanny, she lay there covered in goose bumps, she had nipples that were almost an inch long, she lay there still trembling and growling

"What the fuck did you touch up there? "She finally managed to say Her body was heaving as he looked down at her. Billy was sat on his haunches, he gripped her hands and pulled her up and into him, he pulled her hips close to him and she used a trembling right hand to guide his knob between her swollen fanny lips, she sank down on his thick hard cock, she groaned out loud as she was stretched more than she had ever been stretched before, she then moved herself into a more comfortable position and placing her hands behind his neck, she began to ride his hard thick cock.

Billy grabbed her ass cheeks and encouraged her to rise higher and drop quicker, she was soon moaning out loud again and clinging onto him for all she was worth, she pushed her forehead against his forehead and stared deeply into his eyes, he could tell that she was coming, her breath was hot and sweet as it hit him in the mouth, she suddenly stopped and rubbed herself frantically against him, all of the time she was making lots of unfamiliar noises, she stopped again and sank down as hard as she could and moaned out loud with a growl

"Oh fucking hell, I really wanted that" she cried out. She looked into his eyes again

"What now?" he lifted her from his cock and moved her around, he placed her on her hands and knees and moved into position behind her, he used his right hand to guide his cock into her waiting fanny, she groaned out again as she was yet again stretched beyond belief. Billy gripped her hips and began fucking her, Patsy now met every one of his thrusts, he helped her by pulling her backwards every time he rammed his mighty cock forward, he watched her body as it vibrated as their bodies slammed together as he took her though each of her orgasms, he let her cum three times before he slowed to a stop and pulled out of her, she turned around and smiled at him, he sat down on the blanket with his legs stretched out in front of him, he pulled her backwards so that her bum was in his lap, he moved her fanny onto his knob and eased her down, when she was fully mounted she leaned forward and gripped his shins, she moved her knees and began moving backwards and forwards, he gripped her hips and helped her. Patsy was almost crying with pleasure, she had never had sex like this before and she knew that she would never have sex like this ever again.

Patsy was getting tired, she was not used to such fucking as this but still he pulled her back hard onto his huge cock, she was beginning to think that she could not come any more, she began to slow down and finally stopped, her head hung down and she was blowing hard

"Are you all right Patsy?" he asked slightly concerned, she looked back at him

"I'm not used to this Billy that's all" he pushed her forward off his cock, he stood up and looked around for something, anything and then he saw it, he grabbed her hand and pulled her up onto her feet, he dragged her laughing along to the golf buggy, he turned her around and bent her forwards so that she gripped the front of the golf cart, he used his feet to spread her ankles, he pushed his cock back into her and gripped her hips, he gave her a few practice thrusts then said,

"Now it is my turn, I am going to fuck you to a standstill and then I intend to shoot every drop of spunk that I have as deep inside you as I can" he began slowly and gradually built his speed, he was soon going flat out, now this was his time, he had pleasured her fully, now this was for him. He could hear her making noises but he did not care, nothing would stop him now, he began calling out and finally he sounded like a bull in a field, finally he shot his hot spunk deep into her body, he realised that she was crying out loud, yet he still pushed forwards trying to get that tiny bit deeper.

Patsy had her head hung down and her back heaved as she cried out loud, he pulled her back and gave her another thrust, she screamed out "please don't, please stop I have had enough". Billy pulled his cock out of her tortured body; as soon as he let her go she slipped down to her knees and rested her head against the side of the cool buggy.

Billy picked her up and carried her to the blanket, as soon as he laid her down she curled up into a ball, she had stopped crying but her body still heaved. Billy took a beer from the basket and downed it all in one go, he then lay back on the blanket, he closed his eyes and within seconds he was asleep. He was woken by her mouth moving up and down on his limp cock, he looked at her questionably; she stopped what she was doing and looked up at him smiling, her hand still moved up and down his thick shaft when she said

"There is no-way that you can fuck me again, I'm too sore and I hurt deep inside, I think that you may have split me up there, but so that you never forget me I will give you the best blow job that you have ever had". Patsy true to her word did give him the best blow job of his life and when he came she swallowed every single drop of his cum, she sucked his cock until he was limp. Now they could rest, they lay there like long term lovers hand in hand, Patsy did drop off for a few minutes, when she woke she turned to him and said

"Am I bleeding?" he lifted his head and looked down there and sure enough a thin line of blood was oozing from the bottom of her opening.

On the train heading home Billy fell into a deep sleep and dreamt of Patsy and the sight of her head bobbing up and down on his cock, it is a vision that will stay with him forever. When he woke his mind soon dived into the depths of self- hatred, if he was a woman he would be called all sorts of things, from a slag, slut, tart even a dog. What was the matter with him, he seems to always have his cock out and there always seems to be a willing fanny in which to stick it into.

Billy thought about getting back to the farm and Emma, she will want him as soon as he gets back and then there is Ellen he had promised faithfully that he would call on her, he was glad in a way that Shirelle was staying away but saying that if she came calling, he knew that he would fuck her if possible. His thoughts turned to Jo and Stella, both maybe pregnant by him, but they still wanted him to meet up with them again and Patsy he had hurt her but if he was passing he would definitely send her a message and maybe she would bring her step daughter.

He arrived at his stop and climbed down from the train, waiting for him was brains, he was glad it was not a female, he got into the car and brains said "Are you in a hurry to get back to the farm, only I have found something that you may be interested in for the band", Billy said

"Lead on" they drove for 45 minutes along the highway, brains pulled off at a bar that looked like a barn, parked outside were all sorts of farmers beat up trucks, there were a few trucks and around the side of the building were a row of chopper bikes, they walked into the smoke filled bar, country music from a juke box blasted out, they bought a beer and stood at the bar, Billy looked around the large room and wandered what brains was up to. The music stopped and a man in a big wide cowboy hat, jeans and a silver waistcoat shouted from what was the stage

"I would like to introduce Dana Parks "he began applauding as he walked off the stage, a curtain moved to the side and a beautiful young woman sat in front of an electric organ, she was a real country singer, she was dressed in denim, cowboy boots and a beat up old cowboy hat, under which hung curly red hair, she began playing #homeward bound# Billy was in love again, her voice was pure smooth honey.

Billy wanted her in the band but where would she fit in and what would Emma say, he did not want to upset her, he turned to brains and said

"She is bloody good brains, but where would we put her?" brains suggested that they call a meeting back at the farm, but he said

"You will have to be careful how you put it across to the others" Billy nodded and ordered another beer. When they were back in the car heading for the farm, brains phoned Emma and asked her to call a meeting in the big barn for 1 hours' time. Billy and brains walked into the barn and looked around to make sure that everyone was there, when he went up onto the stage and sat down on his stool, brains was doing something on his sound equipment, Billy waited for him to nod, saying that he was ready. Billy took a deep breath and began

"Hi everybody, firstly it is great to be back amongst you all, when I got down from the train, brains was waiting for me, he said that he had something interesting to show me, he took me to a bar and in this bar a young woman was playing an electric piano, but it was her voice, she sounds just like an angel" [brain's played Dana Parks singing] everyone in the barn was caught up in the special moment, brains played three songs, at the end of the last song everyone applauded and Billy began again

"I take it you all agree that she is special and I would like to ask her to join us but the problem is where will she fit in?" he looked around the room hoping that someone would come up with a suggestion. In the end it was Emma that had an idea and said

"What if we keep the show just as it is and give Dana the interval slot, she could accompany us throughout the show and when we come off at half time, she can then do half an hour on her own", every-one around the room nodded in agreement. Edd spoke up by saying

"That sounds good to me; I say that we have her, if she will come".

Billy and Emma headed back to the bar, when they entered Dana was on stage, they stood at the bar and listened to her sing and Emma had to admit that she was very special, she took hold of his hand and squeezed it, he looked at her and smiled. When Dana had finished her set, Emma went and found her and asked her to join them for a drink, Billy watched her walk towards him and he had to admit that she was stunningly beautiful, she sat down at the table and Billy held his hand out to her

"Hey Dana, my name is Billy and this is Emma" Dana looked from one to the other and said

"Don't I know you two?" he smiled and whispered

"I'm Billy Ridge and this is Emma May Harris and we would like you to join our show, but first we would like you to come to our farm and meet everyone, that is if you are interested?" Dana sat there looking hard at Billy, and said

"Are you really Billy Ridge?" he smiled and nodded but still she looked doubtful. He whispered into Emma's ear and sat back looking at the beautiful Dana, the cowboy whose job it was to introduce the acts called for silence, when the room fell silent the cowboy then said

"It appears that we have the greatest country singer of our time in the room with us tonight and he has agreed to sing us a few songs, put your hands together for the fantastic Billy Ridge" he went to stand up but bent over and asked Dana what her favourite song was, without hesitation she said

74

"I just love the way you sing #good ole boys# Billy went up on stage and sang a dozen songs, he was joined by Emma and they sang duets together. They left the stage to another standing ovation and went back to Dana, as they approached her table she gave them her own round of applause, when they sat down he said

"Well, do you believe us now?" Dana nodded and said that she would be honoured to join them and they arranged for her to be picked up at midday the following day.

On the way back to the farm Emma wanted to make a detour to the hills for some outdoor sex, but he put her off by saying that he desperately needed to sleep. She accepted this and said that she would go to him later if he wanted, he smiled and said

"Maybe, I will text you", he leaned back and closed his eyes. Back at the farm Billy headed for his cabin and Emma spread the news about Dana joining them. When Billy walked into the cabin there were two wrapped parcels lay on the dining table, both with a red bow on top, one parcel was maybe three feet long and the other was a large book size. He opened the card and read #I will love you forever, Em# he smiled and open the smaller parcel, it was a book, a book called #Birds of America# he flicked through the pages and smiled to himself, he reached for the bigger gift to find that it was a telescope, aptly called

"The Birdwatchers Telescope" he smiled and took out the instructions and, began setting up the tripod, when he had the telescope put together he took it out onto the porch and stood the telescope in front of his rocking chair, he sat down and adjusted the height, the end of the telescope that you looked through was built the same way as a pair of binoculars, he looked into the distance and chose a tree maybe 800 yards away, when he adjusted the lenses, he could even see the cracks in the bark of the tree. Billy looked down onto the water below and there were lots of different birds feeding, he adjusted the scope again and he was hooked, he could even see the makeup of the bird's colourful feathers. Billy is still looking at the wildlife when Emma walked up to him

"Ah, do you like my small gift then Billy" he looked up at her and said that it was the best gift that anyone had ever bought him, he sat back in his rocker and using his feet he began to rock back and forth, Em went to him and when he stopped rocking, she then sat on his lap and placed her arm around his shoulders, they sat like this for a while, both enjoying the peace and quiet.

"I love it here Billy, this place is very special, and you are very special" he never even looked at her when he said

"Me, I'm just a country boy who sings country songs, and I don't deserve you Em" she smiled to herself; she is very happy and very contented and maybe very pregnant.

CHAPTER 13

Emma had collected Dana and all of her belongings and took her back to the farm, he had introduced her to everyone, they were talking to the backing singers, when Em said

"We will have to find somewhere for you to sleep until your trailer arrives, as quick as you like Grace, the taller of the The Dark side spoke up quickly

"She can bunk with me, I have plenty of room" Dana looked at Grace in the eyes and then dropped her eyes down to her ample tits and back again

"I think that I would quite like that" Grace took her hand and led her to her trailer. They gave Dana time to settle in before Em put her on the spot, Em arranged for everyone to be in the barn at midday, brains had setup her electric piano upon the stage and he had done his thing with his wires and knobs, Dana sat on the stage and did 45 minutes keeping her audience spellbound, a round of genuine applause erupted when she had finished, When she left the stage every one either hugged her or shook her hand and welcomed her to their little group.

Two days later Billy was sat in his rocker and was just gazing into space when a movement in the distance caught his attention, he moved the telescope and adjusted the vision adjusters until two women came into view one tall the other short, Grace had her arm around the shoulder of Dana and Dana had her arm around the tall girls waist, both women wore long flowered summer dresses and strolled carefree through the lush grass. When the tall girl turned her head and kissed the other woman on the forehead, that was enough to make them stop walking and for them to begin kissing deeply, he watched as the tall girl rubbed her right hand over the other girls breast.

Dana pulled away from her tall lover and lifted her dress up and removed it to show him her naked body, he gasped at her beauty, her firm breasts were the perfect shape and she had a small tuft of pubic hair at the top of her slit, she reached forward and gripped the edge of the tall girl dress and lifted it up, the tall singer lifted the dress over her head and dropped it onto the grass, she has smaller tits but her fanny had not got a single hair on it, Dana lowered her mouth to her lovers right breast and began sucking, her other hand fondled the other breast, she began kissing the black gleaming body and moved slowly down over her stomach, when Dana dropped to her knees, she reached around and gripped her lovers ass cheeks and pushed her mouth to the hairless fanny, Grace lifted her face to the heavens and spread her legs, he watched as the black hands were gripped in the long red hair and pulling her harder into her fanny. Billy was rock hard, as he watched the women, he could not hear what was happening but by watching Grace open her mouth and thrust her hips back and forth he could tell that she was in mid orgasm.

Billy continued to watch as the tall girl stepped away and the redhead lay down in the lush grass, he could just about make out the top of the red heads body, he saw her lift her knees and let them flop open, the tall girl dropped to her knees and lowered her head between Dana's legs, he watched closely as he could see the black head moving back and forth as she pleasured her lover, he could see Dana's hands as they pulled her tits each and every way. Dana came by lifting her head and by the look on her face as she was growling out loud.

Grace lifted her head and sat up and shuffled forward, he watched as there was a shifting of legs, he had never seen this before, he held his breath as Grace took her weight on her left hand as she rubbed her fanny against her lovers fanny, he was fascinated by the scene in front of him. Dana lifted her head and looked at her lover and held her hand out, Grace reached forward and they locked fingers as the fanny rubbing continued. Billy almost shot his load as he watched the women bring each-other to orgasm, a sated Grace flopped back into the grass but he could just imagine that their fannies were still pressed firmly together still twitching, both pairs of hips gently rising and falling.

The lovers lay together in the lush grass, all he could see now was the back of the dark woman as she lay on her side doing whatever she was doing, he did see a white knee for a couple of minutes which set his mind off again. It was some time later that they stood up and pulled their dresses back on, they held hands and began slowly walking back towards the farm. His cock was throbbing as he watched the women as they walked and chatted. His phone buzzed on the table, he picked it up and read the message, and it read simply

"Are you hungry?" he smiled and sent a text back simply saying

"Yes please", he waited and continued to watch the lovers as they stood still and hugged, he heard a car engine stop behind the cabin, Ellen came up to him carrying a basket, she walked into the cabin and began setting out plates and food, Billy walked up behind her and put both of his hands on her breasts, when she did not object, he pushed his hard cock against the ass, feeling his hardness she pushed back at him, he pulled her dress up and bent her forward he then pushed her pants down to her ankles,

Ellen kicked them off and opened her legs, he bent her over and using his right hand he pushed his cock into her. Making Ellen groan deeply as his length stretched her, he closed his eyes and pictured the two lesbian women as they made love, he had gripped her hips and he was giving her a right fucking, it seemed that Ellen liked it a bit rough as she was calling out loudly as he rammed his giant cock into her

"Harder, harder "she shouted pout, as her orgasms came and went, on and on he rode her, now flat out eventually he grunted out loud as he shot his hot spunk deep into her body making the cook scream out loud. When he was done and his limp cock had slipped from her, Ellen still stayed in the same position; he could see her back heaving as he watched lines of live juice running down both of her legs. She finally spoke and said

"You bastard, that was the best fuck ever".

CHAPTER 14

On the bus heading for Kentucky, Billy was asleep when his phone buzzed in his pocket, he took the phone out and read the one word message, it said

"Bastard" but it was followed by a smiley face, which made him smile. Dana came and sat by him and began talking about being nervous about performing in front of such a large audience, his thoughts went back to the last performance that he had witnessed and he had to admit that he had bit of a twitch in his jeans, she reached for his hand and held it tightly, she looked into his eyes and asked him

"Will you stay on stage and sing the first song with me please, Billy?" he nodded and assured her that he would, she kissed him on the cheek and looked at him a fraction to long before she went back to her seat. If he had have just met her, he would have took that look for come here and fuck me but then she was a lesbian, wasn't she?

The show went very well again and Dana was a great success, everyone had decided to book a restaurant and go and celebrate, Billy was sat chilling in his dressing room when a member of security knocked on his door, Billy called for him to enter, the man stuck his head around the door and said

"There is an Isobel out front and she has asked to see you" Billy remembered the last time that he had seen her and said to let her in. Isobel bounced into his room and threw herself into his arms and kissed him hard on the mouth, when she pulled away she was smiling

"Hello Billy, I think that you owe me a good fucking" she said and dropped her hand to his cock. She began rubbing him through his jeans, but he stopped her, and asked her

"Have you got a hotel room?" she nodded, he asked for the name and number and said that he would be there soon, she looked all disappointed and folded her arms around his neck

"I don't think that I can wait that long Billy" and she began to rub herself against him, he explained about the whole crew going for a meal and he had to be there. She said

"At least make me cum just in case you don't make it later "she took his hand a pushed it between her legs, when he began rubbing her fanny through her dress, she hitched her dress up and pushed her pants down, he pushed his fingers into her and frigged her to an orgasm, she soaked his fingers with her cum, then bent down and pulled her pants back up, she wrote the name of the hotel down and the room number, she then kissed him hard on the mouth. Isobel went to leave but stopped at the door and turned back and said "by the way, did you fuck my step mother, only she gave birth to a baby boy, just about 9 months after you played at our house, and the baby looks a lot like you" and with that she was gone.

Billy washed his hands and tried to forget about Isobel, but he slid the address into his pocket just in case he was feeling horny later on, he then left the room and headed for the crew bus. Emma had everything organised as usual and the restaurant was perfect, Dana was the toast of the evening and the crew did their best to get her drunk, she even got into a drinking contest with Edd, let's just say that Edd came off second best and had to be carried back to the bus. They all slept on the journey to their next gig, Emma stayed in her seat on this trip, he put it down to her time of the month, Dana went and sat by him for a few minutes, again she held his hand and said that she was to excited to sleep and that she was buzzing.

Billy thought about trying his luck with her but he remembered what he had seen in the lush grass that day and gave up on the idea. They checked into their hotel at 4 in the morning, everyone was dog tired and went straight to bed, when they woke the next day and had eaten, Emma has arranged for brains and his crew to set up for the show that evening, and as a surprise, everyone else went to the track and watched the horses racing and lost a few dollars. The arena was full and while they played people danced in the isles and sang along to their songs, again the evening went well, Emma came rushing into his dressing room and said "Feel like signing a few autographs only the mayor and his wife are in reception and asking for you, also Diane Riscoe is down stairs and we were running short of merchandise and she said that she would send some along, but she has come herself.

Billy did his thing for the mayor and his group which took best part of an hour, Diane Riscoe had sat patiently waiting for him, they smiled at one another as they hugged, he invited her to join them for the after show dinner, she had not booked a room anywhere so he got Emma to book another room at their hotel, Diane sat next to Billy and by the way she kept touching him he knew that he would have her later, as the meal drew to a close and they made their way to their hotel, Diane walked along with her arm through his, when she thought no-one could hear she asked what room number he was in, he told her and she smiled and whispered that she would see him later. Billy was lay on his bed in his boxers because of the heat, his eyes were beginning to droop when he heard the door handle turn, Diane looked around the door, seeing that he was on his own she entered and locked the door behind her, she had on a white hotel dressing gown, she walked over to the bed and removed it and dropped it onto the floor leaving her standing there naked, she reached over and gripped his boxers and pulled them off. Diane closed her hand around his cock and began wanking it, when she began to get a response she lowered her mouth over his knob and used her mouth to get him hard, she climbed onto the bed and straddled him, she used her hand to guide him into herself.

Diane rode him expertly as she gripped her hair and bounced up and down, Billy lay there with his hands behind his head and watched her tits as they bounced up and down. Billy did not get involved at the beginning, he watched her take herself through her orgasms, when she began blowing loose hair from her face, he knew that it was time to help her, he took her hands and pulled her forwards and placed her hands either side of his chest which lifted her ass into the air, now he bent his knees and began thrusting upwards. Diane closed her eyes and let her mouth drop open and began whimpering, but still she bounced up and down on his mighty cock, after her third orgasm she sat down heavily on his big cock and ground herself into him, she was now blowing very hard as she stared into his eyes.

Billy lifted her from his cock, she looked down at her cum, which completely covered his mighty knob and did not hesitate when she lowered her mouth over his knob and slid her lips a long way down his shaft, when she sucked it made him sit up and growl, Diane gripped his shaft with her lips and moved her head up and down, giving them both a lot of pleasure, when he lifted her head from his cock she looked disappointed and whispered

"Didn't you want me to make you cum? "He shook his head and said "I have other ideas" and got off the bed and dragged her laughing into the bathroom, he jumped into the bath and stood there he held his hand out to her, when she was also standing in the bath, he turned her around and pushed her forwards making her grip the taps, in order for him to be able to mount her, she had to force her knees sideways, once he was inside her she closed her knees slightly, he gripped her hips and fucked her hard, she wanted to open her legs wider and ended up with her right knee resting on the side of the bath. Billy fucked her through another earth shattering orgasm, when she was the other side of her orgasm she asked him to

82

stop, when he stopped she said

"can we try another position?" he asked her what she had in mind, she pulled herself off his big cock and went back into the main room and looked around, she decided on the table and leaned her back against it when he approached her she lifted herself up and sat on the edge, when he pushed his cock back into her she laid down and lifted her legs high and rested them on his shoulders, in this position she could grip his cock hard with her fanny muscles. Billy liked this a lot and fucked her very slowly but ever so deeply, Billy finally shot his seed into her making her scream out loud, Diane even asked him to keep his limp cock inside her, she wrapped her legs around his waist and held him in place, he looked down at her quizzically, she smiled up at him and said

"I hope that I became pregnant this time Billy, I so want a child, your child".

With Diane finally gone back to her room, Billy stood looking out of the window at the night sky, not thinking about anything in particular, his mind totally blank, he was not sure how long he had been standing there but when he finally shivered from the cold, he then turned and climbed into bed, finally feeling totally exhausted. Billy slept the sleep of the dead, and had to be woken by Emma banging on his door. Everyone was seated on the bus and when he walked up the steps, he received a cheer and a few detrimental comments. When they were under way Emma went and sat by Billy and passed him a hot bacon sandwich that was wrapped in tin foil. He was happy that they were heading back to the farm. He had ordered some bird feeders to be placed by his cabin and taking the advice of the retailer he had ordered lots of different foods, to attract lots of different birds, hopefully all of them the feathered kind.

Hiding himself away because Billy just wanted to be left on his own, he was sat on his rocking chair strumming his guitar and thinking about nothing particular when he saw a lone figure walking along the tree line at the edge of their land. He stood up and looked through his telescope to see Dana walking slowly along, as if sensing that he was watching her she stopped and turned to face him. Dana undid the belt at her waist and opened the dress to reveal her naked body, she looked in his direction before she spread the dress on the grass and lay down.

He watched as she lifted her knees and let them flop open, Billy did not need much imagination to know what she was doing. He fought with himself for a few seconds and then went out to his dirt bike; he started the bike and headed for the naked woman. Billy stopped not far from her and leaned the bike on its side; he walked over to the naked woman who was smiling up at him, the fingers of her right hand lazily rubbing up and down her slit

"You saw me then?" she asked, Billy sat down besides her and looked all over her young firm beautiful body, his eyes glued to the little tuft of pubic hair at the top off her slit, she reached out and stroked his cock through his jeans

"Don't you want me Billy?" she asked, he looked into her eyes and thought about saying no, but she had managed to get her hand into his jeans and was rubbing his growing knob.

Dana smiled and said

"I see that you do want me then Billy, is it true that you have a giant cock?" he smiled and said

"Why don't you get it out and make up your own mind?" she sat up and pushed him down and undid his belt and then the button at the top of his jeans and undoing the zip, she pulled his jeans open and reached in and pulled his giant cock out, and exclaimed

"Fuck me, that is the biggest cock that I have ever seen" in a split second she had her mouth over his knob, her hand moved up and down his shaft as her head bounced up and down, she stopped momentarily to move her body around and lower her fanny onto his mouth. Billy was by now rock hard, he could tell that she had sucked a cock before, and he proved to her that he had kissed a fanny before as well, he took her to a hip bouncing orgasm, she lowered her fanny even harder and moved her hips back and forth.

As soon as her pleasure moment was over, she lifted her fanny from his mouth and moved forward so that she had gripped his shins and her fanny was hovering over his giant cock, she waited for him to place his cock at her entrance before lowering herself down, slowly taking his cock inside her body, when he was fully embedded, Dana adjusted her position and began bouncing her lower body up and down his mighty cock. Billy lifted his top half up onto his elbows and watched as the tight skin of her fanny moved back and forth over the base of his thick shaft. Dana made a lot of noise as she was fucking herself, the only way to describe the sound that came from her throat was, if you took a deep growl and added humming at a high pitch you would be getting somewhat close.

As soon as she has cum on his cock she ground her orgasm to a finish and lifted herself from his mighty cock and turned and looked down at his hard manhood and said

"Fucking hell Billy, that feels good when its inside, which way do you want me now?" she asked, he told her to get on her hands and knees and in a flash he was up and behind her, when he roughly pushed his cock back into her he almost lifted her off her knees. He then gripped her hips and began riding her hard. Billy went through a period of self-loathing, and the way that he fucked her, he could have been raping her, suddenly he did not want to be here any- more and thought about pulling out of her and going back to his cabin, but when she began coming again he seemed to snap out of it and fucked her even harder.

Dana screamed out her orgasm and really began thrusting back at him, when he began to meet her stroke for stroke he felt himself heading for his own orgasm, he grunted out loud and pushed forward as hard as he could. Dana began screaming at the top of her voice and as she began grinding against him she shouted for him to pull out, he thought to himself

"It's a bit fucking late now" but still she continued to grind herself against him, all of the time she moaned in a deep guttural voice. Billy gave her a lift back to the cabin and she walked back to the farm on her own, when he went back to his rocking chair, there was a written note stuck to the telescope on it was one word, and that word was #bastard#.

CHAPTER 15

The day was drawing near for him to appear on the Carson show, the last thing that he felt like doing was flying to New York but he had agreed to appear on the show, and so he would go. Emma went to the cabin to see what he wanted to do about flights and car hire. Em did not seem to be herself today maybe it was Emma that had left him the one word note. Billy asked her if she would go to New York with him but she said that she didn't want to go. He asked Dana if she wanted to go, but again he received a refusal. He decided that he had best make the trip alone and that is what he finally did. Billy appeared on the show and it was watched by all of the crew back at the farm. Billy was not looking forward to returning to the farm because he knew that he had caused a lot of problems by fucking three of his friends and work colleagues. When he arrived back at the farm he went straight to the cabin, lay on the table was a note that said

"A very important meeting to be held in the barn, at lunchtime tomorrow. All to attend, no exceptions!"

Billy walked into the barn at midday, Edd nodded a welcome but no-one else did, he took a seat on the side of the stage, Emma had called the meeting and she walked onto the stage and began

"Thanks for everyone turning up today, I will be honest with you, I think that this is a make or break meeting, when we walk out of here today it will be one of two ways, together or apart. We all know that there are problems and those problems are being caused by you Billy, you are either with us or we will find ourselves another lead singer because we held a meeting while you were gone to New York and we decided that we are all basically happy with one-another. As I see it, you have a problem with either depression or low self-esteem and we want you to seek help. Mac here knows people and is willing to help, but at the end of the day it is up to you" everyone was looking at Billy and he looked slowly around the barn at each of the Stoney looking faces and nodded, he said

"I know that I have caused a lot of problems with the ladies of our crew, and I regret not being stronger, but at the end of the day I am only human and the ladies involved are as much to blame as I am, each of you know that you handed it to me on a plate and being a weak man, I ate off that plate, if you want me to leave I will, but I don't want to, I think that we have a long way to go yet and I would like to take that journey with each and every one of you, if you will have me" most people in the barn were looking at the floor, one or two people were nodding. Emma said

"So will you get help, Billy?" he nodded, knowing that he had no choice. Betty walked into the center of the barn and looked at Billy

"I for one am very pleased with your decision because you are a world class singer, the only thing that I ask is this, I for one would like you to find your pleasure away from this group, this may come as a surprise to you Billy Ridge but two of our group are with child, and they both say that you are the father, one of the women wants rid, but the other woman wants to keep the baby but has agreed to come and live here with us, so that she can have the child and keep her job. We as a group at our meeting have agreed that we will take care of her for as long as we are together. Now Billy Ridge I want you to take up your guitar and join us in a song, [she waited for him to take a seat on his stool] she began to sing #Amazing Grace# she was joined by Shirelle and Grace, initially and then everyone stood facing Billy and joined in enthusiastically. When the song ended everyone applauded with not only with relief but with joy and happiness.

Billy knew that it was Ellen that wanted to keep her baby, but which of the other two was pregnant as well, he didn't know. Mac came to see him at his cabin and told him that he had an appointment for him for the next day.

Doctor Alison Sheldon stood maybe 5ft 10, she had long brown hair and deep chocolate coloured brown eyes, she was neither slim nor homely, she was just right at the age of the early thirties, Billy could not take his eyes from her braless tits and in the end she was forced to cross her arms, therefore covering her tits. The doctor asked him questions and wrote down his answers, the appointment lasted for two hours, at the end of the meeting she sat back in her chair and twiddled a pen between her fingers and looked at him until he looked away. The doctor closed his file and said

"I have made my diagnoses Mr. Ridge and to put it quite simply, you sir are a sex addict, a nymphomaniac is what a woman in the same situation would be called, as for a cure, there are drugs on the market these days that can help, but a bit of self-control would be the best way forward. Now you say that you are spending a lot of time alone in your cabin, personally I don't think that that is at all healthy as deep dark thoughts can do a lot of damage, I think that you need a hobby of some sort, painting or pottery something constructive to occupy your mind.

Song writing may not necessarily be the right thing to concentrate on as it can be stressful. We will start with a sleeping pill, it is only a small dose so will not harm you in any way, but it may suppress your sexual urges, which from what you have told me may not be a bad thing" she was writing out his prescription and he was noting that she was not wearing a wedding ring, and her nipples were still rock hard. Alison passed him the prescription which he took and looked at, he looked into her eyes and invited her to their next gig

"If it is an overnight gig why don't you come on the bus with us, we have a great time plus you will see what this life is really like on the road".

The doctor agreed to go to the gig

"If you let me know the date I will book the day off" and that was how the situation was left. The next gig was in Nashville and the doctor arrived early and was taken under the wing of The Dark Spirit, he didn't know what they were talking about but there was a lot of laughter coming from their seats. Emma went and sat by him briefly, just to talk about times, she was about to leave her seat when she put her hand into her pocket and brought out a box of condoms and passed them to him, she said something about horses bolting and gates and left him to his own deep thoughts.

The gig went well and Doctor Alison enjoyed every second of the show, he tried to mess with her mind by singing each song to her, she may be a doctor but he could tell that he was having the desired effect on her. After the show they all went for their usual after show meal and Alison was full of praise for everyone, but by the way that she looked at him, he knew that he could fuck her, but he would refrain for the moment as he needed to concentrate on his crew.

CHAPTER 16

Billy took the doctor's advice and took up painting, but he only painted birds, birds that he had seen from his cabin. When Emma went to see him about a gig, she was astounded at the beauty and detail of his paintings, the colours were exquisite. She asked him if he would hold her, just for a minute, nothing else just a hug. She folded herself into him and breathed in his body scent as she held him, she had to admit that she missed him and his big cock, but they had all agreed that they would abstain from sex with him, just for the sake of the crew.

But she was so wet; she would cum at the slightest touch from this man that she loved with all of her heart. Emma left him and went back to her trailer and took out the biggest vibrator that she had and fucked herself rigid. She had just sorted herself out when there was a tap at the door; she opened the door to find Grace standing there, this was a first as Grace has never visited her before. Emma invited the tall backing singer into her home, she sat on the settee and rung her hands in her lap. Emma went and sat by her and asked her whatever was wrong, the tall woman said

"You will think that I am stupid but I can't help myself, you see I love her", Emma said

"What are you talking about Grace, who do you love?" Grace looked at her

"Dana, I love Dana, you see I went looking for her, I looked everywhere on the farm, as a last resort I went to Billy's cabin, she was not there but I saw something in the distance and when I looked through his telescope, well he was doing it to her from behind and she was loving it Em, I don't know what to do, that is why I came to you, because you will know what to do" But Em didn't know what to do at all, so she put her arm around the dark skinned girl and pulled her to her, "a good cry usually works for me " she said, the tall girl allowed herself to be held and folded herself into the blonde haired woman.

Grace sat up and blew her nose and lowered her head

"I'm sorry for troubling you Em only I needed a friend, I feel so alone at times I just need someone to hold me, I know that I am not beautiful like you and I have not got your confidence, but even I need to be loved" Emma didn't know what to say, because she knew that she could fall into a trap quite easily, she took a breath and said

"But Grace, who has told you that you are not beautiful, because you are

a beautiful woman and when you sing, you have the voice of an angel"
Grace looked at Em

"Do you really think that I am beautiful Em?" Em smiled and nodded
"And I can come anytime for you to hold me from time to time?" she asked

"I suppose "said Em. Grace kissed Em on the cheek before she left, she
was a lot happier than when she had arrived, and when Em went over the
conversation in her mind and hoped that she had said and done the right
thing.

Later that day, the crew had eaten together and Grace kept smiling at Em,
a few of them were sat in the barn chatting and Grace went and sat down
by Em, Em had never been with a woman and had never even thought
about it before now, but Grace was making it obvious what she was after.
But with Billy off limits any port in a storm will do, so they say, But could
she do it with a woman?

Apparently Dana goes both ways, at least with a woman she wouldn't get
pregnant again. On her way back to her trailer Em convinced herself that
she had read the situation wrong and nothing would happen, she asked
herself if she was disappointed?, she may be disappointed but she was
definitely a tiny bit wet between her legs just thinking about it.

Em was lay in bed, not tired, sexual thoughts rushing through her mind,
there came a tap at the door and the door opened and Grace walked in,
she never said a word she just opened her dressing gown and climbed
naked into her bed, she folded herself around Em's body and turned Em's
face to hers and kissed her hard on the lips, and when she pushed her
tongue at Em's lips, the blond woman shocked herself when she opened
her lips and let the pink tongue enter her mouth. The next instance Grace
slid her hand under Em's nighty onto her naked tits, she fondled her breast
and twisted her nipples until they were rock hard, Grace whispered

"Shall we take it off" the blond woman sat up and let the other woman
remove her nightshirt, as soon as it was off, Grace was on her tits in an
instance and Em had to admit she liked the feel of those soft thick lips on
her firm tits, Em just seemed to be powerless as the dark skinned woman
made love to her, when she slid her hand into her pants and felt her naked
fanny Grace moaned out loud, she didn't mess around as she pushed her
fingers deep into her fanny and began finger fucking her, Em had never
felt fingers this long before, she had her legs wide open for this tall thin
woman. Grace lifted her mouth from her tits and whispered

"You can do the same to me if you want to" Em had never felt another woman's fanny before, she knew what she liked when she touched herself, so she supposed that this woman would like the same things, and she was right as Grace began moaning out loud as she began moving her hips back and forth.

Em had never cum as quickly as Grace had, the dark woman had soaked her fingers within seconds of her pushing her fingers inside her, the dark woman's cum ran through her fingers, as she had cum so much. Grace pulled the hand from between her legs and threw the bed clothes back, she then moved around the bed and gripping the sides of Em's pants she pulled them slowly down her legs and threw them onto the floor, she opened the blond girls legs and pushed them up towards her tits, now with her sex at her mercy Grace lowered her mouth the hairless fanny.

Em had never had her fanny kissed with such tenderness and feeling. The black woman kissed all around the crinkly fanny lips before going around again this time sucking the lips into her mouth. Em was on the verge of her first female made orgasm, Grace reached up and parted the thick fanny lips and placed her lips over the blond woman's clit. Grace sucked her clit into her mouth and flicked it with the tip of her tongue, Em came straight away and released a flood of her female cum, Grace moved her mouth lower and pushed her pink tongue deep into the blond woman's fanny in search of the pale fluid.

Em held the back of the dark girls head to keep her in place. Grace had drank her fill and lifted her mouth back up to her new lovers clit, at the same time she pushed two fingers into the blond girls fanny but this time she held her fingers upside down. She frigged Em again until she was close again; she then turned her fingers upwards and searched out the hidden ridged place, which hides just behind the mound. Grace located it first time and as soon as she began stroking her finger tips along the hidden ridges Em called out in another intense climax. The dark girl continued to rub her fingers along the ridges, Em was lost as she was coming continuously, she had never cum like this before, she could die now and she would be eternally happy.

It got to the point where the blond woman could take no more and snatched the dark hand away, but Grace was not quite finished yet as she placed her mouthy over the other woman's opening and sucked hard, Em thought that the thin black woman was sucking the very soul out of her because she could hear the other woman's throat working as she swallowed her flood of warm love juice.

Grace finally lifted her head and smiled at the blond woman and said

"You taste nice Em, now it is your turn to taste me" with that she lifted her knee over the blond woman's head and lowered her dark fanny onto the white mouth. Em didn't have time to think about it, she thought about what had just been done to her and returned the favour, the only difference being that the inexperienced woman had to search for the hidden spot. But once she had located the tiny ridges, Grace let her know by coming loudly.

Em drank her cum and had to admit that it was not too bad, she would preferred have had Billy's but he was not here. But this dark skinned woman was here now, as she hovered just above Em's face, her fanny lips just touching Em's lips.

Grace finally crept back to her trailer at 4 am, she had been well and truly fucked, and the woman that she had left behind was having thoughts that she would never have thought possible. Their lovemaking had changed her for the better, and when Em had got her vibrators out, it turned out that Grace had never been fucked with a vibrator before.

Now watching her reaction to the thick rubber made Em smile as Grace tried to pull away from it, as it stretched her insides for the very first time, at one time Em was not doing it fast enough and the dark girl snatched the white hand away and Em sat and watched the other woman fuck herself rigid for the very first time, Em said that In the morning she would go to the local sex shop and by a big strap on cock and then she could show Grace what she had been missing for all of these years.

CHAPTER 17

Mac had come to the farm with the news that they were going on a country wide tour and they would be gone for 4 months, they had a week to get everything ready and sorted out. Em had been very busy; she seemed to be spending hours on the computer or phone. They were leaving on the Friday morning and so they had a final rehearsal on the Thursday, the whole crew was full of excitement. Billy had studied the route carefully and he soon realised that they would be playing close to where Patsy and Isobel lived, so he had a word with Em and said that he had some family close by and would like to go and see them, so could she arrange for a hire car to be ready at the nearest venue, and he would catch up with them at the next venue. And so it was arranged, he texted Patsy and told her of his plans and could she meet him. Within seconds a text came back saying "Yes I will arrange something and let you know, can't wait" he smiled to himself, neither could he.

The tour was completely sold out and each venue brought a standing ovation, merchandise was flying out at every venue and arrangements had to be made for stocks to be replenished at every other gig. Patsy had booked a hotel and when he arrived at the hotel Patsy was already in the room, she had left a message for him at reception telling him the room number. Billy knocked on the door, Patsy in a silk dressing gown opened the door, and she then placed her finger to her lips and took his hand and led him into one of the bedrooms. A child lay asleep in a single bed; Patsy placed her lips next to his ear and said

"This is your child Billy, her name is Elenore, she will be known as Lady Elenore", she took his hand and led him from the childes quiet room. As soon as the door was closed she placed her arms around his neck, and placed her lips onto his, as they kissed she rubbed he mound against him, she took her mouth from his and looked him deep in the eyes and said

"Give me another baby please Billy", he untied her belt to find her naked, she dropped her dressing gown onto the floor and led him into the bedroom. She then sat on the edge of the bed and watched him remove every item of his clothing, when his cock came into view; she reached out and gently gripped it and began wanking his cock to full hardness. As soon as he was hard, she lay back and opened her legs, she did not want any foreplay this time she wanted to be well and truly fucked. Billy pushed his cock slowly into her willing body, and as before she arched her back as his sheer size stretched her, she wrapped her legs around his back and held him firmly in place.

Billy rode her and rode her, he took her through each orgasm as they came along, Patsy held a pillow over her face and screamed each time she came, when he finally shot his hot seed deep into her body, she received each spurt with a silent prayer that one of his tiny soldiers did its job. Now that he had fucked her she began to relax and now she had become touchy feely, meaning she wanted to be touched everywhere and kissed everywhere and Billy did his best to please her. Just the same way that she had pleased him before, when she given him the perfect blow job,

"To remember her by", she said, the only difference being this time she took him to the verge and asked him to cum inside her again, just in case the first two shots had missed their target. Billy had promised to keep in touch and if he was ever within a hundred miles of her, then he would text her, with a view to meeting up again.

Billy met up with the crew as promised and continued the successful tour, the next venue being in Denver, Colorado. The promoter invited Billy to a party to celebrate the success of his show. The invite was put to him in such a way that he could not really refuse. Billy even said that he had to take the bus with the rest of his crew, but Simon Day the promoter said that his driver would take him wherever he wanted to go, when the party finally ended. Billy mingled and listened to praise from every quarter, a pretty woman with long blond hair, blue eyes and a figure to die for was wearing a blue trouser suit and seemed to be the only person not drinking. She kept glancing at him as if she knew him, he made his mind up and went to speak to her, he held his hand out

"Hi, I'm Billy" she took his hand and held it rather than shook it, she stared into his eyes

"Bob, and when you are ready I'm your driver, I have instructions to take you to anywhere that you want to go" he smiled and said

"Anywhere?" she smiled back and said

"Anywhere!". Billy then said

"Give me ten minutes" she smiled and nodded her readiness.

The car that they were travelling in was very large and very expensive but he didn't have a clue as to what make it was. Bob handled the car confidently, she had removed her jacket and with the air con switched to high, it was having a fantastic effect on her nipples. She would glance down at them from time to time and she knew that he was keeping his eyes on them as well. She went to turn the air-con down a bit, but Billy said

"Please don't, I like the view to much" she glanced at him, but she never blushed. He looked at her again and she turned and said

"What?" he said

"Can I see them?" she looked down at her hard nipples again and then at him

"Help yourself if you must" she said, he reached over and undid the buttons on her blouse and pulled the thin material open, he looked but she had a bra on, he tried to pull it down but her seat belt was in the way, so he slid his hand inside her bra and fondled her left breast. She looked down at his hand in her bra, she lifted her knee and held the steering wheel still and moved the seat belt and pulled her bra down and released both tits

"Happy now?" she asked, he smiled and leaned over her and flicked his tongue over the nearest hard nipple, he heard her moan deep inside, he lifted his head and she looked at him and said

"Show me yours and if it is worth it I will pull over" he stretched his legs out and undid his belt and then his jeans, he lifted her hand and placed it inside his boxers, she gripped his thick limp cock and looked him in the eyes. She kept her hand on his cock and when it began to grow in her hand she pulled it into view, he watched her swallow deeply.

Bob pulled of the road into a disused car dealership, she climbed out of the car and got into the back, and he did the same. She stripped herself naked in the confines of the backseat, she watched him as he stripped off, she reached for her bag and after a brief search she passed him a condom. He bit the end of the wrapper open and pulled the slippery out and rolled the condom as far down his cock as it would go, happy she said

"Do you want me on top of you, or are you going to take me from behind?" he pulled her into his lap and said

"Why can't we do both?" she smiled and reached between her legs and gripped his thick cock and guided it between her fanny lips, she then sank down and gripped him around the neck, she looked him in the eyes and said

"If you last long enough, we can fuck in any position you want". Billy had

95

to move forward slightly so that she could place her knees in the correct position, she began to ride him with confidence, stopping now and then to grind herself against him, when she did this he would fondle her firm tits or twist her nipples, Bob began grunting, the grunts became louder the closer she came to her orgasm, her mouth opened wide and she closed her eyes, now she began using her fanny muscles to intensify her moment of pleasure. At the crucial moment she slipped fully down his length, and gripping the base of his cock as hard as she could, then she would lift herself slowly all the way to the tip of his giant cock and groan deeply as she sank back down again, after grinding against him again she shuddered violently and began riding him hard again. She followed the same ritual this time, only after her shudder she sat still with his giant cock fully embedded inside her, her hips moving slowly back and forth, her eyes closed and with her mouth egg shaped, Bob's mind was in her special place, a place that only she knew about.

They looked at one another and she said

"Your turn Billy, how do you want me?" he looked around and said

"Get off and I will show you" she lifted herself from his huge sticky cock and waited, he turned her away from him and bent her forward, he placed her right knee against the back of the seat and her left foot on the floor, he moved up behind her and entered her again, placing himself in the same position as her, he gripped her hips and began riding her. Bob began grunting from the very first thrust from him, he was soon into his stride and fucked her with long deep strokes.

He could tell that Bob was on the verge of another glorious orgasm by the animal like noises that she was making, so he changed his speed and took her through her orgasm and then slowing down again, he began riding her at his normal pace. She glanced back at him and smiled her appreciation, she then began thrusting back at him as hard as she could, between them they drove her to another earth shattering orgasm, she was now panting heavily and asked him to stop. Billy knelt there with his cock buried deep inside her waiting until she had calmed down, she looked back and said

"Where did you learn to fuck like this?" he smiled at her and said

"It is a gift, are you ready now?" She shook her head and said

"Take it out Billy", he pulled his cock out of her and she turned and looked at his hard cock and then up into his face

"Put your boots on Billy "she said, he did as she said, she opened the car door, the one out of sight of passing vehicles and nodded for him to get out, she turned away from him and still on her hands and knees she backed towards him, he pushed his cock back into her and pulled her back until he held her in the correct position, he spread his legs and gripped her hips and now he began to fuck her hard.

Billy pulled her back hard to meet each and every one of his forward strokes, Bob had begun to shout out all sorts of sexual things but he took no notice of her now, this was his time and he was riding her to a finish. Billy new that he was close, and when he grunted out loud she felt his cum shoot from his piss hole, he pulled her back hard and pushed forward harder. Bob was screaming out loud and the screams brought him back to reality and he let her go, she pulled herself from his cock and lay down across the back seat and cried.

Billy held the distraught woman, he rubbed her back and talked gently to her, she eventually calmed down and rested her head on his chest. Bob looked up and smiled at him and said

"You can take that off now" she said, nodding at the condom, Billy slid the condom of his now shrunken cock and dropped it out of the car window. Bob reached over and lifted his limp cock, as her hand moved lazily up and down his cock, she lifted her lips to his and they began kissing passionately, lips only at first and but then she introduced tongues. He dropped his hand to her tits, Bob began moaning gently and lifting her left hand she began kissing him more urgently, her hand was moving quicker now as it went up and down his cock, when he lowered his hand to her swollen sex, she opened her legs and pushed her hips forward, he slid two fingers into her fanny and began finger fucking her.

Bob began moaning into his mouth as she moved her hips back and forth, she suddenly stopped kissing him and held her breath, a great deep rumbling began in the back of her throat, she closed her eyes and began thrusting her hips faster and faster, when she soaked his fingers, she let out her breath and began mumbling, but her fanny muscled had his fingers gripped tightly. Bob looked at him and said

"Fucking hell Billy do you have this effect on all your women?" he smiled and said

Mostly yea" she looked at his cock which was by now three quarters hard and said

"If I suck your cock will you kiss my fanny" he smiled at her again and said

 "Most definitely". She made him lie down on the back seat and she moved over the top of him, she opened her legs and placed them either side of his head and lowered her fanny onto his mouth, at his first touch of his feather lite tongue, she gripped his cock and exposed his knob, she lowered her mouth over his knob and continued to expertly suck his cock. Billy had to admit that she really did taste nice and each time she orgasmed a tiny amount of her cum would reach the tip of his tongue.

Billy concentrated on his own release, but he had to admit also that she gave great mouth sex; she used her tongue a great deal in her pleasurable efforts. Billy grunted out loud and as he came, he lifted his head and lifted her bottom end clear of the leather seat. Bob swallowed all that he had to offer, when he began to wilt she lifted her mouth from his limp cock and licked her lips and smiled at him

"Billy that was the best sex that I have ever had, if you ever feel like a repeat performance just call me, and I will meet you anywhere in the world".

Back on the road she wanted to talk about sex, she wanted to hear him tell of a few of his conquests, so he told her about Dana and about his three some, he finished up telling her about Patsy. When he had finished she did not look at him, when she said

"I wish that I had another condom, because I want you to fuck me again, real bad" Billy reached over and stroked her fanny through her clothing, she opened her legs wide and let him continue what he was doing, she slowed down and looked down at the fingers as they rubbed her fanny, he watched her smile and pull just off the road, she undid her seat belt and undid the button on her trousers and pulled the zip down, she then lifted her bottom and pushed her trousers down to her knees and turned to face him

"Please make me cum again Billy", Billy reached forward and slid his fingers down her slit to her soaking wet opening, when he pushed two fingers into her fanny, she leaned over and pressed her lips to his. She kissed him hard and the more his fingers moved inside her the more enthusiastically she kissed him, when her final climax happened, her hips were bouncing wildly, she snatched his fingers from between her legs and pushed them into her open mouth. She licked and sucked them clean; she placed his hand back in his lap and readjusted her clothing.

Back on the road Bob was very quiet for many miles, she finally said "No man has ever had that effect on me before Billy, will you make a promise to call me sooner rather than later?" he took her hand and made the promise. She kissed him long and hard and gave him her card, when he got out of the car, she opened the window and said

"Promise me Billy" he leaned into the window and kissed her again and said

"I promise", Smiling, they waved to each other as she drove away.

CHAPTER 18

Billy lay on his hotel bed and smiled as he thought about Bob, he could love Bob, he thought that he could even marry her and happily spend the rest of his life with her. He fell asleep with that same pleased smile on his face. Emma woke him at lunch time the next day, she stood outside the shower while he dried himself and told him that the venue for that nights gig was fully booked and everything was set up ready, she added

"When you are ready, the whole crew are meeting for lunch and tonight after the show a reporter from #Country Now# magazine would like to interview you, I have the number to ring if you agree" he nodded his agreement and she left him to get ready,

"I will wait downstairs for you" she said, and when he did not answer she left him to whatever it was that he had left to do. When he walked into reception, Emma watched him take every step as he neared her table, they joined the crew for lunch and an air of excitement seemed to travel from person to person. Billy tapped his glass to get everyone's attention; he looked at Em and asked

"Is everything ready for tonight?" when she nodded, he said

"Then I suggest that you all take the afternoon off, to do whatever you want, but be back here at 6 pm at the latest, if you need money see Em, now have a good time and I will see you all later".

After the show had ended Billy is sat in his dressing room drinking a bottle of iced water, when a knock on the door surprised him, he opened the door to a tall well-dressed man of his late fifties, and he had grey hair and bushy eyebrows. He also had the longest face that Billy had ever seen, his pointed nose made him look quite threatening. When he spoke, Billy smiled as the man had a very high voice as he introduced himself as Martin Walking, Editor of Country Now.

Billy had forgotten that he was coming, he stood to the side to let him in, he walked in followed by a fit woman of 40 plus, she was smartly dressed in a Blue jacket. She wore a white blouse and a grey skirt, her hair was pulled back severely and held in a bun, she was slightly built with a good handful of tit, her smile turned her from ordinary to very pretty, she smiled at him as she entered the room. Mr. Walker introduced her by saying

"This is my assistant Jean; she is here to take notes". The editor sat opposite Billy and Jean sat well back from them but in Billy's eye line, he asked his questions and Billy answered them, getting bored Billy began looking at Jean and her body, when he looked back into her face she was blushing and looking at him shaking her head. Billy gave her a quizzical look and she mouthed the words

"Stop it", Billy smiled at her, she shook her head again. Mr. Walker was looking down at his list of questions when Billy looked at her knees then back at her eyes and then back at her knee's, Jean looked at her knees and mouthed "what?" Billy chose his moment when Mr. Walker was looking down at his papers again and mouthed the words
"Show me".

Jean blushed again and mouthed
"No" he kept watching her, she was trying hard not to look at him, but he knew that she would eventually look; when she did look at him he mouthed the words

"Go on, please show me" and he looked down at her knee's again. Again she shook her head, but he could see that she had begun doubted herself, she looked up at her boss and then at Billy. Billy was smiling at her; she looked down and opened her legs just long enough for him to see her stocking tops and her white pants, before she crossed her legs again. Jean was bright red now and she was shaking her head, obviously never having done anything like that before. When she looked up again Billy mouthed

"Very nice", she looked down quickly and carried on writing, Billy was in his element now that he was having a bit of fun, when she looked up again, he looked directly at her breasts and raised his eyebrows, she shook her head again but he knew that she would show him something. Jean looked down at her work for a fair while and when she glanced up at him, again he was smiling, she unbuttoned her jacket and let him see the size of her tits through her blouse, she looked up again and mouthed the words

"Happy now?", Choosing his moment again he mouthed the words

"Show me" again, Jean was now blushing down to her tits, she was definitely a bit flushed by now, she reached inside her jacket and did some fumbling about, she did this thing with her right shoulder and then looked at her boss, sure that she was not going to get caught, she opened the right side of her blouse and showed him her exposed breast with its rock hard nipple, in a flash she had put the breast away.

At the end of the interview, the two men shook hands, the editor went out first, as she stepped in front of him Billy felt her ass, he stopped the pair by offering them back stage tickets for the following evening [he took his time explaining what the tickets would entitle them to, all the time he had pushed his hand under her ass and he was trying to rub her fanny, she had parted her legs just enough for him to reach, she ever so slowly pushed her hips backwards]. The editor said that he was busy but Jean took him up on his generous offer and said that she would look forward to seeing him then.

The following evening when Billy went on stage, Jean was where he had asked for her to be seated and that was in his direct eye-line, he smiled at Jean and made it obvious that he was singing each song just for her. He remembered what Jane had said to him all that time ago about the effect his voice had on women and he could tell that it was working very well on Jean. Jean stared into his eyes every second that he was on stage and when the show ended she stood and applauded along with everyone else. Security took her to Billy's dressing room, she walked in and closed the door behind her, she stood leaning against the door looking at him, she then finally spoke and said

"I want you to know Billy Ridge that I am a happily married woman, and I don't know what came over me last night, but I want you to know that in all of the years that I have been married, I have never been as wet between my legs as I have been for the last 24 hours, Now you have promised a lot Billy Ridge and I hope that you can deliver" she turned the lock on the door and began undoing her blouse one button at a time, she removed the blouse and reached behind her back and undid her bra and took it off and dropped it on top of her blouse, she showed no sign of bashfulness as she reached for the button on her skirt, she then undid the button and looked at him and said

"Take your clothes of Billy", when he began to undress she had finished stripping herself naked. She walked over to him and gripped his big cock and began wanking it, he pushed his hand between her legs which she opened wide for him, he pushed two fingers deep inside her and began to frigg her. As soon as he was hard she snatched his fingers away and moved to his dressing table and leaned back against it.

Billy moved to her, as he neared her she opened her legs and reached out for him, she held his giant cock in such a way that she could guide it straight into her waiting fanny. Jean groaned out loud as he entered her as she was stretched for the very first time in her life. She lay back and wrapped her legs around his back; he held her under her ass cheeks and rode her hard. Jean had her eyes closed and gripped the edge of the dressing table, he watched her soft tits as they moved back and forth with his thrusts. She began making grunting noises and unlinked her ankles and held her legs wide open, he took the opportunity to take the weight of her legs on his arms and ram his big cock into her harder. Jean opened her eyes and looked up at him, her mouth dropped open and she began moaning out loud

"I'm coming, fuck I'm Coming" she took a deep breath and began bouncing her hips up and down in orgasm. Jean sighed deeply and looked forward to the next orgasm that she knew was coming, Billy took her to two more orgasms before he stopped and moved his hips back and forth at a very slow pace, he finally stopped altogether and pulled his giant cock out of her body, when she looked up at him he held his hands out to her, she took his hands and he pulled her up. She stepped into his arms and began kissing him. Jean did not hesitate in pushing her tongue into his mouth and grinding her mound against his hard cock.

Billy pulled his mouth from hers and turned her around, he did not have to tell her to bend over, she bent over and opened her legs, he mounted her again and gripped her hips and began fucking her hard. Jean liked this lots and pushed back at him enthusiastically from the off, he was now at maximum depth and each thrust made their bodies slap together. Jean had become very vocal as she was having the fuck of her life, she liked the way he took her through her orgasms at greater speed. Jean had had orgasm number 4 and was heading for number 5 very quickly indeed.

Jean did not want him to pull out, she wanted to feel him cum inside her, and she wanted a child to remind her every day of this monumental fuck. It seemed to her that his knob was getting bigger and bigger as it ploughed her insides, she could tell that he would not last much longer and she held her breath in expectation. She was not disappointed, she heard him grunt out loud and then she felt his red hot spunk explode into her body, she could hear herself screaming out loud but she did not care, each spurt was greeted with a grateful scream. When he had shot the last few drops into her body he pulled her back hard, Jean had her eyes closed and was moaning out loud as she used her hips to grind against him.

When they finally came apart she flopped forwards and breathed heavily, she looked down at the warm cum running down both of her legs and smiled to herself. Not only was this a first for her, she had never cum with a cock before and now here she was having cum at least 6 times. Jean slowly turned around and looked down at his thick limp cock as it hung down with its big purple knob exposed, a huge drop of his cum hung from the tip. She had never had a cock in her mouth before and had always refused to do it to her husband. But right at this moment she wanted to please this sexy man. Jean dropped to her knees and lifting his thick jerking cock she licked her lips and placed her mouth over his big knob, she used the knowledge that she had learned from the internet and sucked his cock for all she as worth.

When he began to get hard again, she was shocked as her husband had never done it twice in one night in all of their married life. She was not sure whether to stop using her mouth or not, the decision was taken from her, when he lifted her head from his cock and smiled down at her, he moved behind her, dropped down onto his knees, he pushed her down onto her hands and knees in front of him., She was shocked as had never done it this way before. When he pushed his giant cock back into her, he seemed to go even deeper if that was at all possible. He gripped her hips and began fucking her hard.

Jean began calling out as he seemed to be touching her very soul, she came and came and came, she had almost had enough, she was not used to being fucked like this. She was sore and she was beginning to hurt deep inside, but she was determined not to give in, she loved the feel of his big cock as it slammed into her body. Billy called out and grunted, he shot his seed into her again and again she received every last drop thankfully. They pushed against each other and when he slipped from her he slipped back onto his haunches exhausted. Jean moved around on her hands and knees until she was facing him, she had tears running down her cheeks as she lifted his cock to her mouth once again.

Jean lay on the floor with her head in his lap, tears still rolled down her cheeks, her fanny was sore she hurt inside but she was so happy, she looked up at Billy and said

"Do you know Billy, I have never cum with a cock before, I have never had cum running down my legs before, I have never been fucked twice in any session in my life, I have never sucked a cock before and I have never been fucked from behind like that before.

Billy I want to thank you for the best fuck of my entire life, now sore or not, I have to go home and fuck my husband, because I know that I am pregnant by you, I just know it and it makes me so happy Billy Ridge" Jean dressed and just before she left she asked him to kiss her one last time, and with that she was gone out of his life forever, very sore but very happy.

CHAPTER 19

Mac Johnson, Billy's manager had called a meeting in the barn for all personnel. He stood on the stage and asked for quiet, when he was happy, he began >I have to report that all of our reviews are first class and from the time Billy appeared on the Carson show, inquiries for bookings have been phenomenal, so much so, that next year in March we will begin a world tour, countries yet to be specified. We have in 4 weeks' time, another country wide tour again,[venues still to be confirmed], but I can say that Madison square Gardens and Caesar's Palace have both confirmed. I now have a team working solely on bookings, which includes booking hotels, restaurants, dry cleaning and anything more that needs doing.

Which hopefully will take the burden from Emma, but she will still be in charge of finance. Talking of finance I have spent some of our money, on which I will show you in a few minutes, but first I want to introduce you to Ronnie Brown and his team, as you know at each venue we attend, we have to rely on that venue's own security, well from now on we have our own. [With that a team of 8 burley men and two women walked in, they stood in front of Mac and they did look impressive dressed all I black, compete with communication equipment]. Now if you would all come outside I have a surprise for you all".

Outside stood a state of the art sign written coach, by the side stood a brand new transporter vehicle again sign written. Mac asked everyone to board the bus, when everyone was seated he began talking again

"At the back of the coach are toilets, a fully stocked fridge with everything from water to beer, from cold meats to microwaveable meals, there is a work surface for food to be prepared and if you look at the back y, I would like to introduce Mell, now Mell will be in charge of this coach, she will be on the coach when you are on the bus, Mell will prepare sandwiches and bring you whatever drinks you require, hot or cold.

Now in the storage lockers above you are blankets and pillows for the overnight road trips. Now in the past as you all know we have had speakers, instruments and all sorts in the empty seats of the coach, but now brains has his own vehicle [he pointed to the transporter] as well as all of the instruments, there are also enough seats for all of his crew and all of the merchandise will be on the same vehicle. Now over the next few days some of my staff will come to each of you to check on passports and any other problems or inquiries, that you may have and please don't be bashful, if you want anything at all, please ask". Mac nodded to Mark Foster the driver and he started the engine of the bus. Mac continued, each seat has its own air conditioning, each seat has its own DVD player and head phones, each seat has its own digital radio. Now if you look up at your control panel you will see a button marked; CALL; if you press this button Mell will know that she is needed. And as expected nearly every man on board pressed the call button, Mell sat there smiling broadly.

Mac asked to speak to Billy on his own, when they were stood outside Mac said

"We have had quite a few inquiries for you to do private parties, now I know that you are not to interested, so I have doubled the price from the last time and still people want to book you. We are talking about serious money here Billy". Billy asked for time to think about it. Billy was about to head for his cabin when Mac stopped him,

"Hm, Billy I want to ask you a favour, it is my brother in laws 60th birthday on Friday, and they have asked me if I could ask you to attend and sing a few songs, we can get Mark to drive you, I will be there so it is not as though you won't know anyone, and you will be paid". Billy agreed to go to the party and sing only for his supper.

CHAPTER 19a

Mark dropped Billy at the front door of the Sea View Mansion, before he could knock the door it opened and a butler opened the door, Billy told him who he was and he was led into the library and asked to sit. After a while the library door opened and a woman aged in her late 30s breezes in,

"Ah, you must be Billy, I'm Ann, Mac's sister, thank you so much for agreeing to do this, it will mean so much for Michael my husband" she held his hand all of the time that she spoke. He muttered something about being happy to be there and glad that he could help. Ann seemed like a lovely person, she was neither slim nor fat she was somewhere in the between, she had plenty of tit and she was pretty enough to look at. She stepped a tiny bit closer and touched him on the arm

"I have heard quite a bit about you Billy Ridge and I hope that it is all true". Coffee was brought in and they sat and chatted about the evening ahead and the 60 or so guests. She also told him that there was to be a sixties disco. But that he was to be the star for the evening and she was so looking forward to him performing. Billy was not slow in coming forward but he could not believe that this nice woman had meant anything by her comment. She also asked him to sing #good ole boy's # for her husband as the song was his favorite. She especially wanted this evening to be memorable for him, an evening that he will never forget.

Billy sat in the late evening sun and watched the guests arriving. He would be glad when he was back in his cabin, lay on his bed in the dark. Ann took him a beer and sat by him looking out over the blue sea, he was not looking at her but he could feel her watching him. Without turning his head he asked her

"Is there something you need Ann?" he turned and looked at her, she dropped her eyes into her lap, she hesitated before she spoke

"I do not want to offend you Billy, but I need to ask you something that is very personal, you see I have heard that you are a prolific lover and also very big down below. When I asked Michael what he wanted for his birthday, he said that all he wanted was to see me happy and as he has not been able to manage to, hm well you know perform in the bedroom for a long time. He wants me or rather you to do it to me, the only thing is he wants is to watch from a secret place. A place that you would never find or see him, you won't even know that he is there. I must admit that at first I was disgusted with him, but the more that I thought about it, the more I liked the idea and now that I have met you I must admit that I am liking the idea even more. To be frank Billy, I have been ready too, well, you know ever since I first set eyes on you". He turned to look at her

"Look Ann, I have come here tonight to sing a few songs for a friend, not to get involved in some other man's fantasy" She had made a great effort with her makeup and her evening dress. She suddenly looked absolutely devastated, he then realised how much bravado it had taken for her to even ask him such a thing.

Billy stood up and pulled her up and took her into his arms and whispered

"Let me think about it, ok Ann?" she lifted her face to his

"At least kiss me Billy" he kissed her hard on the mouth, she instantly began moaning and rubbing her mound against him, he placed his hands on her ass and pulled her hard against him. Ann began urgently rubbing against him. He knew that she was trying to give herself an orgasm; her moaning was becoming more and more urgent. He gently eased her back to the door and leaned her back against it, he used his left hand to hoist her dress up, he reached for the top of her pants and pushed his hand down to her hot swollen fanny.

Billy soon found that her fanny lips were swollen to twice their normal size, he slid his hand along her wet lips to her opening, he then pushed two fingers into her and began to finger fuck her. She opened her legs wide and reached for his giant cock, as his fingers took her to her orgasm she squeezed his cock hard, and whispered

"Please put it inside me Billy, put it in me now" he looked around and said

"But it is not safe, anyone could walk in on us" she looked around and pulled his hand from inside her pants; she held his sticky fingers up and licked them clean. She then took his hand and led him to the back of the room, she pushed a hidden button and a wooden panel clicked open. She then pushed the panel inwards and entering and pulled him after her. She switched on a row of lights and walked down a narrow passageway. She stopped and moved a tiny circle of wood and looked through a spy hole, happy she moved to a panel and touching another hidden button, another panel clicked open.

Again she pushed the panel inwards and stepped into what was obviously a woman's bedroom. She closed the panel and turned around, she reached behind her back and pulled a long zip down, she shrugged her shoulders and the dress dropped down to the floor, she stood there in a wet pair of white silk pants. She pushed them down to her ankles and stepped out of them, she reached for his belt, having undone it she opened his trousers and reached into his boxers and pulled his limp cock out, she began wanking him in earnest with her right hand, her left hand went between her legs and she began rubbing her finger back and forth along her fanny lips. Billy was getting hard, he reached out for her ample tits and began fondling them, when he gripped her thick nipples and began pulling them she began moaning again

"Hurry up Billy get it hard, I want this big cock inside me now".

Billy took her hand from his cock and turned her around and bent her forward, she gripped onto the arm of a chair and opened her legs wide. He put his knob at her entrance and pushed forwards. She gripped tho arm of thc chair and arched her back, he stretched her inner workings to the maximum, making her moan out loud, he then gripped her hips and began ramming his giant cock in to her. Billy showed no finesse, this was a desperation fuck for her, he wanted to make it quick for her, he was due on stage any time now. He was ramming his cock into her for all he was worth when he suddenly looked around the room,

"Maybe her husband was actually watching them now, as they fucked?", Ann had called out twice in orgasm, he was getting close himself, he grunted and shot his seed into her rippling body. She looked at a picture on the wall and screamed out loud, and each time a spurt hit her insides she screamed loudly at the picture. She pushed him back and out of her fanny, she turned on a sixpence and dropped to her knees. She lifted his cock and licked its thick shaft from the base to the tip of his knob, making sure that she had covered all of his shrinking cock. She slipped his knob into her mouth; she made a point of giving him a good blow job. She stopped after a couple of minutes and kissing the tip of his cock she stood up and dressed. She waited until he was decent and then she kissed him again, and asked

"Can we do it again later, please?" he smiled at her

"Certainly we can". Ann took him back to the library and looking at the clock, she said

You are on in ten minutes, just enough time to change my pants and sort myself out" she smiled and she was gone, leaving him standing there slightly shell shocked.

Billy sang his sad songs and looked at Ann as she stood swaying at the back of the room; she was stood next to a portly man whom Billy took to be her husband. Had he already watched him fuck his wife, or was that pleasure yet to come? Maybe he could get away before she traps him in that room again.

At the end of his last song a loud cheer erupted from all around the room. Billy signed some autographs, shook lots of hands and smiled a lot. He went to leave the room when Ann took his arm and led him back into the library. She closed the door and took him back through the hidden panel, along the passage and into the same room where they had fucked in earlier. She checked that the door was locked and proceeded to remove her clothes. She stood there naked looking at him,

"Are you going to strip off Billy?" she asked him, he looked around the room and his eyes studied the picture that she had looked at earlier. When he stood there naked, Ann walked over to him and held his limp cock,

"I had better persuade this chap to grow "she said, and went down to her knees and began sucking his cock to full hardness. When he was hard she took his hand and led him to a deep leather chair, she sat down in the chair and moved her bum towards the edge, she then lifted her legs and placed them over the arms of the chair. Billy went down to his knees, he gripped his hard cock and was about to placed it at her entrance, when she placed her hand over her fanny and shook her head, he looked at her and she made a licking jester and looked down at her fanny.

Billy did as he was bid; he just hoped that his cock did not shrink down to nothing in the meantime. He closed his eyes as he gave Ann her much needed pleasure, when she had cum, she smiled at the large painting of a man of some importance from a bygone age. He straightened up and placed his semi hard cock at her entrance and pushed forward, he gripped her inner thighs and began riding her, at that moment he hoped that he did not embarrass himself by going soft.

He need not have worried as she was soon moaning out loud as his now giant hard cock, was stretching her again. He suddenly found renewed energy and began fucking her with passion, if her husband was watching them fuck, Billy promised himself that he would show the older man how his wife should be fucked. Billy rode her hard and her orgasms were fierce, he slowed down and took her gently to her next orgasm. She had kept her eyes closed until now, but now she looked at the picture and smiled. After her second orgasm with his cock he stopped and pulled his giant cock out, he stood there with his cock on full display. He reached his hand out and pulled her up out of the chair, he turned her around and encouraged her to kneel in the chair and rest her hands on the back of the chair, he pushed his cock back into her supple body and gripped her hips, she was now facing the picture and as he fucked her he had the chance to study the picture. Billy studied every part of the picture while he fucked the other man's wife.

He was so intent in studying the picture that he had missed her climax and she had gone through it on her own. He began riding her hard again and she was soon on the brink again. Ann had been pushing back at him from the off but now she was flagging a bit. He looked around the room and not seeing much to help him, he took the easy option which would show her husband his wife having the fuck of her life. He waited for her to finish her next orgasm.

He then stopped fucking her and pulled is cock out of her again. He helped her from the chair and moved her slightly across the room until she was facing the picture, he bent her forward enough to get his cock back into her, he then pulled her up to standing. Now her husband could see all of her naked body as he was fucking her, she reached up and folded her hands behind his neck. He reached around and played with her tits, he began fucking her hard and she used her hips to fuck him back. They fucked as if they had been fucking each other for years, when she came he pulled her nipples hard, she stopped moving and closed her eyes and let him take her there.

Billy was getting close as he rode her at the same rate, she could tell that he was close and began pushing back harder at him, he grunted out loud and squeezed her tits hard enough to make her scream out loud. She continued to scream out loud, only now it was because he was shooting his cum into her, she moved her hips against him up to the point that his cock slipped from her body. A loud fanny fart erupted from her and a mixture of their warm juices ran down her legs and pooled on the wooden floor between her feet, she turned around on the spot and stood there in front of him, she looked into his eyes and said

"I think that Michael will be happy with his birthday present, I know that I am more than satisfied. [She then glanced down at the floor between her feet] Can we book you for next year, or in two months' time on my birthday?" he smiled at her and said

"But you have not quite finished yet, have you Ann?" and he looked down at his cock, Ann smiled and said

"It will be my pleasure" she went down and licked his cock clean again and as before she took is giant knob into her mouth and sucked him until he surrendered.

They dressed and sat on the couch and drank a glass of first rate port wine, she looked at him and said "For the first time in my life my fanny is tingling after a fuck and I can still feel your hot cum inside my body, thank you Billy, if any time you are passing and you fancy a fuck, just call in" he smiled and held her to him.

Billy climbed into the back of the car and let Mark Foster drive him back to the farm and then to his cabin, and then rest, peace and quiet.

CHAPTER 20

Billy had had the sort of day that he relished; he had not seen a soul all day, he had spent the day painting, strumming, watching and cooking. He was now lay in the pitch black, it was so dark he could not even see his hand in front of his face, he liked it like this, this is how he imagined being dead must feel, or so he thought. Billy had closed his eyes and was trying to sleep when he sensed a movement in the dark room, his eyes searched the darkness for any other slight movement, he then began to relax again after telling himself that it had all been his imagination. Having closed his eyes again and trying to sleep, he suddenly held his breath when he heard someone take a breath, again his eyes searched the darkness, he could see no-one but he knew that someone was there.

He physically jumped when he felt a slight movement somewhere on his bed, he looked down the length of his bed but again he could see nothing. Billy gave a start when a hand touched his leg under the bedclothes; he held his breath and stared into the darkness. The small hand then moved and gripped his cock through the thin material of his boxer shorts. The hand began wanking his cock, when it began to grow, the hand moved faster up and down his thickening shaft until he was hard. The hand moved to the top of his boxers and made its way inside, when the hand discovered his size, the owner of the hand gasped in the darkness.

Again the hand began wanking his cock, the persons other hand began pulling the boxers down his legs; he did his best to help whoever it was, when the hand had taken his boxers off. The hand then threw the bed clothes back, exposing his naked body. Billy reached out into the darkness, but a unseen hand slapped his hand away.

Billy lay there not knowing whether to be afraid or not when the bed moved. A body had climbed onto the bed, he went to reach out again but his hand was slapped away again. The body straddled him; he felt a small hand grip his cock, the next thing that he felt was a hot fanny pressing against his knob, the fanny slid down his cock until the whole lot was deep inside her. Unseen hands reached out to his hands and pushed them down by his sides, whoever it was patted his hands telling him to keep them there. Billy felt the woman's hands on his chest; she then moved her knees closer to his sides and began riding him, hard and fast.

When he tried to get involved by moving his hips the woman stopped. When he was lay still again she began riding him again, he heard her breathing change and become quicker. When the woman moaned under her breath and began pushing urgently on his chest. Billy took this as his signal to get involved, so he began ramming his hips upwards; the woman sank down on him and ground her hips against him. Her orgasm now over she sat still until he again lay still, she checked his hands were down by his side and began riding him again. She rode him with long deep strokes, when her moaning began again, her body movements became much quicker and shallower as her second orgasm closed in on her. This time when she sank down taking all of his length, she gripped his cock with her fanny muscles. Now when she moved slowly up and down she was now moaning out loud as her pleasure intensified, she sank down again and ground herself against him.

When she was done she lifted herself from his cock and climbed from the bed, nothing happened for a few seconds, when a hand took his hand and pulled, he climbed from the bed into the total darkness, her hands reached out and turned him around, the mystery woman placed her hand on his chest and kept it there for a few seconds. The next thing he knew a hand had gripped his cock in a strange way, the hand gripped him from underneath with the thumb nearest to his body. After a few more seconds he felt her trying to get his cock back into her fanny, he pushed forward and his cock slid back into her fine body, this time when he gripped her hips she did not object and she so let him fuck her.

She let him fuck her, and he did a good job to, when he tried to touch her tits, twice she slapped his hand away. Billy fucked her and fucked her some more, the woman whomever it was, was really enjoying herself but she had continued to be in control. Billy grunted and shot is cum into her body making her moan out loud. They pushed against one-another for a few seconds until she reached behind her and placed her hand on his chest, he moved back and stood still, nothing happened for a few more seconds and then a warm mouth closed over his still hard cock. The mouth slid down his length and gripping his shaft with her lips she pulled her mouth slowly up his cock, she lifted her mouth from his cock leaving him standing there.

Billy stood there in the pitch black waiting to see what would happen next, and the truth was nothing happened. She had left him standing there on his own. Billy moved to the bedside cabinet and switched the light on. A pair of white pants lay on the floor. He bent and picked them up and sniffed them deeply, not recognizing the scent he looked down at his cock. Three quarters of the way down his length was a red lipstick ring, all the way around his cock. He stood there totally confused, he looked around the cabin and back to his cock, he felt as though he had been used, almost raped. Maybe that was the message that he had just been given, maybe

114

someone thinks that she had been used and did the same to him, because if he is honest he did feel as if he had been used. Billy sat down on his bed and held his head in his hands and asked himself

"Have I been such a selfish bastard?"

CHAPTER 21

Billy became withdrawn and reclusive and would not go near the farm; the crew were very concerned and sent Emma to talk to him. When she turned up at the cabin, he did not want to let her in, but she pushed her way past him and sat down on the couch. He was standing looking out of the window at his bird feeders when Em asked

"What's going on Billy?" he turned and looked at her and said

"If I tell you something will you promise not to say anything to the others?" Em promised not to say a word, so he told what had happened on that faithful night when his night caller had come calling.

"And you really have no idea who it was?" he shook his head and said

"It's driving me nuts Em, I mean it almost feels as though I have been violated in some way". She sat and looked at him,

"You can't go on like this Billy, to many people rely on you, we will have to get you some help" she said, with that he lay down on his bed and faced the wall, and no matter what she said he would not talk to or even look at her.

Emma called Mac and arranged to meet in town A,S,A,P. Mac was seated in the diner when she walked in, she sat in front of him and made him swear on his mother's grave that he would not repeat what she was about to tell him, especially to Billy. Mac listened to Emma as she told him what Billy had told her. Mac shook his head and said

"Fucking hell Em, it must be driving him mad", they talked for a while longer before Mac told her to go back to the farm and he would be out there as soon as possible. Mac returned to his office and made a lot of phone calls, he took advice from the best people in America, a name had come up four or five times and her name was Dr. Leslie Cottonward. Mac had tracked her down to her home from which she was working; he explained the situation and the urgency of the situation. The doctor lived in Colorado and she said that she would hop on to the next plane available; Mac said that their driver would collect her from the airport and take her to the farm.

Mark Foster collected the doctor and took her to the farm and then to Emma's trailer. When Em saw the doctor she almost called Mac and told him that he had made a huge mistake, you see the doctor was maybe 30 yrs. old, she had long blonde hair and sparkling blue eyes, her body was so perfect that Em even fancied her. Em sat the doctor down and told her everything, even about the members of the crew that he had been with, herself included. Em warned the doctor that Billy was very easy to fall in love with, and that he was a fantastic lover.

The doctor assured her that she was immune to such things and not to worry. When they arrived at the cabin Billy was sat in his rocker with his guitar singing a song called Amanda, the sound of his voice made the two women stop still and listen. When Em looked at the doctor, she had her eyes closed, and her small nipples were rock hard, when she saw Em looking, she crossed her arms to hide her embarrassment, Em smiled and said

"Immune eh?" the doctor blushed deeply and shrugged her shoulders. Em introduced the doctor to Billy and when he spoke to her in his deep gravelly voice, Em thought that the doctor had just climaxed, Em turned away and left them to it.

Em sat outside her trailer and watched the cabin, she was desperate to know what was going on, Em even wondered if he had had her yet. Mac turned up and took a seat next to Em, he asked her what was happening? She passed him a beer from the cool box by her side and shrugged.

Billy sat and listened to the beautiful doctor; he shrugged and nodded in all of the right places. They spent most of the day in the cabin and only the Doctor and Billy knew what had happened between them. The doctor walked back to the farm from the cabin. She saw Em watching her and walked over to her, she said hi and then went on to say that she would need somewhere to sleep, as she would need more time with Billy. She asked Em if there was somewhere for Billy to stay for a while, that is if she can convince him to leave the cabin for a short while, Em said

"there is room in the farm house or if he needs to be with someone, he can come and stay here with me, or I am sure there are plenty of people that would welcome Billy to stay with them. The doctor said

"We need to get him out of that cabin, he can't stay another night in that cabin all alone. He desperately needs to be with other people". Em drove over to the cabin. Billy was filling his bird feeders; he did not even look around when he said

"Hi Em, so have you come to save my sanity them?" Em walked up to him and took his hand in hers, and said

"We are all worried about you Billy, we want you to get better, and we all want to help you" he never even looked at her, but she saw a tear run down his cheek. Em said

"You can come and stay with me if you want Billy, I will look after you", Billy nodded

"Ok, Em whatever you want".

Billy moved in with Em, he slept at one end of the trailer and Em the other. She lay awake and could hear him muttering to himself, she walked to his door and listened, when she heard him still muttering she opened the door a crack and looked in at him. He looked like a small boy as he was all curled up in the fetal position. Em went to him and sat and held him, she sat there all night with him as he slept restlessly in her arms. The next morning he seemed to be a tiny bit better, the doctor came around and had coffee with them; she then asked Billy if he had a car, when he said that he had she said

"Right then, get the keys, we are going to have a day away from here."

Billy drove out to the nearby lakes; the pair spent hours strolling around a large calm lake. He would point out different birds that he had spotted, and impress her by telling her their names. Somewhere along the way she had slipped her arm through his, the doctor talked gently to him before she asked him to tell her about the night visitor that he had had. Billy asked how much detail she wanted, the doctor said

"Tell me everything Billy" they sat down on a bench looking out over the lake and he told her everything, even about the red lipstick mark around his thick cock.

Leslie slipped her fingers through his and looked at him and said

"Billy I have listened to you for 24 hours now and I can tell that the night intruder has had a profound effect on you, but I think that I have a solution if you want to hear it, [he nodded without looking at her] I think that you need to get back in the saddle so to speak, I think that you need to find a woman and make love to her but with you being in control. You will need to show her that you are in control of what is happening" he lowered his head and said

"Will you be that woman, doc?" she sat looking at him, chewing her bottom lip

"If that is what you want, then yes I will be that woman". Billy stood up and without a word he pulled her up and the continued strolling back towards the car. The pair were now seated in the car heading to nowhere in particular, a sign came up for a motel, he looked at the doctor and she looked back at him and nodded. Billy drove into the parking lot, he walked into reception and booked a room for the afternoon, he then parked outside the room and sat there with his hands on the steering wheel and asked

"Are you sure about this doc?" she sat looking at the door and said

"I am if you stop calling me doc", he smiled and said

"Sorry doc" and climbed out of the car, he unlocked the door to the room, he stood to the side and let the pretty doctor enter the room, she stood and looked around the well -used room, her eyes finally stopping when she looked at Billy.

They stood looking at one-another and it was the doctor that spoke first, she said

"You are in control, Billy", he walked over to her and removed her jacket and dropped it over the arm of a chair, he then began undoing the buttons on her blouse, he began at the top and took his time, with all of the buttons now undone, he pulled the blouse open, and looked at her ample tits as they spilled from the top of her bra. He then reached behind her and unclipped the white bra, he pulled it from her shoulders and eased it from her firm tits, he dropped the bra on top of her blouse, he looked from one breast to the other, before lifting both hands and fondling both firm breasts. He lowered his mouth and in turn sucked both nipples.

He then reached behind her and undid her skirt; he pulled the zip down and eased the skirt over her hips. She wore a tiny pink silk thong that was very damp, he eased the skirt down her legs, he held the skirt while she stepped out of it, he looked up into her eyes as he gripped the side of her thong and pulled the tiny piece of material down her trembling legs. The first sight of her fanny made him gasp, she was hairless and has a gold ring through the top of her crinkly fanny lips, he then touched the ring with the tip of his tongue which made her moan out loud.

He eased her knees apart and dragged the tip of his tongue along the

119

whole length of her fanny lips, she lifted her head back and moaned to the heavens and she then gripped the back of his head and held him in place. She pushed her knees further apart and then pushed her hips forwards. Billy licked her fanny from end to end, again and again, he kissed everywhere that he could reach, he then sucked her tiny clit taking her to her first orgasm. He then pushed his tongue deep into her fanny in search of her sexual fluids. He located her cum and took his fill, when he had finished, the doctor was desperate to be fucked.

When Billy stood up she grabbed his head and placed her lips onto his and forced her tongue deep into his mouth, searching every hiding place for a taste of herself. All the time she was pushing her mound against him, he reached down and gripped her bum cheeks and pulled her harder against his growing cock, the doctor was now grinding her mound against him, he turned her slightly and pushed his hand between her legs, he pushed two ringers deep into her fanny and began to finger fuck her. He then lowered himself down to his knees to get a better angle for what he had planned.

Leslie rested her hands on top of his head and closed her eyes, as his fingers pleasured her; her knees became even further apart. When she began to moan out loud and move her hips slowly back and forth he changed his angle of attack. He bent his fingers and turned them slightly, now his fingertips were directly behind her mound, he looked up into her face, when he touched her most sensitive hidden spot, she orgasmed instantly. Now her hips were making deliberate movements and she was moaning continuously, he stroked the ridged place with his fingertips, and drove her wild, so much so that she was now sinking down even lower as she went through the most intense orgasm of her life.

Leslie had begun to lose all control as she was almost openly crying and screaming at the same time, when she came this time, she screamed out loud and sank down to her knees. Her fanny juices ran down his fingers into the palm of his hand and down his wrist. Now when he looked up at her, she was pulling her tits as hard as she could. Billy slowed his fingers down, now he was gently stroking her secret spot, she gained some composure and began to calm down, her eyes finally went to his, she said

"Fuck, Billy I hope that when you fuck me, it will be every bit as good as that was" he smiled and said

"Better" she looked doubtful and began pulling at his clothes

"C\mon then Billy prove it to me" she said. Billy helped her to get his clothes of, he let her pull his boxers down, when his giant cock came into view, she gripped it and held it up, her eyes looked up into his

"I have never had anything this big before Billy [she then began wanking his cock] I can't wait to get it inside me" As soon as he was almost hard she moved to the bed and lay down looking at his giant cock. As he approached she reached up and taking a pillow she placed it under her bottom, when he knelt on the bed she opened her legs wide and waited for him to mount her, he eased himself forwards and placed his big knob at her entrance. When he pushed forward it was like losing her virginity all over again, only this time she was really being stretched to her limit. She groaned out loud and forced her legs even wider apart trying to ease the most beautiful pain that she had ever endured. He gripped her thighs and began riding her; she grunted at every thrust, he fucked her to a most enjoyable orgasm. She looked up at him and smiled, the lovers stared intently at one another as they fucked.

Leslie cried out as her orgasms grew in intensity, she had never been fucked like this before, he was better than she had been told. And the size of his cock, she would happily let him fuck her every hour of every day. Billy took her to another glorious orgasm, he slowed down and stopped, when she looked up at him, he told her to turn over and lift her bum in the air, she sat up and turned around she then folded the pillow in half and placed it against her stomach, she then leant forwards and lowered her top half onto the bed leaving her ass stuck up in the air. She spread her knees and waited, when she felt his knob as her opening she held her breath as his mighty cock stretched her all over again.

When his big thick cock was pushed to its fullest depth she thought that she would choke, he gripped her inner thighs and began ramming his cock into her as hard and as deep as he could, on and on he rode her, orgasm after orgasm flashed through her body. Billy was relentless as he fucked her, she changed position slightly when she lifted herself on to her all fours, now she could push back at him, and the doc was soon in time with this beautiful man with his mighty cock. Leslie liked to be fucked like this, she liked the feel of her tits swaying in time with the thrusts, and she would occasionally lift a hand and pull her right nipple as hard as she could.

She could feel herself getting closed again; she then closed her eyes and welcomed the wonderful sensation. Billy was indeed a special lover, on and on he fucked her, she so much wanted to feel, him cum inside her. She tried something that she had thought about but never tried, she suddenly gripped his cock as hard as she could with her fanny muscles, the first thing that this did was drive her over the edge and give her another earth shattering climax.

Leslie was tiring fast, but he was relentless he slowed down again and stopped, he pulled his cock from her and climbed from the bed, he pulled her after him. When she was standing in front of him he pushed her down to her knees, he held her head and pushed his cock towards her mouth, she looked up at him and said desperately

"But I want to feel you cum inside me" he gave her that smile again and said

"Don't worry doc, I will give you what you want, now open wide" she held his thick cock and lowered her mouth over his knob, tasting herself as she did so. She had sucked a cock before but nothing this big, she almost had to stretch her mouth to accommodate him. She gripped his shaft with her lips and sucked hard, all the time her head moved up and down. He began moving his hips back and forth, when he gripped the back of her head she thought that he may choke her, so she gripped his cock at the base and held him tightly. Billy had begun to moan as his pleasure increased.

Billy stopped her and pulled her up, he turned her around and bent her forward, she then gripped the end of the bed and spread her legs wide. He pushed his cock back into her and spread his own legs, he then gripped her hips and began ramming his cock into her, and she then began to cry out, shouting something totally ineligible. But he was too far gone by now, he grunted out loud and when his first spurt of red hot spunk exploded into her body she screamed out at the top of her voice. For the next minute it was a spurt followed by a scream. He finally pulled her body back by her hips as he pushed forward.

She thought that she would faint, as the pressure built in her head, finally he released the pressure that he had on her hips. He stood there holding her hips and breathed hard, Leslie released her hold on the bed and flopped forwards, he held all of her weight in his hands. His knees began to shake and he lowered them both down onto the floor, they stayed that way until his limp cock slipped from her tingling fanny. She grunted as a fart escaped from her fanny, spraying him with her warm fanny juice, he sat back on his haunches and she flopped down onto the floor besides him.

Billy finally had enough energy to stand up; he reached down and pulled the doctor to her feet. She looked down immediately to see love juice, not only running down her legs but dripping from her fanny; she looked up at him and asked

"Do you always fuck like that?" he smiled an answered
"Usually, but the second fuck usually take longer" she blew loose hair from her face and said

"Does that mean that I will have to go through all that again?"

he smiled

"In a minute when I have had a rest, but first you have a bit of cleaning up to do" he looked down at his sticky cock. Leslie took him to the bed and told him to lie down, she spread his legs and knelt between then, she lifted his limp cock and pulled the skin down which exposed his big purple knob, she looked at it as if inspecting it.

She then pushed the tip of her tongue into his piss hole and wiggled it about, making him groan and when she closed her hot mouth over his knob and began sucking, he thought that he had died and gone to heaven.

CHAPTER 22

The lovers lay on top of the bed and folded themselves around one-another, lay holding hands as they should be after perfect sex. Un-lady like Leslie is now lay on top of a bath towel as the cum is still oozing from her sore tingling slit. She is lay with her eyes closed lazily twisting her fingers in his chest hair, as for Billy he has his arm around her shoulder and his finger and thumb absently twisting her nipple. They lay like this until she suggests getting back to the farm, he looks across at her

"But I have not finished with you yet, doc, I think that you need an internal inspection by my one eyed probe" she smiled up at him and lifted his limp cock and says

"Do you mean this excuse for a probe?" he shrugged

"Give it a bit of hand friction and we will see what happens next" he smiled. The doctor administered a lot of hand encouragement, but it was her mouth that finally worked in getting him hard, she kept her hand moving up and down his mighty cock as she smiled at him, proud of her achievement, he said

"Do you think that you could ride that?" she looked at his big knob and said

"I don't see why not" she positioned herself above his cock, she reached under herself and gripping his mighty weapon, as she moved herself into position.

Leslie eased her fanny down his full length and then moving herself into a comfortable position and used her thighs to move her body up and down his length. Billy reached up and took both of her breasts in his hands and fondled then, meanwhile Leslie had her fingers wrapped in her hair and with her eyes closed she rode his big hard cock. When her orgasm grew close she would lean forward and take her weight on her hands and use her thighs to ride herself to her orgasm. She rode him until she could go no further, she slowed down and finally stopped, but her hips were still moving back and forth, she rested her hands on his chest and said

"Will you do it now Billy, I'm fucked, but I will do it any way you want?" he looked around the room, his eyes stopped at the table, he looked up at her and said

"Ok you get off, I have a plan" she lifted herself from his cock and climbed from the bed, he slipped from the bed and with a pillow in one hand and her hand in the other, he took her giggling to the table, he laid the pillow lengthways on the table and told her to lay on the pillow frontwards, she did as he asked and looked back at him quizzically, he moved up behind her and looked at her position and went back to the bed and took another pillow, he asked her to stand up again, he then laid the second pillow across the first pillow. Now when she laid down her fanny was at just the right height. Now when he mounted her again he actually lifted her feet from the floor, after a few strokes, she knew that she had to grip the edge of the table to stop herself from sliding around, he gripped her hips and began to fuck her hard.

Billy was deep inside her in this position and each stroke seemed to take him deeper, he did smile to himself when he noticed that if he did stop fucking her and gave her individual strokes, he could watch the rippploo movo up her back, but she didn't seen too happy with this game so he went back to fucking her normally. Her orgasm this time seemed subdued when it hit her because now when she came she screamed into the pillow. He took her to two more orgasms in this position when he stopped, he stood there with his cock still buried deep inside her, and again he looked around the room and decided to try something else.

He withdrew his mighty cock and she turned and looked at him, he beckoned her with his forefinger. She stood up and followed him, he took her back to the bed and laid her down again, he turned her onto her side and pushed her top leg up towards her chest, he pulled her into position and pushed his big cock back into her, she moved slightly, getting into a more comfortable position. Billy gripped her thigh and fucked her hard, she had not done this before and she was not too sure about it, but as long as his big cock was inside her she did not really care which way he fucked her.

Billy had had enough and rode her for broke, he stopped and pulled out to the edge of her fanny, he lifted her bodily and placed her on her hands and knees again. He pushed back into her, gripping her hips, he fucked her hard and he pulled her back just as hard. Leslie began moaning; her orgasms came and went, as soon as one had finished another one would start to build. She knew that he was on his race to the finishing line. She hoped that he wasn't cured and would need some more convincing, she heard him grunt and readied herself, his burning hot cum exploded into her, forcing her to scream out loud and just as before each spurt brought the same glorious reaction from her.

As soon as he had finished shooting his cum into her she pushed him out of her body, he looked slightly disappointed. But she turned and dropped to her knees, she desperately wanted to taste him, she closed her mouth over his big knob and sucked for all she was worth. She smiled to herself when she was rewarded with a few drops of his pale cum and became enthusiastic about giving him mouth sex, she took her time and gave him as much pleasure as she could as a thank you for the amount of pleasure that she had received from him.

Finally spent they lay on the bed; she had the biggest smile on her face. He reached for the phone and called reception and asked them to order two pizza's and a bottle of red wine, he also told the receptionist that they wanted the room for a while longer and he would pay him later. The food and wine arrived, they sat naked on the bed and ate, when they had opened the wine, she asked him if he felt any better, he looked at her

"You are the best fucking doctor in the world, but I'm not quite sure that I'm cured properly yet. I think that you may have to give me a little bit more reassurance", she gave him a sideways glance, and said

"You seem fine to me MR. Ridge, but if you are sure you need to continue your treatment, who am I to argue" they both chuckled at that. With most of the wine consumed and both of them rested, he switched the tv on and took her hand. They lay like this for a couple of hours, it finished up with her head in his lap and him casually running his fingers through her hair.

Billy felt that he was ready for round three, he had thought about how he would fuck her this time and he had made his decision. He put his feet onto the floor and sat up; now standing he held his hand out to her. She smiled up at him knowing that she was about to be well and truly fucked again. Taking her hand he pulled her from the bed and took her into the shower room, he turned the water on and eased her into the hot water, he poured shampoo onto her head and took his time washing her hair, he then poured some shower gel onto her shoulders and ever so slowly he washed her body, taking extra care with her tits.

He then poured some more gel into his hand and placed his flat hand on her fanny, he rubbed his hand along her hot swollen fanny and when he bent his middle finger upwards it slipped easily into her well lubricated fanny. Using his single finger he began to frig her, he watched as her whole body became covered in goose bumps, when he added a second finger. She reached up for her tits and pulled both hard nipples outwards. She began moaning out loud and moving her hips.

She suddenly groaned and soaked his fingers; he continued to use his fingers on her for a minute or so. He then removed his fingers and held them to her mouth, giving her the option to lick them clean or to reject the offer. Leslie opened her mouth and he placed the fingers into her mouth. When he felt her silvery tongue move all around his fingers he felt his cock jerk as she searched out her own cum.

Leslie picked up the shower gel and washed his chest and his stomach, she filled her hand with gel and gripped his cock, she twisted her hand all around his slowly growing member, she had worked up quite a lather as her hand moved up and down is now hard cock. He turned her around and bent her forward; she spread her feet and gripped the taps. Billy entered her slippery fanny, he gripped her slippery hips and they began fucking, both very enthusiastically.

They met each other stroke for stroke, Billy watched her carefully and made this last fuck very special, he fucked her harder through her orgasms. He rode her hard in between her orgasms. He stopped fucking her just long enough to pull her upright, still deep inside her he pushed her against the cold tiles, he threaded his finger through hers and held her hands out wide, and used his hips to fuck her. The doctor liked this position the best of the day because she had always fantasizes about being raped and this was the closest that she had ever been. She closed her eyes and took herself to a place that only she knew existed.

She had convinced herself that the rape was real and began making a lot of noise as she was now in a continuous state of orgasm. She didn't know if it was the warm water running from her fanny or whether it was her fanny juices. Finally Billy shouted out loud as he shot his hot cum into her, the doctor reacted for the first time since he had pushed her against the cold tiles of the shower wall. She was now thrusting her hips back at him as hard as she could, they were now coming together and both making a lot of noise.

Billy's treatment seemed to have worked as he was now full of himself, because he knew that he had satisfied both the doctor and himself. They eventually finished their shower, this time he let her use her hand to clean his cock. They dried each other and went back to the bed, rather than getting dressed they lay on the bed and shared a special sensual moment. They could have been a newly married couple. Late into the night they dressed and headed back to the far. Billy dropped her at Emma's trailer and he walked back to his cabin, not feeling tired he picked up his paint brushes and set to work.

As for Doctor Leslie she crept into the trailer and crept to her bed, she had just got into the bed, when a voice said

"Have you cured him Doc?" Leslie switched her light on to see Emma leaning against her door
"Well, have you?" she asked, the doctor looked at her trailer mate

"I have done my best Em" she said, Em stood looking at the young doctor and said

"I told you he was a good lover, didn't I?" with that she went and sat on the doctor's bed and took her hand,

"Thanks doc, we all owe you one, anything that you want, you only have to ask and it is yours".

CHAPTER 23

The doctor looked at Em and said

"Anything?" Em nodded, Leslie said

"I have had a lot of sex today, but what I would really like is to share my bed with someone, just to be close to someone, just someone to hold", Em climbed into bed with the woman and she could smell him on her, and just the smell of him was making her wet between her legs. The doctor lay with her back to Em and Em had folded herself around the doctor, she placed her arm over the other woman's waist. Leslie reached down and folded her fingers in between the other woman's fingers. They lay like this for a good few minutes before the doctor began trembling, Em whispered

"Are you ok, Les?" the other woman did not answer her, she just continued to tremble, Em was having some strange thoughts, the main one being she wondered if she could get her tongue into her fanny, would she still be able to taste Billy. Em lifted her hand to the other woman's right breast, nothing happened at first, then the doctor released her fingers from Em's fingers leaving the hand on her breast, Em fondled the breast making the nipple stand out hard. When Leslie did not object, Em reached down to the bottom of the other woman's night shirt and moved her hand up to the naked breast, as soon as the hand touched her tit. Leslie gave out a tiny moan.

Em fondled the breast and twisted the hard nipple. Em lowered her hand down the other woman's body to the top of her pants. She slipped her hand inside the Doctors pants down to the hairless fanny; she stopped momentarily when she felt the ring that was through her inner lips. She then rubbed her fingers along the swollen fanny lips, Leslie lifted her top leg up which allowed Em access to her fanny. Em slipped a finger into the other woman's fanny and began frigging her, the doctor began moaning out loud and placed her hand onto the hand in her pants and pushed it harder against herself.

The doctor began moving her hips as the finger took her ever closer to yet another orgasm, how many times she had cum today she didn't know or care, she only knew that she was going to cum some more. She turned her face towards Em and they began kissing urgently, their tongues fighting with one-another. Leslie reached behind her and found her way into the other woman's pants, she went straight for her fanny and began finger fucking her. Leslie turned herself around to face the other woman, she removed her fingers from her fanny and pushed the other woman's pants down and removed them, now Em opened her legs wide, the doc placed her hand onto her fanny and pushed two fingers as far into the other woman's fanny as she could get them and instantly began fucking her with her fingers.

Em moved onto her back and reaching down she gripped the edge of her night shirt and pulled it over her head and dropped it onto the floor. Now naked she began to enjoy this other woman who was giving her so much pleasure. The doctor moved around and got herself in between the other woman's legs she took her fingers from the wet fanny and lifted the woman's legs and pushed them open. Now that the naked fanny was at her mercy, the doctor lowered her mouth to the swollen fanny, at the first lick Em reached down and held the woman's head in place.

Em could tell that the doc had kissed a fanny before and closed her eyes and allowed herself to be well and truly pleasured. And pleasure her she did, she took an age before she closed her lips over the tiny clit, the doctor sucked Em to a climax as strong as any other that she had ever had. The doctor lowered her mouth to the other woman's fanny and pushed her tongue deep into the void and located the salty warm fluid. The doctor took her fill, she lifted her mouth from the fanny and moved her mouth to the other woman's mouth, and when she opened her mouth, the doctor pushed a folded tongue into her mouth and released some of the woman's own cum onto her flat silky tongue. Em sucked and licked the tongue thankful for the offering.

Em pulled at the other woman's nightshirt and within seconds the doctor was lay on her back naked. Em began on her tits, sucking and slowly nibbling her hard nipples, she moved slowly down the fine body kissing as she made her way lower, she moved herself between the doc's legs which she opened wide and lifted up her hips, she offered her fanny to the other woman. Desperate to see if she could taste Billy, she pushed her tongue deep into the naked fanny and searched every crevice, she finally located the taste she was after at the limit of her tongue. The back of her tongue ached from the effort of her search.

Em returned the favour of an orgasm through some clit sucking. Em moved up the other woman's body and placed herself between the other woman's legs. Em moved into a position where she could get her fanny against her lover's fanny; they sorted their legs out and began a session of frantic fanny rubbing. The women stared at one-another as they gave each other a vast amount of pleasure, at one stage they linked hands to allow them to assert even more pressure on the others fanny. Both women had multiple orgasms, before they both fell backwards exhausted, they may have been lay on their backs breathing heavily but their fannies were still pressed firmly together and their hips gently moving against one – another.

CHAPTER 24

Mac had contacted Emma to find out how Billy was doing, she assured him that the doc had said that Billy was back to his old self. It had taken a lot of effort and self-sacrifice on her part but she seems to think that it was all worth-while. Mac asked her if she would go and see Billy to find out if he was up to a family show on the next Saturday evening at Maple Cross. If he will do it, I will get Mark to pick him up and bring him back. Emma walked to the cabin, it was a sweltering hot day and Em had on a thin flowered summer dress and a pair of flip-flops. When she reached the cabin Billy was in his boxers, stood painting a fluorescent blue humming bird. She stood there watching him work; she even thought that she was in love with him.

If getting wet between her legs just looking at him was love, then she was definitely in love with him. Em gave a tiny cough, he turned and smiled at her, with the sun behind her he could see straight though her thin dress, and he liked what he saw. Em went into the cabin and took two beers from his fridge, she opened them both and passed him one, they touched bottles and she stood looking at the painting, he really was a very fine artist.

Em sat in his rocker watching him work; she asked him about the gig on Saturday night, he never took his eyes from his work when he said

"I will do it if you drive me" she sat thinking about the doc who was now on her way back to the airport, she made a decision and said

"Ok, I will drive you, only if you will sing with me?" Billy agreed and placed his paintbrush down and sat down on the floor by her, he was looking at her, he had already noticed that she was braless, he could now see her hard nipples, he asked

"Will we be staying over on Saturday?" she shook her head and said

"No it is only an hour away, we should be back by midnight", he looked out across their land and said

"That's a shame, Em" They sat quiet for a while, he eventually asked
"Is the doc gone?" she told him that she had, knowing the answer she asked

"Did you fuck her Billy?" he looked at her

"Why do you ask Em?" she sat for a few minutes thinking about how to answer him,

"I just wondered if you were back to normal, that's all" he asked her what she thought normal was, Em just shrugged in answer. Em wanted him to fuck her so she took the bull by the horns and said

"The Billy I know and love, would have noticed that I was naked under this thin dress" he never looked at her when he said

"I noticed Em, but I thought it was hands off each other around the farm, I mean you came up with the rule Em", what could she say, in the end she said

"I suppose", she placed her beer on the floor and stood up, she stood in front of him for a second, she let him see her naked fanny, then turned and walked deep in thought back to the farm.

Em called Mac and told him what Billy had said, Mac said that he would e\mail her the details, Em had moved to the window and was standing looking out at the cabin. She had crossed her legs tight, she could get a vibrator out and fuck herself or she could go back to the cabin. A light tap on her door broke her thoughts. She opened the door to the tall dark backing singer, Em stood to the side and thought

"Maybe there is a god, after all", Grace sat down on the couch and began ringing her hands in her lap again. Em took the tall woman's hand and took her into the bedroom and closed the door, she reached down and gripped the hem of her dress and pulled it over her head, she stood naked in front of the backing singer who looked all over the blond woman's body, Em moved forward and placed her naked fanny within easy reach the backing singer's mouth. Grace lifted her hand and ran a long finger along the swollen fanny lips. She moved the finger slowly back and forth all the time she was looking into the other woman's eyes.

When Grace slipped a long thin finger into her fanny Em closed her eyes and lifted her hands to her tits, while the dark skinned woman used her finger to fuck her, she pulled her nipples painfully hard. Grace added a second finger into the blond woman's hairless fanny; she intended to take this beautiful woman to her orgasm. Grace reached behind the white woman and pulled her hips closer, now that she was using her fingers in a straight line. Em began moaning out loud and moved her hips back and forth. Grace received her rewards when the blond woman soaked her long thin fingers. She continued to use her fingers until Em was past her pleasure. Grace stood up and removed her clothes, now both women were naked things seemed to take on a life of their own. Grace was definitely the dominant partner because she now had Em on her back with her legs bent up to her chest and holding her legs wide open. Grace was lay on her stomach with her mouth on the white woman's fanny, she was holding the fanny lips open and her tongue was licking between the pink lips, she stabbed the tip of her tongue at her lovers clit, bringing deep moans from E.

Grace then closed her puckered lips over the tiny white button and sucked as if she was sucking up liquid with a straw. Em was close as she gripped the curly black hair of her lover and held her mouth in place until she finally reached her climax. As soon as she had cum she moved the woman's mouth to her fanny opening and held the thick lips against her and waited to feel the pink tongue as it entered her, in search of her salty fluids. Just like a limpet, Grace covered the hairless fanny with her thick lips and sucked for all she was worth. She was soon rewarded with a few drops of her lovers heavenly cum.

Grace was now lay on her back and Em had her mouth around her lovers clit and two fingers deep inside the pink fanny. Em wanted to bring her orgasm on quickly as she had a surprise for the tall woman. Grace lifted her head and hissed at Em as she came, Em went in search of her cum but did not waste much time in the search, as she wanted to give her surprise. Em lifted her head and looked at the smiling backing singer,

"Do you want to try something else, Grace?" when she shrugged Em took this as a yes, so she climbed down from the bed and went to her dressing table and opened the bottom draw and took out a box that was wrapped loosely in brown paper. She then placed the parcel on the bed and began unwrapping it. Grace watched with interest as what was inside the box came into view. Em picked up the long thick strap on cock and looked at the straps to figure out how it went on. She eventually sorted the straps out and slid the straps up her legs, she tightened the straps so that when she let go the thick rubber cock stayed in place.

Grace had a look of terror on her face. Em reached into the parcel and took out a small plastic bottle, she read the instructions and squirted some of the clear liquid along the length of the rubber cock. Em rubbed the liquid all over the cock like length of rubber. When she was done she looked at Grace who was staring at the rubber cock petrified

"I never have Em that is why I am gay because I am terrified of having anything up there" she said with her hand over her mouth, Em looked disappointed and suggested

"Why don't we try it and if you want me to stop I will, but I promise you Grace that you will love it, just relax and let me make love to you, I promise that you will enjoy it" Grace was not sure as she still looked terrified at the thick rubber cock. Em knelt on the bed and eased the dark skinned woman down onto her back, she reached out and took a pillow and placed it underneath her lovers bottom. Em lifted her lovers long legs and held them up and open, when she let go of the right leg, it stayed where it was. Em gripped the rubber cock and placed it at the black woman's entrance, Grace put her hands over her eyes as the blond woman pushed forward. Grace gave a tiny scream as the first few inches slipped inside her easily, Em pushed again and the rest of the rubber cock disappeared inside the tall woman's body. Em said

"Tako your hands away from your eyes Grace", the black woman shook her head, Em said

"But it is all over now, it is all inside you" Grace moved her hands and looked shocked, not believing her lover she looked down to see that it was true, the whole length of rubber cock was inside her

"Now for the nice bit" said the blond woman, she gripped the tall woman's thighs and began to make love to her. Grace grunted a few times but Em used her previous knowledge that she had gleamed from the internet. She read the tall woman's signals and as she neared her first ever climax with a cock, Em fucked her harder until Grace called out, and lay there gasping as Em continued to ride her, now that she knew what to expect, the tall woman began to enjoy it and move her hips in time with her lover. Em took her to another orgasm before she stopped, Grace turned in panic

"Please don't stop now" she said, Em smiled and said

"Turn over Grace, now I will give you a proper fucking" Grace was placed on her hands and knees and the blond woman entered her again. Now she gripped her thin hips and gave her the fucking of her young life.

Grace called out for the first two orgasms and then for the next two she screamed out her pleasure. Em rode the thin singer to a stand-still; Grace had fallen forward and curled into a ball. She had tears rolling down her cheeks; the blond woman sat by her side and rubbed her back

"What's wrong Grace?" she asked, Grace shook her head and said

"I feel such a fool Em, I was terrified of having anything inside me, and now that I have had that rubber thing inside me, I am wondering what I have missed up to now and how can I make up for lost time?" Em said

"What you need to do now, is have a real cock inside you as soon as possible" Grace nodded and then sat up and took hold of Em's hands,

"But what about you and your pleasure, Em? take that thing off and let me have a go with it, I want to do it to you so that I can see what goes on back there". Em went to the draw again and took out a larger red strap on cock, she helped the tall woman to strap it onto her hips, she then showed her how to lubricate it, when all was ready Em got onto her hands and knees. She talked her lover through what she needed to do to get the cock inside her and then how to grip her hips and finally how to fuck her. Em helped her by speeding up on her backward thrusts when she was close to her climax. It took Grace a few minutes to get into a good rhythm, but she was a fast learner and was soon fucking her perfectly.

Grace rode her white lover until she had had enough. Em was now lay on the bed breathing heavily while Grace was taking the big rubber cock off, when she had got it off she was trying to get it up the blond woman's legs. Em looked up to see what Grace was up to,

"I want to try this big one, c\mon Em, help me" she sounded desperate. Em pulled the red cock into position and clipped it all together. Grace was on her hands and knees, ready and waiting. Em took up position behind her lover and when she pushed the head of the thick red cock into her. Grace grunted out loud and arched her back, the blond woman pushed a bit further to more grunting and groaning, Now Em took hold of her lovers hips and pushed forward and sending the rest of the thick cock deep into her lovers body, before she could object.

Em began to fuck her hard, Grace was soon on the verge of another orgasm, the only difference was this time was the orgasm was a lot stronger and lasted a lot longer than any other orgasm that she had ever had in her life before. Grace took that thick cock until she was too sore to continue. Both women lay on the bed and held hands, both now sated, both now sore, both now very very happy.

Em is driving the car to the birthday party with Billy in the back seat, he had positioned himself so that every time that Em looked in the rear view mirror, she saw his smiling face. He began playing a little game with her, every time she looked back at him, he would then either smile or make a stupid face. They had been on the road for maybe 35minutes when he asked,

"How long till we get there Em?" she looked in the mirror and said

"Maybe 25 minutes, why?" he moved his bum forward and undid his jeans and pulled his big cock out, he was shaking his cock back and forth when he said

"I have a gift for the little lady if she wants to take it", Em looked back at him and down at his cock just as he had uncovered his big knob. She looked forwards and concentrated on her driving. She is so wet between her legs; she takes another look at his now almost hard cock and decided to pull over. Em pulled off the highway and before she had set the brake she had the door open. Before she climbed out of the car she reached under her dress and pulled her pants down and took them off, she reached for her bag and searched inside, she found the box of condoms and passed him one. She climbed into the back seat and looked down at his big cock just to make sure that it had its cover on. She did not get a choice of position, he pulled her into his lap, she straddled his lap and reached under herself and gripped his hard cock and guided it into her fanny, she sank down and instantly began using her hips. Em reached up and lifting her top and her bra at the same time she released her perfect tits.

Em linked her fingers behind his neck and began riding him; he fondled her tits and pulled her hard nipples. Em used her strong thighs to ride him to her first loud orgasm. Billy stopped her and slid his body sideways, so that he could lie down, she changed her position and now they helped each other as she rode him. He bent his knees and waited for his moment, he waited for her to lean slightly forward and rest her hands on his chest. She closed her eyes and began moaning, now he could join in. He began ramming his giant cock upwards as she dropped down, this was all too much for her and she cried out another orgasm, she sank down a ground her fanny against him, she then said

"I've missed your big cock Billy" and began to ride him again. Em rode him to her third orgasm before she lifted herself from his cock. She checked that the condom was still in place, she pushed his long legs off the wide seat and getting on her hands and knees she turned away from him. Billy moved around and got in place behind her and pushed his giant cock back into her, as soon as he began fucking her he could hear her nails as they scratched the leather seat. They were in such a rhythm that the big car was rocking from side to side. Billy was on the verge of shooting his load, as he increased his thrusts, she began sliding across the seat until her head was pushed against the door.

Billy was in the final throws of his journey and he was ramming his big cock into her. Em was banging her head against the door but he did not care. He finally shot his load deep into her and as he pushed forward her head was now pushed flat against the door but still she managed to push back at him, giving herself another wonderful orgasm. While they pushed against each other Em could see the clock and they were now running late. Even though she did not want to she pushed him back and out of her, she pushed a bunch of tissues between her legs and pulled her pants on, she put her tits away and climbed back into the driving seat and resumed their journey.

When they were maybe only half a mile from the house, Billy was still lay naked on the back seat of the car, she looked at him and his limp cock as it lay across his thigh

"Get dressed Billy, we are almost there and we are late" for the first time, Billy was not really interested and would have liked nothing better than to have returned to his cabin and locked himself away, then the beautiful doc would come back. Em encouraged him to dress and take up his guitar, she sat and listened to him sing his sad songs. The woman whose birthday it was was 50 years old on this very day and she was in love with Billy. She sang along to each of his sad songs, which she had listened to a thousand times before. Em collected the rather large cheque and they began their journey back to the farm. Billy was covered with a blanket in the back seat, snoring lightly.

Em stopped the car by his cabin, she woke him and told him they were home, he sat up and looked at the cabin and asked

"So you want to stay with me then, Em?" she was tempted but she had no-more condoms with her and she knew if she slept with him, she would let him fuck her with no protection and she did not want to end up pregnant again, so she sadly declined the offer.

CHAPTER 25

The cook Ellen Burrows who now had an assistant named Mary because Ellen was over 8 months into her pregnancy and was having trouble reaching anything, she was that big. Mary way 18 years old, pretty and petite with tiny tits, the first thing Ellen had said to her was to give her a warning about Billy and his lecherous ways. But she knew that once he has clapped eyes on her he would want her.

Plans were being made for a nationwide tour, Mac, Billy and Em were sat in Billy's cabin sorting out the best route to take, that would take them from venue to venue. Mac told them that he had requests for 8 individual nights during the tour if Billy was interested, and they were all top dollar events. The only problem being that they would have to take a car on tour with them, to get to these venues. He went on to say that they could share the car driving between them or they could take on another driver, it was up to them. Billy's thoughts turned to Bob, Simon Day's driver, yes that would be good, he thought to himself. But he would sound her out before he said anything; instead he asked how they were doing financially. Em said

"I often wondered when you would ask, only you never have, in all of the time that we have all been together, not one person has asked, I could have taken millions and no-one would have been any the wiser. But seeing that you ask, you are already a very rich man, and the rest of us are doing ok as well, the financial situation is due to be checked soon, for the IRS, but there is nothing to worry about. I have everything under control, the only thing that they will not know about are the private function's that you attend, all of that money goes into another account that we use for running the farm. All in all we are doing very nicely thank you" Billy nodded and thanked them both for what they had done.

Em came rushing into the cabin slightly out of breath, calling

"Billy, Billy where are you?" he was lay on the bed with his eyes closed, at her shout he opened his eyes and when she entered the room and walked up to him. He reached out and grabbed her and pulled her down onto the bed, in a flash he had his lips pressed against her and her tits out, he was rolling her nipple when she pulled herself away from him. She stood with her hands on her hips looking down at him,

"Get up Billy we have an emergency job on, we have got to get into town as soon as possible to open a mall. They have been let down and are willing to pay well, providing that we get you there in 45 minutes" she said all of this and he lay there with a smile on his face

"Are you going like that?" he asked, she realised that she standing there with her tits out. Within five minutes they were in the car and heading to the mall. They were met by a smartly dressed woman, with short blond hair, the brightest blue eyes that he had ever seen and she had a body to die for. On her name tag it said #Milly Revell. Store Manager.# she took his arm and led him into an office. She stood close to him and adjusted his string tie and said

"All I want you to say is. I declare this mall open. And cut the ribbon, smile for the cameras and that is that. Then you can go or you can join myself and the management team for drinks up here in the offices", he looked around her office and saw a door off to one side, he walked over and opened the door, looking inside he saw a washroom and a dressing table.

Billy walked into the room and stood looking at himself in the mirror. She came in and stood by his side also looking in the same mirror. She bent forwards and was doing something to her eyelashes. Billy stood up and looked at her rear end as she was bent over. He placed his hands on her hips and rubbed his cock against her ass. She looked at him in the mirror, but did not move, he reached under her and felt her firm breast, she looked down at his hand as it was trying to get inside her blouse. Milly did a quick turn and spun away from him, she was blushing when she said with a croaky voice

"I am a married woman, thank you" she said, he moved a step towards her and pushed her against the dressing table and said

"I saw the ring [he took her hand and placed it on his cock] but I bet he ain't got a cock like that, has he?" she was holding his cock through his jeans, her hand was moving but only slightly. Billy was hitching her skirt up to above her hips and she was letting him, he and his hand between her legs and was rubbing her fanny lips through her pants, her hand was now moving quicker on his growing cock when a voice called out

"Milly, are you in there?" she pulled her skirt down quickly and called out

"I will be there in a second" she ran her fingers through her hair and looked down at his almost hard cock; she reached out and felt it again and then turned and walked out of the door. He could hear them talking but could not make out what they were saying. Milly knocked the door and said

"Are you ready Billy?" he held his hat over his slowly shrinking cock and followed the two women down to the entranced to the mall, it seemed a bit disorganized at first but Milly soon had everything under control. Billy did what he had to do and told Em that he had to meet the management team for drinks but he wouldn't be long.

Drinks were flowing freely and everyone was full of excitement about the opening, after a reasonable amount of time Milly took his arm and said

"Let me show you around" she took his arm and led him from the party. They walked down a flight of stairs and into the mall itself, they intended to sell everything that you could possibly think of. Milly took a ring of keys from her bag and opened a white door, she held it open and let him walk in, she then closed and locked the door behind herself and placed her bag on a table

"This is the security room" she walked over to him and placed her fingers at the top of her blouse and began undoing the buttons she pulled the blouse open and reached for the button on the back of her skirt, he reached and pulled her bra up and released s nice pair if firm tits. He fondled both tits and rubbed his thumb over both nipples bringing both to full hardness. She let her skirt fall to the floor and leaned back against the table

"Show me your big cock then, Billy" he stood back and undid his belt and the top of his trousers, he pulled the zip down and pulled his jeans open, he reached inside and pulled his giant cock out and watched her eyes grow very big. She reached out and took it from his hand and began wanking it, he reached forward and gripped the side of her pants and pushed them down, for him to get them to fall down her legs she had to open them slightly. Her red pants fell to the floor and she lifted her feet from them and parted her legs slightly. His cock was growing nicely in her hand and her eyes were locked onto his giant knob which she had uncovered.

Billy lifted her bum onto the desk, she opened her legs wide and he stepped between them, she lifted her knees and held them wide open, meanwhile he was rubbing his big knob up and down her fanny lips. When his knob moved over her entrance she pulled him forwards, his giant cock slipped inside her, she lay back and let him push his massive cock into her. She groaned out loud as he stretched her wide. She stretched her legs out and folded her ankles behind his back, he gripped her thighs and began to really fuck her hard, her eyes closed and she said

"That's it Billy fuck me as hard as you want, I'm on the pill so fill me up with

141

your cum". Within a minute he had her on the verge of her first of many orgasms, she groaned all of the time that he fucked her, she arched her back and began to thrust her hips up and down as her violent orgasm came and went. Billy took her to three orgasms before he stopped and pulled out of her, she lifted her head and looked at him

"You haven't cum have you?" she asked, he shook his head and smiled, he then held his hand out to her, he pulled her up to standing and said

"Take everything off, I want you naked" she stood there and removed every item of clothing, he looked at her perfect body and turned her around, he pushed her top half forward and he pushed his big cock between her legs. She began rubbing her fanny along his thick shaft, he stopped her when he gripped her left hip, she spread her legs and pushed her hips back, he entered her again and gripped her other hip.

Now Billy rode her hard, he pulled her back as he thrust forwards, he could see her reflection in a screen that was in front of her. Milly was having the time of her life, she was not used to getting fucked like this and she hoped that it would go on for hours yet. Billy took her to more orgasms in this position; he stopped and pulled her up to standing, when he began to fuck her again she pushed her hips back, he could see her watching them fuck in the screen in front of her,

"Play with your tits "he whispered, she did not hesitate and took a tit in both hands and began fondling them, he watched her closely, choosing his moment he whispered

"Now open your fanny lips and rub your clit" again she did not hesitate and did as he asked. Milly was now into this form of voyeurism, she was doing things with this stranger that she would never ever do with her husband, never in a thousand years. Her thought returned to the fuck when she sensed that he was about to cum, his knob seemed to have swollen to twice its normal size as it stretched her even further. She knew that he was holding his breath, suddenly he grunted out loud and pushed hard into her, his cum when it erupted inside her was hot, and with each spurt she felt the warmth spread through her body, sending a warm feeling spreading around her heart.

He finished spurting and stood there with his huge cock still buried deep inside her, she was grinding back against him trying to give herself another beautiful orgasm. It came but only just before his big cock slipped from her fanny, she felt his cum running down both of her legs onto her feet, he turned her around, she then looked into his eyes and said

"Thank you Billy at last I can say that I have been properly fucked, will you come and see me again, I will be here most days, we can do it here or we can go for a ride somewhere, where ever you want day or night" just before he pushed her down to her knees, he said

"I will come and see you Milly, maybe sooner than you think " she looked into his eyes as she let him push her down, she had never had a cock in her mouth before, but for this man who had given her so much pleasure, she would do anything because she wanted him to come back and fuck her again. She closed her mouth over his giant knob, she had seen some woman on her husbands DVD doing the same thing, so she did as that other woman had done and hoped that it was right, he spread his legs and gripped the back of her head, he began moving his hips back and forth, she was really enjoying this and was letting him go further and further down her throat, when she thought that she may choke she placed her hand on the base of his shaft to stop him going to deep. Milly wasn't sure but she thought that he was getting hard again, when he began stretching her mouth she lifted her mouth from him and replaced her mouth with her hand, her hand moved up and down his cock, as she looked up at him expectantly.

Billy removed her hand from his cock and moved behind her, he pushed her forwards onto her hands and knees. She knew what was coming and parted her knees and waited to be mounted again, he pushed his cock into her tender body; she arched her back again and groaned out loud. He seemed even bigger this time and he was definitely deeper. This time it was all about him, he had given her her pleasure, but she would take as much pleasure as she could. So she closed her eyes and drifted to a place that she had never been to before. Her orgasms were strong but were over to quick as the next one built, he never changed pace at any time during this fuck. When she heard him finally grunt and begin shooting his hot spunk into her now tortured body, she wasn't sure whether she was relieved or not.

She ground herself against him and hoped that her cum glands or wherever the cum comes from had just one more orgasm left, as she was trying her hardest to bring it forth. She got her wish and her last orgasm was slow and long, and when his cock slipped from her, she turned at once and took him into her mouth, suddenly she was desperate to taste his cum. She sucked a few drops from his cock and savored the taste, it was a taste that she would never forget, but she would only ever suck this beautiful man's cock.

CHAPTER 26

Billy lay on the backseat of the car as Em drove back to the farm, she was extremely jealous as she knew that he had been fucking someone else. She had been hoping that he would fuck her on the way home. They never spoke a word on the journey back to the farm, she stopped outside the cabin, he sat up and looked out of the window. He thanked her but she did not answer him, he stood and watched her drive back to her trailer, he saw her look back at his cabin before she turned and went inside. Billy lay on his bed with a smile on his face, he could quite easily fall in love with the lovely Milly, Billy knew that she was already in love with him. Billy fell asleep thinking about Milly, in his mind's eye he could still see her perfect naked body bent over in front of him.

Billy stayed in his cabin and painted, he had begun a portrait of Milly, to remember her he only had to close his eyes. It took him hours to get her eye colour right, but when he had the colour right it was as if the painting had finally come to life. He would not embarrass her by putting her trimmed fanny hair in the picture so he used a discreetly placed hand, but he knew it was there and he planned on seeing it again, very soon. The next day Billy took the car and went to the Mall, he had timed it so that he arrived just before closing time. He asked a member of staff to let the manager that he was there. He was told to wait and she would be down shortly, he waited as the store closed.

Milly came and let all of the staff out, she said goodnight to each member of staff, the lovers walked around the building checking that the mall was securely locked. Finally happy she placed her arm through his and led him towards the back of the building. She took him through a door marked; #staff only;# inside was a large area where the staff made up the furniture, against the wall were a small pile of mattresses, she stopped by them and began removing her clothes, he stood and watched her remove each article of clothing, she sat on the edge of the mattresses and opened her legs

"Will you do something for me Billy, only I may never get the chance again, will you kiss my fanny, I have always wanted someone to do it, but no-one has ever offered" he looked at her swollen fanny lips and said

"It will be my pleasure mam" he went down to his knees in front of her, he gently pushed her legs further apart, he moved his head forwards and gave her a slow lick with a flat tongue, starting at the bottom by her opening, moving slowly upwards to where her slit ended, she moaned out loud, so he repeated the action over and over again. He stopped and reached up and parted her fanny lips, he sucked the crinkly inner lips into his mouth, he moved his mouth around so that each part of her lips had been in his mouth. Billy then began flicking the tip of his tongue at her clit.

Milly gripped the back of his head and opened her legs as wide as she could, he reached up and pushed two fingers into her fanny opening, he began moving the fingers slowly back and forth, at the same time he closed his lips around her tiny clit and began sucking. Milly had suddenly become very vocal as she neared her climax; he sucked harder and moved his fingers faster, this action forcing her to scream out her orgasm. Before she had begun to calm down from her pleasure, he had stood up, he still had his fingers buried deep in her fanny, he now turned his fingers so that they faced the back of her mound. He gently touched the secreted ridged place, she moaned out loud and with her left hand she pulled his forehead to hers.

She pulled their heads together and with her right hand she undid his jeans and gripped his hard cock and began to wank it furiously. He took her to two glorious orgasms, she had soaked his hand twice and his palm was full of her cum, he pulled his fingers from her fanny and lowered himself back down, he pushed his tongue into her fanny and tasted her salty cum. She was now lay flat on her back holding her legs as high and wide as she could. She had a deep gurgling sound coming from her throat; he closed his lips over her fanny and sucked for all he was worth.

Her cum was slowly seeping from her and entering his mouth, he took his fill and the stood up, he pushed his hard cock into her, she lifted her legs onto his shoulders; he gripped her thighs and gave her a fucking that she would never forget. He fucked her in this position until he shot his hot seed into her body, she screamed out loud and in this large building the scream sounded so loud that he was sure that it would be heard outside.

CHAPTER 27

Back in his cabin he is working on his portrait, even if he said so himself it was a true likeness. He was getting hard just thinking about her. Billy was standing in his boxers painting; he was humming a tune that his daddy used to hum, but he had never known the name of the tune. Maybe he would get around to writing some lyrics one day, to go with the tune. There was a light tap on the doorframe, he looked to see Grace, the tall thin backing singer, he waved her in. She then walked over and stood by his side and looked at the painting

"She is beautiful Billy, who is she?" he looked at her and said

"This is Milly, I met her two weeks ago and she made a good impression on me, and I decided that I would paint her. I have never painted a portrait before and I must say that I am very pleased with the way it has turned out" she swayed a few times and said

"Would you paint me Billy?" he looked into her eyes and said

"I don't think that I am good enough to paint such beauty as yours" she looked at the painting and seeing that the woman was naked, she said

"You can do me naked if it will help?" he looked at her thin body, his eyes locked onto her hard nipples. Grace gripped the top of her dress and lifted it over her head and dropped it onto a chair. She stood there in a pink thong, she then sat down on his couch and made some poses, he stood looking at her chocolate coloured skin, he nipples were long and thin, he had not realised it but his giant cock was almost hard and pushing his boxers tight. She looked at his hard cock, and said

"I have never had a real one of those Billy, can I see it please" his eyes were still looking at her nipples and without really thinking about it he pushed his boxers down, his hard cock sticking out in front of him, her eyes were like saucers.

Grace had come here hoping to have a real man or the first time, now that she could see his massive cock she was not so confident. He tried to put her off by saying

"But wasn't it agreed between everyone that we stay away from each other" she placed her fingers into the side of the thong and pushed it down her long thin legs

"Just don't make me pregnant and I won't say a word to anyone" with that she lay back on the couch and looked up at him. She had one foot on the floor and one foot on the couch, he looked down at the chocolate coloured fanny, he reached out and held his hand out to her, she knew that if she took his hand, he would fuck her. But then that is what she had come for. Grace reached out and took his hand; he pulled her up and took her into his bedroom.

He closed the door, the backing singer went and lay down on the bed, she watched his hard cock as he went to her, he reached out and gripped her legs and pulled her lightweight body and moved it easily, into such a position that her body was right in front of him. Grace was to low so he reached up and taking a pillow he pushed it under her bum and gripping her left leg with his right hand, he then used his left hand to guide his big cock into her slight body. Grace grimaced hard as she thought a fence pole was being forced up her fanny, her hands were clenched together as well as her teeth, he said

"You can relax now grace, it's all inside you now, now you can relax and enjoy it from here on in "he held her thin legs over his arms and began to slowly move his cock back and forth.

Grace kept her face screwed up for the first few strokes, then she slowly relaxed and closed her eyes, when he began to thrust harder, she was forced to grip the edge of the bed to stop herself from sliding away from him. Her eyes suddenly opened wide and her hips began to bounce up and down

"Oh fuck I'm coming" and she did, she came with such a look of pleasure on her face that it made him smile, he rode her at a sedate pace as it was her first time, she looked up at him and said

"You won't break me Billy, you can do it harder, the harder the better" she closed her eyes again and he felt her body relax, so he gave her a real good fucking, she came and came, he thought about turning her over but he was enjoying watching her small tits bouncing back and forth, her nipples were still the longest nipples that he had ever seen. He looked down at her face and said

"Do you want me to shoot it over your tits or do you want to swallow it?" she never opened her eyes, she just said "tits" he told her to lean on her elbows and watch him cum. Grace was watching him fuck her, this was better than with a woman for her, and there is the risk of getting pregnant. She watched his face as he held his head back, he grunted and pulled his cock out of her and held it over her stomach, his right hand was flying up and down his shaft, he gave a second grunt and he shot his seed up her body all over her tits, she smiled widely as each spurt exploded from his big cock. She used her right hand to rub his cum all over her tits, she closed her eyes and he was sure that she was mid orgasm.

Billy held his still almost hard cock pointing at her, she looked at his huge purple head, he didn't say anything but she knew what he wanted and she was willing to try new things. So she bent her thin body and closed her mouth over his knob, she guessed the rest and what she did not guess he encouraged her to try it, when a few spots of cum came from him she was surprised at the taste and decided that she quite liked it. He had placed her hand around his shaft and had moved it up and down, she was giving him a lot of pleasure and when he pushed two fingers deep into her fanny and began to finger fuck her.

She was suddenly a very happy woman and she wondered what she had been so worried about, but there was one thing for sure, she would not be going back to women, except maybe Emma because she was special.

CHAPTER 28

Em was sat in the cabin watching him as he concentrated on his painting, he was spending a lot of time on Graces hair, Em said

"I told her that she needed to try a real man, what I did not expect was for her to fuck my man" he did not turn and look at her when he said

"I ain't anybody's man Em, you know that, you know that I can't be faithful to one woman, I ain't built that way" he continued to paint when she said

"Will you paint me Billy? "he looked back at her, she was lay naked, she lay on her left side, with her with her right foot resting on her left knee, her naked fanny on clear view. She reached down and lazily ran a finger along her fanny lips

"Is this what Grace did Billy?" she asked, he shook his head

"Why are you doing this Em?" he asked, as a single tear ran down her cheek

"you must know that I am deeply in love with you Billy and I would do anything that you ask at any time, you don't have to love me back, I just want you to come looking for me for a change, instead of me coming looking for you all of the time, I mean it is not much to ask, is it?". He sat down by her and took her hand,

"I am so sorry Em, I never even gave it a thought, you see I think the problem is that I take you for granted, I know that it is wrong. I know that now and I never meant to hurt you Em, I'm sorry". He put his paintbrush down and walked out of the cabin, he suddenly wanted to be on his own; he got on his dirt-bike and rode away, leaving the farm far behind him.

Billy returned two days later, he himself could not even remember where he had been or what he had been doing, he went to his cabin and lay down on his bed and fell asleep. When he opened his eyes Emma was sat looking at him, she asked him

"Are you ok Billy, do you want me to call the doc?" he shook his head, and said

"No need Em, I'm fine but thanks" with that he held his arms out to her; he did not want sex he just wanted to hold her. Em broke the mood when she

149

said

"Have you remembered tomorrow and the interview about the tour?", he stammered that he had not forgotten but she knew that he had and said

"It's with Country Now magazine and we have to meet at the Silver Shoe Hotel at 12am, I will come and pick you up and drive you", he nodded and fell asleep again. Em left him to his dreams and went back to her trailer where Grace was sat on the steps outside her front door; Em sat down by her side rather than take the singer inside. Neither spoke for a while, finally Em said

"I have seen the painting Grace, when I suggested that you try a real man, I didn't mean my man", Grace lowered her head and said

"Where else do you think I will find a man Em, it was only sex and you did tell me to". Em stood up and entered her trailer, closing the door firmly behind her.

Em pulled up outside the Silver Shoe Hotel and let Billy out, he said he would ring her when he was ready, he walked into the hotel with his guitar over his shoulder, he followed the sign for reception, he walked in and a woman with long straight blond hair stood up and smiled at him, they shook hands and said

"Hi, my name is Julie DE Renzo, I have a room booked and the photographer is in there setting up for his shots" Billy followed her up a flight of stairs and along a corridor to room 46, she walked in without knocking, a man with obvious hippy traits was looking down the lens of a camera, he looked up and waved them over. Billy sat down in the chair indicated and a young woman of maybe twenty opened a case and began doing his makeup, he hated this bit and took his mind off things by looking at Miss De Renzo, he put her age at 28, she was slim in a pale yellow trouser suit, under the jacket she wore a white silk shirt, she seemed to have some tits but he could not tell how big they were, when he looked into her face she was blushing under his gaze.

She asked him to strum his guitar while the photographer took more shots. Finally the photographer had taken enough snaps and packed up his equipment and having asked him for his autograph, he left them to it. They sat opposite each other, she asked her questions and he strummed his guitar, he answered her questions as truthfully and with a smile. She closed her note pad and placed it on the coffee table, he looked at the pretty woman and said

"Can we go to bed now, Julie?" she blushed and looked directly at him and said

"I have heard of your reputation Billy, but I can assure you that I will not fall under your spell no matter how big you are down there "he smiled and said

"Not even if I sing to you, tell me your favourite country song?" he strummed his guitar while he waited for her answer, she was blushing again when she said

"I do like the way that you sing #Love, is a Wonderful Thing #", he nodded and tapped the side of the guitar and began singing.

Julio had closed her eyes and laid her head back in the leather chair, her knees had parted slightly and she was tapping her finger on the arm of the chair, her knees opened s little bit further. He might have been imagining it but he was sure that he could see a tiny damp patch, just about where her fanny opening should be. He ended the song and before she could say anything he began another song, then another. Her knees were further apart now and he could definitely see a damp patch now. He stopped singing and she opened her eyes and smiled at him

"You really have got a sexy voice Billy "she said, Billy strummed his guitar and said

"Shall I sing you another song Julie?" she nodded and closed her eyes again, he said

"Undo your jacket Julie and let me look at you" she did not hesitate she opened her suit jacket and pulled her blouse tight over her braless tits, he began to sing # Tulsa Town# her mouth was slightly open as she tapped her feet, he finished the song and she stayed exactly where she was, he strummed his guitar and said

"Undo your blouse and show me your tits " he began another song as her fingers began at the top of her blouse and undid all of the buttons, she smiled and pulled the blouse open, her tits were more than a good handful, her nipples were upturned and hard, he felt his cock twitch for the first time. Billy finished his song and said

"Do you like #good ole boys, Julie?" she nodded and said

151

"That is my favorite song" again he strummed his guitar and said

"Why don't you take all of your clothes off while I sing to you?", she sat up and pulled her jacket off and then her blouse, she kicked he shoes off and then undid the top of her trousers and undid the zip, she then lifted her bottom and pushed her trousers down her legs and left them on the floor, she put her fingers into the side of her white pants and pushed them down to the floor. She sat there naked, he looked at her naked body, a tiny tuft of hair at the top of her slit was the only hair on her fanny.

Billy finished his song and stood his guitar by the side of his chair, he stood up and taking her hand he led her into the bedroom, she stood in front of him as he removed his clothes. When he pushed his boxers down she smiled and said

"It was all true then "and reached out for his giant cock, he placed his hand between her legs and slid his fingers along her slit, he pushed two fingers into her fanny and began frigging her, all of the time her hand was flying up and down his now hard cock. He took his hand from her fanny and turned her around, she bent forwards and gripped the end of the bed, and parted her legs, he stepped forwards and put his knob against her opening and pushed forwards, he giant cock slid into her making her gasp out loud. From his first thrust she met every one of his thrusts, with a backwards thrust of her own, even when he picked up speed to take her through her orgasm, she met him stroke for stroke. Julie had cum three times before he slowed down, he reached around her and gripped her tits and pulled her upright the held onto her tits and squeezes them hard, she reached behind his ass and kept him moving inside her. Billy was getting close and dropped his hands to her hips, he whispered into her ear

"Play with your clit and make yourself cum while I fuck you" she spread her legs wider and reached down and began rubbing her clit at the same time she bent forwards slightly and pushed her hips back. Now Billy gripped her hips and began ramming his giant cock into her, for the first time she stood still and let him fuck her, he could feel her wrist on his hand and her fingers were moving fast back and forth over her clit. And for the first time during the fuck she began to make a lot of noise. It began with a high pitched grunt on every thrust and this turned into a continuous series of smaller grunts until he shoots his hot cum into her body.

She felt the searing hot cum spread throughout her insides; each spurt gave her more and more pleasure. They pushed against each other, both groaning deeply, she was still rubbing her clit only a lot slower now, he was pulling her tits, both had their eyes closed, both in the afterglow of good sex. He finally slipped from her, he tried to get her to suck him clean but she would have none of it and refused point blank.

Billy called Em and asked her to pick him up at the front of the hotel, once in the back of the car; he sat and strummed his guitar, humming along to the tune. He knew without looking that she was watching him in the rear view mirror trying to figure out if he had been shagging again. Billy had agreed to meet Julie at the end of the tour for another interview and he could not wait.

CHAPTER 29

They arrive back at the farm to the sight or the flashing lights of an EMS vehicle. Em parks the car nearby and runs into the house to find out what is going on, other members of the crew are standing around also waiting to find out what's happened. After maybe half an hour Em comes out and walks to the car, she looks at Billy and says congratulations Billy, you the father of a baby girl. She turns away from him and goes to tell the rest of the crew that Ellen has given birth, and that both mother and child are doing fine. It then hit her that if she had not had a termination, then she would be giving birth about now also. And from what she had just witnessed in the farm house she was mighty pleased that she had done what she had done. Em went back to the car and Billy but he was not there, she looked all around to see him walking towards his cabin. She wandered if she should go to him but he probably wanted to be on his own right now.

Em and Billy went to the hospital the next day to see the new arrival; they stood looking into the crib at a sleeping baby. Em looked at Billy to see tears running down his cheeks. They left the baby and went to see Ellen, she smiled as they approached. They both kissed her and Em asked how she was doing, Ellen said that she was fine; she looked at a pale Billy and said

"How does it feel to be a father then Billy?" he had not spoken a single word since they had arrived at the hospital, he finally spoke, and said

"I' m sorry El, sometimes I am such a selfish bastard, but don't worry I will take care of you and, have you thought of a name yet?" she nodded and said

"I'm going to call her Amanda after the song you sang to me the night that she was conceived; she will be called Amanda, Emma". They finally left Ellen and went back to the farm and told everyone the good news. An impromptu party began and carried on until early the next morning. Billy made his way back to the cabin, he lay in the dark and cried at the thought of how many other children that he had and had never seen, all over the country.

The whole crew were in the barn preparing for a county wide tour. Mac is stood on stage running through the itinerary. He tells the crew that up to today he has confirmed dates for #Kentucky, Washington DC, Detroit, Toronto, Chicago, Wisconsin, North Dakota, South Dakota, Nebraska,

Denver- Colorado, Arizona, Amarillo#. These are confirmed dates and most of these venues are two or three nights. In between these dates Billy has private functions to attend, these are all top dollar events, and we will be taking one of the cars, to take Billy to these events, for this we will have to share the driving. The plan therefore is thus Brain's and his crew will set off first thing in the transporter and set up at each venue ahead of the rest of you arriving, and that will happen throughout the tour, we are expecting further conformation's as the tour progresses". Emma shivered violently and had a strange feeling of foreboding, she listened to Mac finish speaking before she went to her trailer and wrapped herself in her quilt, for some reason she just could not get warm.

Emma was busy booking hotels and planning routes, but no matter how hard that she worked she could not shake of the feeling that something bad was going to happen. She threw herself into her work, but the feeling stayed with her for days. Emma made a trip into Kentucky where one of the true fortune tellers worked. Her name is Madame Stella and she worked on Temple street, the building was a two story town house, when Em entered the reading room, which was decorated in different shades of red, net curtains hung from the ceiling and in the center of the room stood a round table again covered in a dark red sheet, in the center of the table stood a clear glass bowl full of strange shaped stones.

Madame Stella was covered in red, over her head was a red head scarf, she had a clear net veil over the lower half of her face, her age showed by the wrinkles around her eyes, her eyes were a light gray colour. She told Emma to choose a handful of stones and to drop them onto the table in front of her, this done Madame Stella waved her hands over the stones and stared at them, she became very quiet as she said

"This is very bad my dear, very bad, you have a trip planned, a trip where you plan to visit many cities, to see many shows, but be warned a great sadness will befall many of your fellow travelers [she placed her hand on Emma's hand] but you dear, you will be safe but there will be a great sadness that will hurt you deep in your heart". Emma sat in her car and cried, when the tears had stopped flowing she began to wonder if she could stop the tour, realizing that there was nothing that she could do and if she said anything they would just laugh at her, so she decided to say nothing.

The day loomed ever nearer for them to leave for the tour, all of the vehicles had been made ready all fully serviced, all of the fridges were full to bursting, Everyone was excited about the tour, the backing group were all practicing their vocals, Dana Parks had her head-phones on and was singing along to the tracks that brains had done for her, Em was on the phone all of the time booking hotels and restaurants. Billy was in his cabin putting the finishing touches to his paintings, everything seemed very relaxed. As they were going to be away for so long Billy went to the Mall to see Milly again, he had chosen to arrive just before closing time, again Milly said that she would be down shortly, she came down and let all of the staff out and locked the doors, she turned and went back through the door that she had come out of, they climbed a flight of stairs, she stopped at a door with Milly Revell. Manager painted on the door, she opened the door and went in, he followed close behind and closed the door, she stood behind her desk and began removing her clothes, and she had her blouse open and her left tit on show, when she said

"Seeing that you will be away for such a long time, I thought that we could fuck on my desk and then when I am a work, I will remember you. She removed her blouse and then her skirt she gripped the sides of her pants and pushed them down, she leaned back against her desk and waited for him to catch up, he stood in front of her, both looked at each other's bodies, she reached out for his banana shaped cock but he stepped back and pulled her from the desk, she stood looking into his eyes, he put his hands on her shoulders and pushed her down she sank to her knees. Wanting desperately to please him he lifted his cock and pulling the skin down she exposed his big purple knob, she licked her lips and closed her mouth over his now huge knob, his knob grew even bigger in her mouth until he was hard.

She looked up into his eyes waiting to see what he wanted next, he had been watching her closely. He nodded that she had done enough and she stood up and then she then sat back on her desk and opened her legs, he stepped forwards and she gripped his cock and guided him into her fanny. She lifted her legs and folded them around his back; she used her heels to make him slip in deeper. Once he was fully embedded inside her she unlocked her ankles and held her legs high waiting for him to take hold of them.

Now Billy held her legs up she gripped the edge of the desk and he began to pump his huge cock in and out if her. She closed her eyes and lay there with a huge smile on her face. He stood there fascinated as he watched her tits bouncing back and forth. It was not long before she was on the verge of her orgasm. He watched her grit her teeth and blow hot air through them, quick, low moans were coming from her throat. She suddenly held her breath and let the feeling wash over her, he was quite happy fucking her like this and she seemed more than happy to just lay there and let him do whatever he wanted. They had been fucking for a while and Milly had cum a few times when she reached forwards and placed her hand on his chest, he stopped and looked down at her, she smiled up at him and said

"Billy I could lie here all day and let you fuck me, but I want you to come back to me so I want to take you in my mouth and suck you to a finish, just so that I can taste you at least once" he slowly pulled his cock from her, she sat up and pulled his lips to hers, within seconds they were kissing deeply. Milly slid down his body and did not hesitate about him fucking her mouth, she met each of his thrusts, if he tried to go to deep she dug in with her teeth. He finally gripped the back of her head and fucked her mouth as hard as she would allow him to; now that he was close she gripped his shaft and wanked him as hard and as fast as she could. Billy held her head still and grunted out loud, she smiled inwardly as he shot his cum down her throat, and Milly was forced to swallow as quickly as she could because there was so much of his warm seed. Now that they were sated she was sat on the floor licking her lips and he was sat in her office chair, she looked up at this man that she loved

"Will you come back to me Billy?" he looked down at her and smiled

You try and stop me, I will text you when we are on the way back, and then we can arrange a meeting place, if not here we can always get a motel somewhere" she nodded and said

"You text me and I will arrange something" they stood and began kissing because he said that he had to go. She asked him to make her cum with his fingers before he went, which he did. Covered in fanny juice he held his fingers to her mouth, she looked into his eyes and smiled, she opened her mouth and let him push the sticky finger deep into her mouth. She took her time as she licked the fingers clean all of the time she simply smiled into his eyes.

Billy was about to leave her at the front of the Mall, she was about to pull the door closed when he held the door and looked deep into her eyes and asked her

"When I come back will you leave your husband and live with me as man and wife?" she looked into his eyes and answered

"Is that your big cock talking Billy or do you mean what you say? [she leaned her heads to the side] I will tell you what, if you still feel the same when you return, ask me again" with that she closed and locked the door and watched him, her perfect lover walk away.

Now that Billy had made the decision to settle down with one woman. He called Em and asked her if he could go and see her, naturally she said yes and told him that she would be waiting. Em had thought that he was going to her for sex. But she was so wrong; he sat down on the couch and began speaking

"I want a house Em, built where the cabin is, I want it built for a country singer, the only thing that I insist on is a room that I can paint in, for that I will need glass on at least three sides. I want a stables built for two horses and a road down to the house, now do you think that your local builder can get it done for when we return from the tour?" Em sat there open mouthed, she finally asked him

"Why did you want a house when there was just you?" he shrugged and said

"Maybe I want to settle down, get married, have kids" Em smiled and asked hopefully

"Have you anyone in mind then Billy?" she sat down by his side and turned sideways and placed her naked legs into his lap. She had on a short skirt and she knew that he could see her fanny lips; she also knew that her pink thong had slipped between her swollen lower lips. When he looked down she parted her knees which gave him a proper look, He placed his hand on her leg and looked into her eyes, he then slid his hand onto her fanny and began stroking her swollen lips

"What about the agreement Em, and I haven't got any protection" he said, she reached out to a draw in a small cabinet and pulled out a large box of condoms, she passed him the box and then lifted her top and exposed her naked tits, she then lifted her right foot and used it to rub his cock through his jeans. Billy pulled the thong from between her fanny lips and pushed two fingers into her fanny and began to frig her. Em lifted her right leg and placed it behind his head, her left foot she placed on the floor, now her legs were wide open which allowed him to do whatever he wanted to do.

He pulled his fingers from her fanny and undid his belt and jeans, he lifted his bottom and pushed his jeans and boxers down to his knees, his giant cock was ready and straining. When he turned sideways she took to pillows from behind her head and put them under her bum, therefore lifting her fanny to the correct height. Now on his knees he pulled her thong off and dropped it onto the floor. He ripped the condom box open and rolled a condom down his length, he moved slightly and was able to push his giant cock into her willing body, there was no finesse, no thought of her pleasure, it was just a fuck, plain and simple. He gripped the insides of her thighs and fucked her hard, he rode her flat out.

Em had her fingers in her hair and was making all sorts of noises but he didn't care. He only had one thought and that was his own pleasure, he shot his load and pulled her hard against him. When he looked down at her she was lay there limp and moaning, he eased her down and slowly pulled his still hard cock from her, he moved out from under her and lay her legs 0down, Em was still limp and moaning. He was worried that he had hurt her, he put her tits away and pulled her skirt down, he then sat down by her side and stroked her forehead and asked

"Em, are you all-right, do you want me to get someone, one of the other girls maybe?" she shook her head

"Am I bleeding?" she asked quietly he looked under her skirt and could see that a small amount of blood had come from her and was lay on the bottom of her skirt

"just a tiny bit Em" he said

"Get something to put under me" she instructed, he looked all round and took a load of kitchen paper and placed it against her fanny and under her bottom, she groaned out loud when he touched her fanny

"I'm so sorry Em, I don't know what came over me" she never opened her eyes

"that was almost rape Billy, do you hate me that much?" when he did not answer her she whispered

"That was the last time that you will ever fuck me Billy, now go and let me sort myself out".

Em had to go to the emergency room and be stitched up, she was asked a lot of questions and the doctor wanted to get the police involved, but she insisted that it was all her fault. Em shut herself away in her trailer and used the excuse of sorting out the tour. Billy kept well away from her, but he convinced himself that she had started it and she did not complain while he was fucking her, he was convinced that he could talk her around and decided that he would leave it a few days and see what happened.

CHAPTER 30

They were on the bus heading for Kentucky, the band were all playing cards, Dana and Emma were going over a pile of papers, as for the backing singers, he looked at each of them in turn, Shirelle walked up and sat down by him, she looked at him and smiled, she said

"You know that you wanted me badly when we first met, and I well played hard to get, well I have a confession to make Billy Ridge I have to tell you that you have had me, I was the night caller and if you want me on your terms now, just ask me. But I have to ask, did you enjoy it Billy?"

Before he could answer her she was gone back to the other singers, leaving him gob-smacked, he looked back at her, she winked at him and then smiled broadly. Billy had got bit of a stiffy just thinking back to that night. He took his mobile out and texted Patsy Himes the wife of Sir Walter, and mother of his child, the message said simply "call me if you want to meet early next week. B."

Within a milli second his phone vibrated in his hand, Patsy had rung him back and said that she would meet him when and wherever he wanted, and she hoped that he would ring, as she had something to show him. The date was arranged and Billy had something to look forward to, he looked down the list of venues and wrote another text to Diane Riscoe and tells her that he will passing close by in two weeks and would she like to meet up.

Again the answer came back in seconds that she will meet him anywhere he wanted. He sent a text to Bob the woman driver of Sir Walter Himes, asking if she was available to meet up in three weeks' time, he would let her know where nearer the time. Again a text came back saying that she would meet him on the moon if need be. Billy leaned back and closed his eyes and dreamt of adventures to come.

CHAPTER 31

The tour got off to a great start with a standing ovation in Kentucky, Billy was driving the car as he had told them that he had relatives nearby and he would see then at the next venue, he texted Patsy and she told him that she had booked the same room as before and would meet him there, at the appointed time. Billy arrived at the hotel and looked at the note that had been left for him at reception, it said simply 57, so he took the stairs and knocked at the door, the door opened and he had the shock of his life when Sir Walter opened the door he said

"Ah Mr. Ridge, come in and take a seat" Billy walked in and sat down on the couch and looked at the older man. Sir Walter stood looking out of the window and said

"Isobel has told me about you and my family and how you have loved both of them and that you are the father of Elenore and the baby that Patsy is carrying now, I want to know your intentions towards my family Mr. Ridge?" Billy sat there looking at the man with his stiff back towards him, what could he possibly say. Sir Walter did not look at him when he said

"you are not the first lover that my wife has had, but you are the first to impregnate her, and for that I thank you, I think the world or Elenore and I will do the right thing for her as long as I know that you will not try and contact her ever again, I mean never contact her, if you agree, then nothing more will be said on the matter, now I want you to leave and never contact any member of my family ever again" Billy did not say a word, he just stood and left the old man standing looking out of the window.

Billy drove the big car carefully as he headed out of town, his mind was all over the place, but it came to him that it must have been Isobel being pissed at him for not going to her when he said that he would, that is why she went to her father and told him everything. He left the town far behind him and he gunned the big engine, he could not see a light in any direction, so he opened all of the windows and turned the music up in volume, he was singing along at the top of his voice, the speed of the car began to creep up to 100 mph.

When he saw the flashing lights in his rearview mirror he cursed out loud, he turned the music down and slowed the car, he pulled to a stop with the police car stopped just behind him, he sat and waited while the officer approached the car, a female officer said

"Sir, show me your hands "he put both of his hands out of the window, the officer came closer but he could see that she had her hand on her gun butt,

"get out of the car and stand facing the car, with your hand on your head" he did as he was told, she came up behind him and pushed him in the back forcing him against the car, using her right hand she frisked him, happy that he was not armed she asked him for his driving license, he went to reach into his inside pocket, he suddenly felt the cold steel of her gun barrel in the base of his neck, he passed her back his license, she took it and looked at it,

"Where's your insurance?" Billy reached into the car and passed it to her. The officer took both items and returned to her car, he looked at her and could see her talking on the radio, after a couple of minutes she came back to him and said "do you know how fast you were going Sir?" in his deepest voice he said

"I guess I was going to fast huh?" she said,

"I could lock you up for forty eight hours and put you in front of the judge, but if I did that I would not hear you sing now would I?" he turned to look at her for the first time and he was not disappointed, she was taller than him and maybe broader, her dark hair was pulled back and hidden under her hat, she was full chested and not bad looking, he said

"You going to Detroit then officer ?" she said

"Sure am, I have been looking forward to it for a long time now" he smiled and said

"How would you like to meet everyone back stage and be my guest?" she said

"there is no need for all that Sir, just sing me a song on the night and I will be happy" he stood leaning against his car looking at her "and what is your favorite song officer Serang?" he asked her, she lifted the right hand side of her mouth and said

"Call me Sue and my favorite song has to be # love me tonight#" he looked around and they were in the middle of nowhere, not a car or light in any direction.

He reached into the back of the car and pulled out his guitar

"how would you like me to sing that song just for you, here and now?" he asked, she looked around at the emptiness all around and said

"let me turn my lights and engine off first", she went back to her car and turned the flashing lights off, leaving her small car lights on, she spoke into the radio for a while and looked at her watch and said a few more word into the radio. She walked back to him and stood leaning against her car, he began singing to her, from the instant he began singing she closed her eyes and pushed her thumbs into her belt, he could see her hard nipples through the thick material of her shirt, he moved closer to her as he sung, he finished up with his hand maybe 1 inch from her right nipple, she could feel his presence and opened her eyes and looked deep into his eyes, he reached out with his little finger and stroked her nipple, she looked down at the finger as it moved over her nipple

"that classed as assault on a police officer?" she asked, he stopped playing and fondled the whole breast, again she looked at his hand "that is definitely an arrest able offence, I may have to punish you for that, Sir" she said, she looked at his fingers as they opened some off her buttons on her uniform, he opened it wide enough so that he could get his hand inside, he pushed his hand inside her bra and fondled her tit, she looked into his eyes as she reached out for his cock, she stroked his cock for a few seconds, she then fumbled for his zipper, she pulled the zip all of the way down and pushed her hand inside his jeans and gripped his growing cock.

He placed the guitar into the car and lowered his hand to her fanny; she opened her legs and let him rub his fingers along her fanny lips. Sue pulled his hand from inside her shirt and walked away from him to the back of her car, she reached into the front of her car and turned the internal camera off, she checked that they could not be detected in any way, then continued undoing the buttons on her shirt, she pulled the shirt open and lifted her bra over the top of her tits, she reached down and removed her utility belt and dropped it on the front seat, she undid her belt and trousers, she then reached down and removed her right boot, she pushed her pants down and lifted her foot out of them.

She turned away from him and pushed her underpants down and took her foot from the thin material, she looked back at him and said "this is the best you are going to get, so get your cock out and fuck me" she leaned her hands on the back seat and waited for him to shove his big cock into her, he dropped his jeans and boxers and pushed his hard cock into her, he gripped her hips and pushed his cock to full depth, the officer did not groan or make any sounds as he entered her, but when he began fucking her it was a different matter, she became very vocal as she shouted out all sorts of things, every swear word that had ever been heard came out of her mouth, she was a strong woman as she pushed back at him, they bounced their bodies against each other sounding as if a lone person was clapping, Sue was loving it, this was not the first time that she had stopped a lone man and fucked him, but this was definitely the best fuck so far and with it being Billy Ridge as well made it even more special, maybe this time she will get pregnant, she and her husband had been trying for years now, that is why she did what she did she was desperate for a baby.

When she had come twice she gradually forgot about her desperate need for a baby and began to enjoy the fuck, she realised how deep he was inside her and how nice it felt, relaxed now she concentrated on her pleasure, her orgasm built again and he fucked her through it and then slowed down he stopped and held his cock inside her for a few seconds, he then pulled his cock from her, she looked around at him and he gripped her hand and pulled her to the front of her car, he picked his shirt up and spread it on the front of her car and laid her back onto it he picked her legs up and pushed his giant cock back into her, as he fucked her she slid back and forth easily on the shirt, he shouted for her to play with her tits.

Sue cried out as she pulled her nipples, suddenly she was really enjoying herself, something that she had never done with a man before, she began bouncing her hips in time with him, this was a first for her, he slapped her right thigh hard, she screamed out into the night sky, he slapped her again only harder this time, she screamed again but did not object so he stopped fucking her and lifted her legs onto his shoulders he now held her onto the car by his giant cock, he looked down at he and slapped her with both hands, she screamed again, each time he slapped her she screamed, his hands hurt so he began to really fuck her hard, Sue was now a demented woman her arm were flailing about, her head was moving from side to side and yet her hips still bounced in time with him, he grunted and shot his spunk into her, she lifted her head and screamed and called him a bastard, each spurt brought forth another curse followed by a scream.

He finally stopped spurting and stood there with his cock still buried inside her, she lay there moaning moving her head from side to side, he lowered her legs down and eased his cock from her, he lowered her feet to the floor and pulled her up to standing, she looked down at his semi hard cock and said

"You have one hell of a long barrel on that gun Sir". They dressed and he promised to see her at the show, she told him to drive carefully, and that was that.

He continued on his way and she turned around and went back the way that she had come from, never to see each other again.

CHAPTER 32

He arrived in Detroit and found the venue quite easily, he walked in to find most of the crew sat down chatting while brains did his thing with his knobs and wires, the Billy Ridge CD was playing and he had to admit the music sounded good in the big hall. When brain's was finally happy, he made sure that the security was all in place and suggested that we all go eat. They all filed into the chosen restaurant and took their seats, as usual Em sat by his side, he waited until they had ordered before he asked her if she was ok, she looked at him and said

"I meant what I said Billy, you hurt me for whatever reason, but you will never hurt me again" they ate their meal in silence. But on stage they were as professional as ever and sang with each other and smiled at each other. It was the same for the next three weeks until Em went to his room one evening, she went to show him some pictures of his new house that was being built, there were pictures of each room, Billy was more than happy and went to hug her but she pulled away from him, he held her arms and said

"look Em, I am sorry for what happened, I think it was because I was so disgusted with myself for being so weak, we both knew the rules that were made but when you showed me your fanny you knew what would happen, you wanted me to fuck you, that is why you did what you did" she had tears running down her cheeks as she quietly sobbed, she stood up and ran from his room, leaving him feeling even more guilty than he did before.

Billy needed some kind of distraction; he took out his phone and texted Bob

"where are you?", his phone rang in his hand, he answered to hear Bob's voice, after a quick chat, she told him where she was and he told her where he was, she said to give her a minute and she would call him back, his phone rang again and Bob gave him the name of a motel on the edge of the city, she told him to go there and she would meet him there in two hours. He watched her pull into the parking lot, she parked near the office, she was in and out in a minute, she smiled broadly when she saw him leaning against her car, she walked up to him and kissed him hard on the mouth, pulling away she said

"Get in" he climbed into the big car and she drove to the back of the motel, the room that she had booked was at the very end of the block. She got out of the car and opened the door, he looked around and said

You want us to be on our own then?", she pulled him into the room and closed the door and said

"I make a lot of noise when I am being fucked, don't you remember?", she began stripping her clothes of, as he stood watching her she went to him and undid his belt and jeans, she pulled the zip down and pulled his jeans down his legs, his boxers followed soon after, she gripped his cock and gave it a few quick wanks, her eyes never left his cock as she finished removing her clothes, he still stood looking at her, she placed her hands on her hips and said

"Do you want to do this Billy or shall I get dressed again?" he smiled and said

"I was just taking in your true beauty, I only saw you naked in the back of a car before" he stripped his clothes off and took her hand and led her to the bed.

She sat down on the bed and he moved up to her, he looked into her eyes and then down to his limp cock, she shook her head and stood up she turned from him and climbed onto the bed, she placed herself on her hands and knees and looked back at him and said

"kiss my fanny and reward me for rushing here to see you, kiss my fanny and then you can do whatever you want to me", he sat down on the bed and she faced forwards again, he reached over and parted her fanny lips, he then took his time to give her as much pleasure as he could with his mouth, he licked and kissed every bit of skin in and around her fanny, he had deliberately not touched her clit, he was saving that until now, now that she was in such a desperate state, he turned her onto her back, she opened her body to him by flopping her legs wide open, he pushed two finger deep into her wet fanny and began to move them back and forth, she was on the point of her climax when he placed his lips on her clit, at his touch she closed he thighs against the side of his head and gripped the back of his head, as her hips began to move up and down.

Bob became very vocal, she began growling at the top of her voice, the growls turned into a low pitched scream and then as her climax hit her she let out a blood curdling scream, her hands were clenched by her side and her hips were bouncing up and down, it was all he could do to hang onto her, he pulled his fingers from her fanny and pushed his tongue as deep as he could inside her, she began moaning again as another orgasm grew ever closer, he pulled his tongue out and closed his lips over her clit again, her whole body seemed to go into spasm, she was suddenly stiff, the only thing moving were her hips. Bob came with a giant sigh, he lifted his mouth from her fanny and looked into her face, she lay there her legs wide open and her fanny twitching, she had a stupid grin on her face

"by fuck Billy, you can sure kiss a fanny" she said, he smiled and stood up, his giant cock now rock hard, she looked at his cock and then back to his eyes

"You can do whatever you want to me Billy, you can even fuck my ass if you want?".

He sat down by her side and looked at her

"anything?" he asked her, she nodded her head and sai "anything that you desire" he looked around the room again and pulled her up, he told her to stand still as he went into the bathroom he came back with a thin hand towel, he covered her eyes and again told her to remain where she was, he went fetched the drawstrings from the window curtains, he tied one to each wrist, he then turned her around a few times, now she was disorientated, he pulled her across the room to a wooden dressing table, he placed a pillow on the top and moved her close, he bent her forwards so that she was lay on the pillow but over the dressing table, he took the free ends of the drawstrings and passed them over the top, down the other side and then underneath the dressing table, he tied the drawstrings, one around each ankle, Bob was now trapped, she was bent over with her ass and fanny at his mercy, he stood silently and watched her straining her ears for any sign of him, when he slapped her ass she screamed out loud and called him a bastard, he walked around the room, she followed him with her ears, he stopped and looked out of the window at a small tree, he could not make out what tree it was in the dark, he looked back at the trussed up woman and asked her

"Have you been naughty Bob?" she nodded her head

"Very naughty Billy" he smiled and said

"Do you need to be punished Bob?" she nodded her head again

"oh yes Billy, I definitely need to be punished, I have been a very bad girl" he went to his leather waistcoat and took out his penknife, he pulled on his boots, in just his boots he went to a tree and cut a thin branch, he trimmed all of the twigs and anything else that could hurt her to much, he swished it through the air and was very happy, he walked back into the room, he watched as she cocked her ears again, she followed his movement around the room, he stopped behind her and stood still again.

She jumped when he touched t her back with the swish, he took a step to the side and gave her a slap across the ass with the swish, she screamed out at the top of her voice, her whole body was trembling, he gave her another slap, only this time it was a little bit harder making her moan out loud, he placed his mouth by her ear and whispered

"Shall I punish you before I fuck you?" she nodded her head and said

"oh yes please Billy" he took up position and gave her six firm slaps, he watched the red whelps appear on her naked ass cheeks, she had gone quiet but her body was heaving, he moved up to her ass and rubbed his hard knob along her fanny lips, he placed the tip of his knob against her bum hole, he saw her tense, he dribbled some spit onto his finger and rubbed it all around her brown hole, he could see her shaking, she mumbled

"please don't split me Billy" he had no intension of fucking her ass but he made out that was his intension, he gave her a few play full thrusts at her ass, but then he moved his knob down a fraction and slipped it into her fanny, she let out a loud sigh of relief, he gripped her just above the hips and fucked her hard, with her trussed up like this he could not read her body language so he didn't know when she was coming, so he just fucked her and fucked her, Bob made all sorts of loud noises from screams to grunts, she was at one stage crying out loud, he grunted out loud "NO, DON'T CUM UP MEEEE" but it was too late he was shooting his seed into her, spurt after spurt shot into her, he pushed hard into her and she was openly crying, great big sobs.

Billy finally slipped from her tortured body, he left her tied up while he went to the bathroom and cleaned himself up, when he came out she was sobbing, he untied her ankles but she just lay there, in the end he had to pull her up, she turned and folded herself around him, he held her tight and let her get it all out of her system, she eventually calmed down enough for him to take her to the bed, he laid her down and lay by her side, she rested her head on his chest and listened to his heartbeat, he lay quiet and stroked her shoulder, he knew that she would speak eventually.

Bob took a deep breath and said

"did you know Billy that the most common fantasy for a woman is to be raped, I guess that what you just did to me was as close to rape as you could get, even when you came inside me, that is what would happen if I had been raped for real, the worst part for me was not being able to push back at you, I don't know how many times I came but it was a lot, I thought that you were going to fuck my ass, I wouldn't mind if you did but I would need to prepare myself, I think that if you had done it then it would have hurt me because I was holding myself so tight and if you had forced your big cock up there you would have split me " she reached down and lifted his limp cock and began moving her hand up and down, she then said

"If we meet up again will you do the same thing to me again"?, he smiled to himself,

"we will meet again Bob, we both know that, if you want I will bring some ropes and things the next time, maybe I will blindfold you and take you somewhere and tie you to a tree or something like that" he said, he felt her nod her head move as she nodded

"whatever you want Billy, now let's see about getting this big cock hard again, then you can fuck me properly, and seeing as though you have already cum inside me, you may as well do it again as often as you like" his cock was beginning to show a bit of interest, she moved her head down his chest all the way to his knob, she opened her mouth and closed it over his big purple knob, she gave him well practiced mouthy sex, her head was bobbing up and down his cock, he had to stop her or he would have cum, she looked a little disappointed,

"I don't mind Billy, if you want me to suck you all the way I will" he said

"but I want to fuck the ass off you, I want you to make a lot of noise, I want you to scream out in ecstasy" she sat up and turned away from him and got onto her hands and knees, she looked back at him and waited for him to push his giant cock into her. Billy rode her for as long as he could, he gave her the fucking of her life, Bob was a most enthusiastic lover and he wondered if he could spend the rest of his life with her, lay by her side holding hands, which to him was the perfect way to end a session of perfect love-making. His thoughts went to Milly and her husband, then her divorce and would the crew accept her knowing that she had left her husband to be with Billy. Then on the other hand, there is Bob, younger, single, beautiful, perfect body and loves to fuck, in all honesty there was no competition, without looking at her he said

"If I asked you to, would you live with me in my new house?". Bob gave a one word answer

"Yes" and they turned and smiled at one-another.

CHAPTER 33

Life for Billy, unknown to him was about to take a strange turn. Em had driven him to country mansion in deepest Nebraska which belonged to a Governor Johnstead. Billy was singing for his supper in a large ball room, in front of a room full of local dignitaries, all dressed in dinner jackets and bow ties, with their wives and girlfriends all in evening dresses. He was almost an hour into the set when Em appeared at the back of the room, she looked very distressed and for her to be in the room in itself was very unusual. The more that he watched her the more agitated she became, he decided to take a short break to find out what the problem was, Em was in his dressing room waiting for him, as soon as he walked in she jumped up and said

"We have to do something Billy, we have to help her" he held her by the shoulders and said

"What's wrong Em?" she opened her hand which held a blue piece of paper, on the paper was written #please help me, I am a slave. Eva# he looked up at Em, she said

"she is only a teenager Billy and she has a black eye, she said if the governor found out about the note he would kill her or sell her to be a prostitute, we have to do something" he stood there in thought and asked

"Where is she now?" Em said "She is hiding in the kitchen, waiting for me to go back to her" he said

"right this is what we will do, you bring the car around to the kitchen door, get her into the back of the car and cover her up, then drive to the front or the house and wait for me to come out, I won't be long. Billy went back and sang some more sad songs, he looked at the governor and wanted to go down and throttle him, he finished singing and went to change in his room, on the table was his payment. He left by the front of the house without a backwards glance, when they were on the open road he said

"you can come out now Eva, you are safe" a young coloured girl of maybe 15 years of age sat up and looked all around her with terrified eyes, she looked at Billy and shrank back into the corner of the back seat looking even more terrified. Em stopped the car and looked at the scared young girl, she turned to him and said

"you drive for a bit" with that she got out of the car and got into the back seat of the car, she took the girl into her arms and held her trembling body tight, talking to her soothingly, he could not hear what Em was saying but it seemed to be working.

They pulled up at the hotel and Em took the girl to her room, she gave him instructions to get the backing singers, he did as she asked, he watched as the dark side singers all entered Em's room. He sat in his room waiting to find out what was happening, when Em came into his room without knocking, she looked white as she said

"Mac has just rung me, apparently the governor from earlier has told him to tell us to return his property as soon as possible or there will be trouble, and Mac wants to know what is going on" Billy told her to get Mac on the phone. Billy talked to Mac for a long time and when he came off the phone he said

"we have a plan, you get the head of our security up here as soon as, I will do the rest. When he returned to the room he had with him a woman of maybe forty years old, she was a big woman with bright red hair, she wore a black trouser suit and on her lapel was a badge that said # hotel security# her name was Heather Tranal, she looked and nodded at everyone in the room, Billy stood in front of them all and began speaking

"right this the situation, first of I need you all to promise that you will say nothing of what we are about to do, [he looked from one to another, each one of them nodded] at the gig tonight Em was asked for help by a very young girl who was being held against her will as a slave, we have her in the hotel at the moment but I think that we need to get her away from here as soon as possible, the man who we played for tonight has asked for his property to be returned and by the sound of it he has a lot of influence around here so what I suggest is this, you two security men and Heather here take Eva the young girl back to our farm and leave her there with Ellen, we will ring Ellen and tell her the situation and I am sure that she will look after her, now Heather says we can use her car because if the local police do turn up they will expect to see our car here and if it is missing then they will want to know where it is.

I think that is everything, any questions?" as he looked at each person they all shook their heads, he told Em to fetch the girl while the security men mapped a route. When the girl walked into the room she looked completely different, the dark side singers had done things to the girl hair and dressed her in a light blue dress, they had done her face over with makeup, now she looked over 20 years old. Em sat the girl down and explained everything to her, Eva grabbed Em around the neck and thanked her, Billy said that they had better be on their way sooner rather than later.

They had been gone maybe 40 minutes, Billy and Em were sat in his room talking about what to do to help the young girl when there came a knock on the door, Em opened the door to see a sheriff and a deputy standing there, they did not wait to be invited in, they just walked in, the sheriff stood looking at Billy while the deputy searched every room, he finished his search and shook his head at the sheriff

"Where is she?" he asked

"Who?" asked Billy, the sheriff stared at Billy and then at Em

If she is here we will find her" he said, he then told the deputy to watch them and then left the room. The sheriff and his men searched every room in the hotcl, they even went through the security tapes, but Heather had seen to that side of things. The Sheriff came back and did some more staring and made some more threats and left, Billy phoned Ellen and filled her in on events, she was only too happy to help and said that she would wait up for her arrival. Em went and sat by his side and said

"Thank you Billy, we did the right thing didn't we?" he placed his arm around her shoulders and reassured her. They spent the night together and held each other but there was no sex involved, but Em knew that if he had wanted to fuck her she would have happily gone along with it.

On the bus the next day Mark Foster was following the transporter that was following their car out of town when they were all pulled over into a side road by the sheriff and his deputies, they made everyone leave the bus and stand by the side of the road, they searched every inch of every vehicle, every bit of equipment and every piece of luggage was piled on the side of the road, the sheriff walked up to Billy and said

"Where is she?" Billy shook his head and said

"Who are you looking for sheriff, tell me and we may be able to help you" the sheriff just stood there staring at Billy knowing that he had been beaten by this singer, he finally said

"don't ever come back here Billy Ridge, your sort are not welcome around here" he gave Billy one last stare then he turned and he and his men all left, leaving the crew to load everything back into the vehicles. Ellen called to say that the parcel had arrived safely.

CHAPTER 34

Billy was en route to Diane Riscoe, she was waiting for him at her home and wanting the evening to feel more like a date than just sex, she had offered to cook for him, she had told him to call him when he was an hour away, which he had done, she was at this moment stood stirring a red wine sauce dressed in a thin white evening dress and literally nothing else. When she heard his car stop outside her house her fanny seemed to begin without her, she felt instantly wet and swollen, she ran and opened the door, as soon as he had walked in she threw herself against him, he lifted her from the ground and swirled her around, both more than happy to see each other. Diane could feel him growing against her, she was tempted to rub against him but she had spent most of the day preparing this meal and she was not going to let it spoil now.

She pulled away from him and looked down at the bulge in his jeans, she coughed and took his hand and led him to the table he sat down but instantly made a grab for her, he almost got his hand on her fanny before she turned away, if he had managed to touch her most intimate place she would have let him fuck there and then. They sat opposite each other and enjoyed the meal together; they sat holding hands across the table, but Billy being Billy had kicked his boot off and had his foot between her parted legs gently stroking her thigh, she was really turned on but she wanted to hold out as long as possible, the main reason being that this may well be the very last time that she sees him so she wanted to make it last as long as she could. Her fanny seemed to take over again as she eased her bottom forwards on her chair, her fanny was on fire, she opened her legs wider as she pushed her naked fanny against his foot, in response he instantly began rubbing his big toe against her slit, they sat looking at each other both smiling.

Diane lifted her bottom slightly and lifted her dress over her head and tossed it onto the couch, he looked from one naked tit to the other and back to her eyes, she looked down at his big toe as it gentle stroked her fanny and said

"I hope that you have something bigger than that to go up there?" he looked down into his lap and after a bit of fiddling about, she saw his naked purple knob appear above the table, she looked into his eyes and said

"that's better" she stood up and went to him, he tried to get her to straddle him but she wanted him to fuck her in bed, like proper lovers do He stood up and reached out for her again, she took a step back and said "take everything off Billy, then you can fuck me any way you want" he stood and removed every item of clothing, she reached out and took his hand and took him into her bedroom, they stood looking at each other, almost touching but not quite, their eyes searching each other's bodies. Diane said

"Billy, would you do something for me?" he nodded

"Anything" he said, she never looked into his eyes when she said

"Rather than just fucking me, can we make love, can you make love to me?". He laid her face down on the bed; he then opened her arms out wide and then did the same with her legs. Billy knelt by her side and began kissing her, he took his time and kissed every single inch of her goose bumped body, he finished at the top of her spine and kissed slowly downwards, as he reached the top of her buttocks she lifted her bum into the air. Julie was moaning out loud and was desperate to be fucked but she would wait, she felt him move his body so that he was now knelt behind her, she did not know whether he was about to enter her or not, when she felt his tongue at the top of her fanny and ever so slowly lick upwards, as his tongue touched her opening it was just that bit too far and she cried out in orgasm, her hips bounced back and forth as well as up and down.

He could not keep his mouth on her fanny so he sat up and grabbed her hips, he placed his giant knob near her entrance, Julie had suddenly become desperate as she forced herself to hold her body still long enough for him to enter her, as his giant cock slid into her body Julie growled out loud and began desperately thrusting her body back at him.

Julie cried out loud as she climaxed over and over again, she was now in a place that she had never been in before or even dreamt existed, she was so desperate for the feeling of her orgasm she was calling out to him desperately, all he could do was keep pumping his big cock into her as hard and as fast as he could and wait for her to calm down, he had never seen a woman react like this before and he was not sure how to react. Julie calmed down so much that she was limp in his hand's, he kept going flat out because he did not know what else to do, her back was heaving and she gave the occasional sob, he slowed down and eventually stopped, he asked her if she was ok?

Her only reaction was to begin crying out loud, he pulled his cock out of her and moved to her side, he pulled her into his arms and held her tight, she sobbed broken hearted and tears dripped onto his chest. Billy rubbed her back and made calming noises, she eventually calmed down and lay there quietly, he eventually lifted her face and kissed her, he pulled his lips from hers and whispered

"Are you alright Julie?" she had tears streaming down her face as she looked up at him

"I don't know what just happened, I have never felt like that before, I felt so desperate while you were fucking me, it felt like 10 men all with big cocks like yours could have been inside me and it still would not have been enough. What's wrong with me Billy, you have to help me" he folded her back into him and lay there and held her, his cock had shrunk back to nothing and he doubted that there would be any more sex this night, mainly because she would be to frightened in case she went back to that terrifying place.

Julie finally fell asleep, he did the right thing and covered her up with her quilt, he wrote her a note saying that he would ring her soon but he knew that he would never ring her again.

CHAPTER 35

In his car heading back to the crew he switched his phone on, to his surprise it buzzed saying that he had a message, he pressed view and the message came onto his screen

"Ring me "and it was from Emma, he pressed the call button and she answered straight away

"Where are you Billy, I have been trying to get you for hours" he made an excuse about being with family and then said "what's so urgent?" Em said

"I can't say anything over the phone but you need to get back here as soon as you can, what time will you be here?", he said that he would be a couple of hours and she said that she would wait up for him. Billy walked into the hotel and Em was sat waiting for him, he went and sat down by her and said

"Well?" she looked all around the reception area and it was a little bit crowded for what she had to say

"Let's go up to my room" he followed her into her room, she locked the door behind herself, she checked the bathroom and sure that they were now on their own she placed her mouth against his ear and whispered

"What I am about to tell you, you cannot say a word to anyone and I mean anyone" he looked at her and said

"spit it out Em, the suspense is killing me" she whispered "it is a case of national security, you see we have been asked to play for the first lady at the Whitehouse in three days' time at her birthday celebrations, Mac you and I are the only people this end that know anything about this and that is the way that it has to stay, any sign of this getting out and it will be cancelled, is that clear?" when she looked into his eyes they were like saucers and he seemed to be holding his breath.

"Say something Billy [she shook him] speak to me" he took a breath and said

"Fuck Em" he grabbed her and they danced around and around both laughing out loud.

  Billy being a man had noticed her braless tits bouncing up and down, his mind told him that he had a load in the delivery shoot and he wondered if he could deliver it into Em, he finally flopped down onto the couch and she flopped down beside him, resting her head on his chest, they could both feel the others heart beating fast. Billy looked at the drinks cabinet and asked her

"is there any champagne in the fridge?" she lifted her head and went and had a look, she turned with half a bottle of Moet, she took two glasses and went and sat back down by him, she passed him the bottle for him to open, she held the glasses out waiting, he opened the bottle and poured champagne into both glasses, they looked into each other eyes and then chinked glasses and smiling at one another they drained their glasses, she held her glass out for a refill and he topped it almost to the brim, she looked at the level of the drink and then at him, she shrugged and drank almost all of the liquid, she took a breath of air and then drank the rest, she looked into the glass and he poured the last of the champagne into her glass, she did not hesitate as she emptied the glass in one gulp. Billy looked into her sparkling eyes, he had noticed that her nipple were now rock hard but it would be up to her if anything happened between them after the last time, she placed their empty glasses on a nearby table and rested her head in his lap,

"who would have thought it, us going there and singing for her as well" she placed her hand under her head, whether or not it was intentional or not she had placed her hand directly on his cock, he rested his hand on her waist and they sat like lifelong lovers, he could just see her hard nipple under her arm, he thought about reaching out and tweaking it but thought better of it. Em made the decision for him when she began using her nail to rub the tip of his cock; his response was instant as his cock began to grow, she continued to scratch his knob as it grew.

She lifted her head and looked down at his hard cock, she placed her mouth over his knob through his jeans, and chewed as for Billy he reached down for her breast and rubbed the hard nipple, he asked

"are you sure Em?", in answer she began undoing things to enable her to get his big cock out, having freed his cock she closed her mouth over his big knob and began giving him mouth sex, he reached down and slid his hand up her bare leg as he reached the top of her leg she opened them wide for him, he rubbed his fingers along her swollen slit, Em had on a tight pair of pants and when he tried to get his fingers under the side of her pants he pinched her skin, she did no more than reach down and pull her pants to the side, he pushed two fingers deep into her wetness and began frigging her. Em had obviously missed him because she was soon on the verge of her orgasm, she turned onto her back and began bouncing her hips up and down all of the time deep moans were coming from her throat, her right hand reached out and gripped his hard cock, she began wanking him but as her orgasm hit her she squeezed his cock very hard making him gasp out loud, she released him and mouthed

"sorry" as soon as she began to calm down she reached under her skirt and pulled her pants off and dropped them on the floor, she hitched her skirt up and sat up she then smiled at Billy and moved into his lap, she reached under herself and guided his big cock between her fanny lips, she held her breath as she slid down his thick cock, she moved her thighs closer to him, she then reached up and locked her finger behind his head and closing her eyes she began to ride him. As she moved slowly up and down Billy undid the buttons on her blouse and freed her perfect tits, he held a breast in each hand and used his thumb to tease the nipples.

Em took herself to another orgasm on his cock, she was happy that he had not tried to ram his cock to hard into her as she was not sure about her insides and whether they had healed properly, she was happy enough and lifted herself from his cock, she climbed off him and took his hand she then led him into the bedroom, she stripped herself naked and then stripped Billy naked, she walked to the end of the bed and gripped the bottom end headboard she bent forwards and looked at Billy, as he approached she opened her legs and waited. Billy mounted her ever so gently and when he began to fuck her he did so very gently, this was the first time that he had made love to her, when she came the climax was also very subdued. She let him take her there again and enjoyed the same type of orgasm, when it was over she turned and said

"ok, Mr. considerate, you can fuck me now" and gave him a few backwards thrusts, he spread his feet and took a good hold on her hips and now he began to give her a good fucking, just like the old times Em called out and screamed her way through her orgasms, he rode her to a finish and this time she did not mind about him shooting his army of little soldiers into her body, she had decided that when she had had a termination before she had been a tiny bit hasty and if she became pregnant again then she would go through with the pregnancy, she knew that she would have to go it alone regarding Billy as a father but she could afford to have a permanent nanny, and she had the girls from the dark-side that she knew that she could rely on them.

Billy went back to his room so he was not seen coming out of her room, he was happy that he and Em had resumed their sex life as he had missed her terribly. When he went down to breakfast the next morning everyone was there except their driver Mark Foster who was checking the bus over. They were chatting between themselves as they ate, when they were resting after the meal, Dana asked Em

"When will we be back at the farm Em?" because they all knew that they were nearing the end of the tour, Em looked at Billy and he looked back at her, she raised her eyebrow and he stood up and waited until everyone was quiet

"first I would like to thank you all for your efforts on the tour, you all have to admit that the tour has gone very well, now Mark is checking the bus over as we have a long journey in front of us, you see we have another gig in two days' time, unfortunately we are not allowed to tell you where the gig is, but when we near the venue it will blow your minds, so today we want you to take the day off and do whatever you want, we have booked this hotel for another night so we will all eat here this evening, but we will have to leave early in the morning, so I suggest that we all pack our cases tonight, when Mark has worked out the route and times we will let you all know what time we will be leaving, now any questions?" it was brains that put his hand up, when Billy nodded to him brains asked

"Are me and my lads not going on ahead and setting up first?" Billy shook his head and said

"On this occasion that will not be possible, we will all have to muck in when we arrive" everyone seemed happy with that and began to leave the hotel.

Billy and Em went out to find Mark, who was wiping his hands on a piece of oily rag, they had sworn him to secrecy about their destination, but they had not told him about the Whitehouse part. Billy and Em spent the day together they had taken the car and driven around taking in the sights, they arrived back at the hotel in plenty of time, Em had gone to her room and had begun to pack her things, Billy was lay on his bed with his eyes closed when there was a light tap on the door, thinking that it was Em he told whoever it was to come in, he was shocked when Dana walked in, she smiled and walked to his bedside, she stood there with her hands behind her back and said

"Can I ask you a question please Billy?" he lifted himself up onto his elbow and said

"Ask away?" she began swaying as she said

"have the rules been relaxed about fucking in the group only I am next door and I heard you and Em last night, if the rules are relaxed will you do it to me again please?" he looked at the beautiful singer and said

"What happened last night was a celebration of our next gig, the one we can't tell you about yet" she began swaying again

"well, can't I celebrate it as well?" she asked, he looked at her trying to decide what to do, she began undoing the buttons at the top of her dress, he watched her undo the buttons to her waist, she stood there still swaying.

Billy climbed from the bed and went and locked the door, he walked up behind the blond singer and eased her dress from her shoulders and let it drop to the floor, Dana stood there naked she reached behind and gripped is cock through his jeans, he reached around her and gripped her tits, how do women do some of the things that they do?

She had her hands behind her back and with no problems at all she undid his belt then his jeans, she pulled his zip down and then got his cock out she even began wanking it perfectly, he took his hands from her tits and pushed his jeans down his legs, he kicked his boots off , then using his feet he got his jeans off, he bent her forwards and parted her lags she gripped the edge of the bed and he put his cock to her entrance, he pushed forwards and it made her arch her back and grunt as he stretched her again, he rode the small woman hard, he took her through each of her first three orgasms, he then stopped and pulled her upright, she was quite a bit smaller than him but he was still inside her, he reached around and gripped her tits, she reached behind him and held on tight, when he began to fuck her again she must have been standing on her tip–toes.

Dana liked this a lot as she had never done it like this before, when he told her to play with her clit, she was not sure whether she would be to embarrassed or not, when he told her again, she lowered her left hand and began to rub her clit, this made it much better for her and soon she was coming, she suddenly became wanton and forced her knees further apart, her fingers were now flying across her clit, she heard him grunt and at the same time as he shot his hot seed into her she had her own climax, they pushed against each other all of the time she was still enjoying her climax, her nipples were the hardest that she had ever known then, this had been the best fuck of her life, she had never touched herself like that before whilst doing it but she was sure that she would be doing it again.

Dana crept from his room without any-one seeing her, she went back to her room and removed her dress, she pulled the tissues from between her fanny lips and watched as the fluid made its way slowly down her right leg, she pulled a chair in front of the mirror, she sat down and opened her legs wide and looked at her fanny, she watched her finger as it moved back and forth along her slit, she pushed harder and touched her clit, she closed her eyes and pushing two fingers together she began to rub her clit, her fingers moved from side to side as fast as she could make them go, it did not take long before she was having another orgasm, she watched herself cum in the mirror, she then searched out her cum with her fingers and then licked them clean, she repeated this until she could find no more.

CHAPTER 36

Mark Foster was leading the way to Washington DC and brains followed close behind and one of the security men was driving the car. As soon as the signs for Washington came into view different members of the crew began speculating as to where they were going, Billy was quite enjoying listening to the banter. Em went and sat by Mark the bus driver; she had her phone against her ear and was telling him which way to go. They all pulled to a stop by a filling station and waited; Em climbed down from the bus and stood looking both ways along the road.

When 4 motor cycle police stopped by her, everyone looked out of the windows to see what was going on, after a brief discussion two of the policemen turned and went to the back of the car, the other two policemen set of down the road, now that we were being escorted by the police everyone had become very quiet, as they continued along the road they picked up another four policemen on bikes, they took it in turns to block roads so that the convoy had a clear path, they eventually entered a large estate through gates that were fit for a palace, as soon as they were inside the gates, they were closed and an army of men emptied the vehicles and searched everything, they even used these mirrors on long sticks to look under the vehicles. With everything once again loaded back on the vehicles, the outriders took them further into the estate, when the rear of the Whitehouse came into view everyone became suddenly silent.

Now parked at the rear of the white building Billy and Em were taken inside and introduced to a colonel Devaroe who showed them the room that they would be performing in, they were also shown a series of rooms that were guarded at each end by armed guards, they were given instructions that they were not allowed anywhere other than where they had been shown. Billy and Em asked for everyone to get onto the bus, Billy stood and told them that they were in fact performing for the first lady and her guests at the first ladies birthday party, he then went on to tell everyone about where the guards were situated and that they would be watched at all times.

They were helped with all of their equipment into the great hall, everyone helped brains and his crew get everything ready, when they were finally ready a man in uniform said that they were all to return to their dressing rooms a gong will sound in one hour and refreshments will be served in one of the dining rooms, they will be shown the way when the time comes.

They were all showered and dressed when the gong sounded, a man led them down a long passageway that was guarded at both ends, they were shown into a room that had a long dining table running down the center, the table was dressed as if royalty was attending, they were served by soldiers in full dress uniform. The meal was first class even though some of the food was unrecognizable.

The time came for them to go on, they were all waiting in the corridor outside the ball room, a door opened and they were waved in, a polite round of applause met them, they all took up their positions, most of the guests were seated and talking quietly, the doors opened and everyone stood, the first lady entered the room, she shook a few hands and took her seat in the front row, she nodded at Billy and gave him a smile. After three songs people at the back of the room began dancing, after five songs even the first lady was standing and having a good time. After an hour Billy said that they were having a short break and the doors opened and rows of butlers entered carrying trays of drinks and finger sized nibbles. Billy and the crew were served refreshments in their rooms.

They went back on and finished the evening with the first ladies favourite song #good ole boys#. The first lady asked to go up on the stage, she took her place on the stage and thanked Billy and the rest of the group for a brilliant show, she then led the rest of the audience in a standing ovation. The first lady asked to see Billy and Emma, they were taken into a drawing room where she was waiting, she greeted them with a huge smile and handshakes, she thanked them for a wonderful evening's entertainment, Billy gave her a bag full of their merchandise, they all sat and chatted for a while and when the first lady said that if there was ever anything that she could do for them, they only had to ask. Billy looked at Em and Em looked at Billy, the first lady asked

Is there something that I can help you with?" Em went on to tell her about Eva and governor Johnstead, the first lady called for a secretary and asked her to take down all of the details. The first lady said to leave everything to her and that she will sort everything out and be in touch in a few days, but the papers for Eva will be in the post first thing in the morning. She shook their hands and thanked them again and then she was gone.

With everything loaded in their vehicles, they headed to their hotel, Emma had arranged for sandwiches and drinks in the breakfast room of the hotel, the whole crew was buzzing, Billy made a grand entrance pushing a trolley loaded with champagne and glasses, and he was met by a round of applause. They were almost at the end of the tour and they were all looking forward to getting back to the farm, Billy had one more private show to do and they had one last gig to perform in Detroit and then home. Billy took the car and headed to Toronto to a young man's 21 birthday party, when he arrived at the ranch he got out if his car to see that the whose farm had been decked out ready for the party, a large man dressed like John Wayne strolled over to him with his hand out stretched, Billy took his hand and they shook hands, the man said to call him Chuck and his sons name was Adam, he led Billy to a large barn that had been completely done out for the birthday party, even to straw on the floor, a skittle band were setting up their equipment, they were all really excited to meet Billy and were looking forward to hearing him play. Chuck took Billy into his huge log built house, he took Billy to a room and said it was his for as long as he wanted, on the bedside table lay a large brown envelope, Chuck pointed to it and said

"Your fee" and feel free to take a look around the house and grounds. Billy took him at his word and strolled around the house, he heard voices so headed in that direction, a tall slim woman was giving instruction to the kitchen staff, she had her back to him and from what he could see she looked after herself, her blond hair had been tied up in a bun at the back of her head, sensing that someone was there she turned sharply and looked him up and down

"And you are?" she asked sternly, he removed his cowboy hat and said

"Billy Ridge mam" her eyes dropped straight to the bulge in his jeans, her eyes lifted to his and she blushed deeply and said

"Ah yes, my name is Beth, have you been shown to your room Mr. Ridge?" he smiled and said

"Yes mam and a very nice room it is to" again she blushes, she walked to him and said

"let me show you around" she gave him the tour of the house and then led him into the grounds, she chatted about the farm and her family, he worked out that she must be just over 40 years old but she looked 30, she was braless and her firm tits were swinging nicely as she walked, she knew that he was watching her tits and it was doing something to her as she had a line of sweat under her nose.

They stood looking at a dozen horses in a coral; she leaned against the rail which accentuated her tits even more,

"Have you met Chuck my husband?" he said that he had, she never looked at him when she said "he loves these horses you know, but it is these bloody horses that ruined his life, you see he was thrown maybe 4 years ago up in the mountains, he lay there for almost 24 hours before he was found, he had broken his pelvis and damaged all of his nerve endings and from that day to this he has had problems down there, and having heard about your reputation and size, it was me who suggested that we hire you for the party, you could say it was for my own selfish reasons, now you know what I want Billy how do you feel about that?" he looked around the farm and seeing no-one near enough to see what they were doing he said

"Show me your tits Beth" she took a glance around and turned back to face the horses, she undid the buttons on her shirt and opened it slightly, just enough for him to see her tits, she did the buttons up and looked at him

"And when would you want to meet me Beth?" she turned and looked back at the horses

"Can you stay overnight?" she asked

Maybe "he said still not looking at him she said

"We could go riding in the morning, or I can come to you tonight?" he looked at his watch and said

"We could go riding now if you like?" she turned and studied his face and said

"Meet me here in half an hour; I will get the horses saddled".

Billy was stood there waiting when she returned, they mounted their horses and she led the way out of the farm, she still had the same shirt on but now she had on a pair of white flared trousers, she knew where she was going as they were riding in a straight line, neither spoke for a while, she stopped at the top of a long valley in which there must have been close to a thousand cattle grazing, they looked out over the most impressive sight

"our main heard" she said and making a clicking sound they moved off again, he watched her tits moving around inside her thin shirt and said

"Open your shirt Beth and show me" she reached up and undid a every button on her shirt and pulled the shirt open and turned to him

186

"Are you as big as they say you are, Billy?" he smiled and said

"yes mam" she turned slightly to the right and headed towards a wooden shack, they tied their horses at the rear of the shack, she entered first and stood to the back of the shack she took her shirt off and looked at him

"Your turn to show me Billy" he undid his belt and then his top button on his jeans, he opened his jeans and reached into his boxers and pulled his big cock out. Beth gasped and began undoing her trousers, she removed her trousers and pushed her white pants down her legs and moved to the table, she leaned back and smiled at him, she rubbed her finger along her naked fanny lips and said

"it has been 4 years Billy, now I want a good fucking" he stripped his clothes off and went to her she reached out and took his cock in her hand, she rubbed his growing cock along her fanny lips she had parted her knees in readiness, she reached up and pulled his lips to hers, they kissed deeply, their tongues doing a lovers dance in her mouth, she pulled her mouth from his and whispered

"please do it to me Billy" he lifted her bottom onto the table, she opened her legs as wide as she could, he pushed his big knob into her, she groaned deeply as his mighty cock really stretched her insides for the first time, she lifted her feet onto the table, so he gripped her hips and fucked her, he took her to many orgasms and when he stopped he asked her if she wanted to change positions, she shook her head

"no I want to watch you cum, I want to feel you cum inside me" so he continued to fuck her, when he grunted she watched him closely, he closed his eyes and shot his hot cum into her, she let out a muffled groan as she felt him explode inside her. He pulled her hard against him as she ground her sex against the base of his thick cock taking herself to yet another much needed orgasm.

Dressed they headed back to the farm Beth looked at him and said

"Can we do it again before you leave please Billy?" he said

"Anytime you want Beth, you just find the time and the place" he could see her plotting in her head as they rode back to the farm. The birthday party went well with almost everyone taking part in line dancing, he finished the evening with #Amanda# which brought forth a round of applause, he had not seen Beth for a while, he went back to his room to find a note, that read >meet me by the coral, B>. he then placed his guitar into the back of his car and walked out into the darkness towards the coral, he found her leaning against the rail, she had on the same green dress that she had on earlier,

"you really are a sexy singer Billy, you were having an effect on most of the women here tonight" he moved to her and took hold of her around the waist, she lifted her lips to his, as they kissed he hitched her dress up, when he placed his hand between her legs to find that she was naked, she parted her legs wide to allow him to get his fingers into her fanny, she moved her hips against his fingers it took him only seconds to make her cum, her fanny juices flooded over is fingers and pooled in the center of his hand, now that she had cum she wanted him inside her, she ripped at his belt and jeans, she reached into his boxers and pulled out his hard cock, she gave his cock a few quick strokes before she turned around and gripped the middle rail of the coral he lifted her dress over ass and gripping his knob he placed it as near as he could to her fanny she moved slightly to put him in line.

He pushed forward and his giant cock slid into her willing body, as they fucked s group of horses came and watched them, one particular horse, the one that she had been riding on earlier sniffed at his owner and snorted, she said something to the horses and they moved away, it felt quite strange to be out here in the darkness fucking this married woman, but they were having a good time, she had had many orgasms and when he finally shot his hot spunk into her, she howled into the darkness as she felt him explode again deep inside her, this was a feeling that she had missed more than any other, she could make herself cum with her fingers or her toys but that feeling was one thing that she could not replicate. As they moved against each other she hoped that it did not take another four years before she got fucked again.

CHAPTER 37

Billy was heading to Detroit for their last gig of the tour ,then it was finally back to the farm and his new house, he couldn't wait to begin painting again, he had visions of painting Beth as she was bent over in front of him holding onto that rail, maybe he could even paint all of the horses in the background. Billy was tired and needed to sleep but he kept driving towards Detroit, in a couple of days' time he could rest as much as he wanted. He found the hotel easy enough and when he entered the crew were having bit of a party, he found Em and gave her the envelope full of money, she looked inside and said that she would take it up to her room and that he could come and help her check it if he wanted, she was a bit disappointed when he declined the offer, he got a drink from the bar and was about to turn around when Grace was standing beside him, she looked deep into his eyes and asked

"Can I come and see you when we get back to the farm only I need seeing to Billy" her voice was so low he wondered how she sang so beautifully he nodded, she then said

If you can't wait Billy-boy I am in room 73 and I never lock the door" with that the tall dark singer kissed him on the cheek and walked away from him back to her friends.

The party lasted until the early hours, Billy had slipped away and was in bed asleep when Em crept into his room, she looked down at his sleeping form and crept back out again, he slept the sleep of the dead for three hours, he woke with a start but did not know why, he looked out of the hotel window at the city below, it surprised him how many cars still there still were moving along the busy streets, he wondered where they were going or where they had come from, he looked at his watch and saw that it was 3.16 am, he went and showered and cleaned his teeth. It was a long time until breakfast but he walked down to reception, there was a bell that had a sign on it #ring for attention#.

He headed back towards his room, he stopped outside room 73and wondered if he should do to her what she did to him, his hand reached out and turned the handle, he crept into the room, Grace's body was mostly covered but he could clearly see her right breast with its long nipple, she looked so peaceful an her sleep, it seemed a shame to wake her so he took a dollar bill out of his wallet and laid it down on her pillow, just to let her know that he had been there,

They played and sang their hearts out in Detroit to another standing ovation, the gig ended at 11.30pm and by the time that they had taken to sign merchandise and load all of the vehicles it was close to 1am, everyone was settled on the bus, Billy asked everyone to get on the bus as he wanted to say a few words, with everyone seated he thanked them all for their effort during the tour and if anyone needed to take a holiday now would be a good time. Em had booked a local hotel for everyone, but no-one wanted to stay, everyone wanted to get back to the farm.

Em said that she said that she would take the car and travel through the night and head for home, brains said that it was a good idea and he would do the same, his crew said that they would stay on the bus and have a beer with everyone else, Dana asked Em if she could travel with her in the car as she did not want to drink besides they could have a girlie chat. Em, brains and Mark Foster discussed the best route to take back to the farm, Mark said that by going over the mountains it would save them hours and that was the route that he intended to take, brains said he would follow him until the other side of the mountain and then he would pass him and make his own way from there. Em said that she would follow in the rear and do the same as brains.

The trip began ok, but became boring on the climb to the top of the mountain, the talk in the car inevitably turned to Billy and his big cock and his staying power, the two women compared notes and giggled with one another, Dana did not know about Billy and Grace, Dana couldn't believe it and said

"But she is so thin he must have split her in two" both women laughed out loud at this. They finally reached the top of the mountain and began to move faster down the other side, she thought that mark was driving a bit too fast so she dropped back a bit, but brains drove his normal way which was close to the bus, something to do with aerodynamics or saving fuel or some such crap. Dana was looking at the sheer drop on her side of the car, it just looked like a black hole and she passed a comment about not wanting to go over the edge as it was a long way down, the bus seemed to be going too fast for the narrow road and Mark kept braking which in turn made brains brake hard, Em kept well back and let the boys play.

The coach and the vehicle that brains was driving went around a sharp left hand bend way to fast it was as if Mark and brains were racing, Em went around the bend at the normal speed to see a sight that did not make sense to her, the rear lights of both vehicles were not where they were supposed to be, Em slammed on the brakes and watched as the lights of both vehicles disappeared into the darkness of the black hole, there was no explosion, no flash and no sound, they were just gone. Dana began screaming out loud as she stared into the darkness, Em was trying to get her phone out of her pocket, she finally managed it and call all of the emergency services, the two women got out of the car and stood listening for any sound of life, a helicopter was the first emergency vehicle to arrive, it shone its strong light onto them, the helicopter then dived down into the darkness of the void, flashing lights seemed to come from both directions at the same time, police men shone torches down into the darkness, all they could see were the flashing lights of the helicopter below.

Policemen were talking on hand held radios as more and more rescue vehicles arrived, a tall man with a white fireman's hat on took charge and deployed men to different duties. Another helicopter arrived and disappeared into the void. The man in charge came over and spoke to them. he said

"We have men being dropped off down there and they will take a look but down expect too much, they have fell as long way" then Em said a stupid thing she said

"But that is Billy Ridge down there and I love him" the wait seemed to take forever until the watch commander came back to them, he removed his white hat and looked from one to the other

"I'm sorry to have to tell you this but there are no survivors in either vehicle, these policemen will take your statements" and then he was gone.

The two women were taken to the police station, they had given their statements and then released, they headed back to the farm, when they arrived they cried with Ellen and Eva, and when Mac turned up they all began to cry again. Mac took charge of everything, he liaised with the police and the coroner, he spoke to Em and Dana and asked if they agreed with him that the whole crew should be buried on the farm,

"We will make a private plot for each of them" they all agreed and a team of grave diggers moved in, when the graves were finally finished the two women were stood looking at the series of holes, it was Dana that broke the mood when she said

"You do realise that there should be another grave out there don't you, if I had not been in the car with you, I would be dead now, dead with the others,[she broke down then] I wish that I was dead and with Billy" she ran away then, ran back to her trailer. With the graves all finished the workmen turned up to put up the white picket fence all around the outer perimeter.

The authorities had finally identified and finished with the bodies, all of the families had been informed and the date set for the mass funeral to take place. Em and Mac had sorted everything out, they had agreed that there would be no fans allowed at the actual funeral, but the farm will be opened shortly after as a memorial for the fans to attend and pay their own respects.

CHAPTER 38

The day for the mass funeral arrived and there were hundreds of people in attendance, each grave had been marked and the respective family members attended that grave, The minister delivered a good service and there was not a dry eye anywhere. Each grave was blessed in turn and then filled in. Billy's grave was the last to be blessed and when they lowered the coffin into the ground, the song #good ole boys # was played through loud speakers.

What happened next took Em's breath away, every single person in attendance began singing along to Billy's favorite song. Em and Dana held hands and cried together as their dead lover was lowered into the ground, they stood and watched as the grave was filled in. The wake was held in the barn with Billy's voice soothing them in the background. It was late the next day when the last family left the farm. Mac, Dana Em, Sue, Ellen and her baby Amanda all sat in a room talking about their futures and what would happen to them all. It was Em that came up with a good idea, she said

"Why don't we make the farm into a tribute farm for all of them, we could use the barn as the museum, we could still sell all of the memorabilia. Ellen Sue and Eva could run a rest room, cafeteria and sell home mad cakes and things. We could charge the fans a small fee to enter the farm We have more than enough money to keep us running for years even if no-one ever turns up" she had just finished speaking when Mac's phone rang he stood up and looked out of the window and into the clear blue sky. He looked around the room and said excitedly

"Bloody hell she is coming, she is coming here now, she is almost here" with that he ran outside and looked into the sky. They all rushed outside and looked to where he was looking. Em asked

"Who is coming Mac?" he never took his eyes from the sky as two small dote appeared in the far distance. They all covered their eyes as the dots grew bigger.

Two helicopters landed side by side. Armed soldiers climbed down from the first aircraft and spread themselves out. All facing away from the first helicopter. The first lady stepped down from the second air-craft. She went straight to Em and took her hand. Em led The Presidents Wife to Billy's grave where she spent a few minutes. On her way back to the aircraft she shook hands with everyone. When she got to Eva she asked the girl if she had received her papers. When she said that she had the first lady said quietly

"And don't you go worrying about that governor Johnstead, we have taken care of him, he won't need any slaves where he is going" Her press agent took lots of photographs which she said that she would send them a signed copy of each picture. It took two months to get everything set up with the barn full of life sized pictures of Billy and the crew. Instruments were laid out in their correct positions. The same control panel that brains used was erected in the correct position. The scene was set. Billy's house although he had never lived in it, became part of the memorial of Billy Ridge and the Ridge Boys. Ellen walked up to Emma and asked her if she had a few minutes because she had received a letter from lawyer in town asking her to contact him. She asked Em

"Will you come with me Em, only I don't know what I have done for a lawyer to want to see me" En smiled and said

"There is no time like the present, let's go" and that is what they did. They sat outside Mr. Saintbury's office looking at all of the official looking certificates on the waiting room walls.

The phone rang and the secretary nodded and said that they could go in, the tiny man sat behind the large oak desk looked at them over the top of his half moon glasses, he said

"Sit please" they sat down opposite him, he looked from one woman to the other and asked

"Which one of you is Miss Burrows?" Ellen put her hand up, the lawyer looked at her and said

"Right then, I don't know if you knew but a Mr. Billy Ridge has left everything that he owned to you and your baby Amanda. There is too much to read out but it is a considerable fortune. [he passed her a sheet of paper, she and Emma studied the paper and both looked up at the funny looking lawyer] If you are happy with what is written, please sign the bottom of the paper. Also you will need to sign these papers as well[he passed her over one paper at a time and she signed where he told her, having signed everything, the lawyer checked everything was correct and finally satisfied, he said] now do you want me to transfer all of the money into your bank account? Or do you want to think about things for a while. You will need someone to act for you as there is a lot to sort out. I will act for you if you so wish on the same terms as Mr. Ridge?" Ellen held Em's hand and looked at the other woman for advice. Emma said

"Leave things as they are until we can go through everything and sort it all out" and that is exactly what happened.

On the way back to the farm Ellen said

"What am I going to do Em, I don't want all of that money, I wouldn't know what to do with it" Em said

"But Billy wanted you to have it El, it is for Amanda's future, you deserve it". The women were quiet all of the journey back to the farm. The next day Mac turned up at the farm and asked to speak to everyone. They all sat in the dining room and the manager began to speak

"I want to speak to you all, about all of our futures, fortunately Em had everyone and all of the equipment involved in the accident heavily insured. Now only this morning I have been in touch with the insurance company and they are going to pay out fully on the claim. But what I need to know is if you all want to start again with Dana as the lead singer. We will have all of the what brains used and all of the instruments and two new vehicles. We have the farm, so all we will need is some musicians and backing singers and away we go. But we will only do all of this if we all agree", Em looked at Dana and said

"What do you think Dana, if you take the lead I will back you up and do whatever to make it work. We could even do some duets?" Dana looked at every face around the table in turn, her face rested on Em and asked

"Do you really think that it will work, am I really good enough?" Em smiled and said

"You are more than good enough. You would have gone on your own, sooner or later anyway so this is the perfect opportunity for you. No it would be the perfect opportunity for all of us", Dana looks around the faces again and nodded and said

"Ok, if you are all sure, then let's do it" everyone began applauding.

Ellen said

"With some help that I could run the memorial side of things, Eva can work the gate and take the money and with a little bit of working out, I can tell you how many staff that we will need. I know some people in town so finding help won't be a problem". Mac looked at Em and asked

"Are you happy with that Em?" she looked at Dana who nodded her agreement. So Em said

"Ok then lets do it" this brought a round of applause and laughter from everyone. Mac finally spoke, and said

"In that case I had better get back and start work again on finding some more, Musicians, backing singers and another brains. And what about finances? How do we stand financially?" Em looked at Mac and said

"We have enough in the account to last us a very long time and we can buy whatever we need to set up the memorial" Ellen spoke and said

"You can have all of my money if you need it. If I can continue to live here with you, I don't need anything else" Em shook her head and said

"What about we leave things as they are for now and if we need additional funds, then I will ask you for it?" Ellen nodded her head in agreement.

With the meeting finally over Dana asked Em

"If they could take a walk as she needed to talk to her" they walked towards the house that had been built for Billy. Once inside they stood looking at the paintings that he had painted, Dana slipped her hand into Em's hand and said

"You really loved him deeply didn't you Em?" Em nodded her head and began to cry. Dana pulled the other woman into her arms and let her cry into her shoulder. Dana was rubbing her hands up and down the other woman's trembling back. Em held the singer around the waist with her head resting on her chest. Her mouth was almost touching the hard nipple of the blond singer. Em pushed her tongue out and flicked the tip of her tongue over the hard nipple. Dana reacted by pulling the other woman's head around so that her mouth was fully on her breast and began moaning out loud. Em lifted her mouth and looked at the other woman's eyes and said

"Please take me to bed and make love to me" The blond woman led Em into the bedroom and stood her by the brand new bed. Em reached out and slowly undressed the blond singer and took a step back. She removed all of her own clothes and climbed into bed, she held her hand out to the singer who took the hand and allowed herself to be eased into the bed.

Em pulled the singer into her arms and pushed her mouth hard against the other woman's soft mouth.

They kissed long and hard, but by now the women were urgently rubbing mounds against each other. Em opened her legs wide and bent her knees up and allowed the singer to use her body and rub their fannies together. Dana knew exactly what she was doing and soon had Em on the edge of her orgasm. Both women were now staring at each other as Dana took her new lover through her orgasm by using long slow hard pushes with her hips. She continued to rub her fanny up and down the other woman's fanny until she moaned out in her own much needed orgasm. Em pushed her hips up high to help the blond singer reach her orgasm. The strokes between them were now slow and deliberate. Dana now had her head back and stared at the ceiling, moaning deeply as her climax shook her whole body.

The new lovers changed position. Em was now lay flat out on the bed and Dana was tenderly kissing every part of her lovers goosed bumped body. She had opened Em's legs wide and she began kissing all around her lovers inner thighs, teasing, intensifying the forthcoming pleasure, slowly moving upwards to her intended goal. Dana was looking at her lover's most private place, the fanny lips were slightly parted and a single drop of Em's love juice oozing from the base of her slit. Seeing the drop Dana pushes her tongue forward and gently took the fanny juice with a single lick of her tongue.

Em almost came at the touch of the silky tongue. Em lifted her knees up to her chest and opened them wide. Dana moved her mouth to her lovers beautiful fanny. Dana is lying on her front with her mouth glued to the naked fanny, she licks slowly from the bottom upwards, again and again. Dana reached down and parted her swollen fanny lips, she then set about sucking every inch of the crinkly inner lips, as soon as she began to tease her lovers tiny white button, Em lifted herself up onto her hands and watched the blond woman as she began to suck her clit.

Em suddenly became very vocal as the pleasure that she was receiving was getting to the point of no return, she began bouncing her hips as her climax made her shiver in ecstasy. Dana lowered her mouth and went in search of her reward, she pushed her tongue as deep into her lovers fanny as she could manage and searched out the salty love fluid. Dana used a stabbing motion which made Em moan out loud and start her hips moving slowly up and down.

The woman lay between her legs had begun to suck as hard as she could,

Dana lifted herself on to her elbows and again began bouncing her hips up and down as fast as she could and moaning in ecstasy. Dana had no choice but to push two fingers deep into Em's fanny and take her to yet another glorious orgasm. As soon as the orgasm had hit her Em called out loudly. She then reached down and began rubbing her clit, her fingers moving as fast as possible. Dana began moving her fingers in and out of her lovers fury purse, fast enough to bring forth yet another earth shattering orgasm.

Em snatched the finger from her fanny and lay on her back breathing hard; she said

"Fuck me Dana, where did you learn to do all of that?" Dana moved slowly up Em's body, she spent a lot of time on the fine tits before she held her lips a fraction away from her lover's lips and whispered

"Your turn lover", Dana turned onto her back and closed her eyes and waited to be pleasured. Em knelt and looked at the blond girls perfect body that was covered in tiny goose bump in anticipation of the pleasure to come. Em did not want to disappoint her new lover, so she used the knowledge that she had learned from Grace. She moved around so that she was knelt between the other woman's legs, she lifted the legs until her lovers knees were almost touching her tits. Dana gripped her own thighs and pulled them apart, leaving her fanny exposed and at the mercy of her new lover.

Em did not mess about she went straight for the blond woman's clit. She parted the naked fanny lips and closed her lips around the tiny button and sucked hard, Dana gripped the bed clothes and lifted her hips up high and moaned at the top of her voice as she orgasmed. Em told her to stay as she was and then she reached under her lover's bottom and pushed her fingers into the naked fanny, using the fingers of her other hand she began rubbing her clit at the same time. This was a first for Dana and she liked it a lot, she moved her hips slowly up and down but Em kept her contact and continued to give her lover as much pleasure as was possible. This time when she came she sank down to the bed and lifting her head and stared at her lover. Em continued what she was doing until Dana came again. Dana growled at the woman who was giving her untold sexual pleasure.

Em moved around and lowered her mouth to the beautiful fanny, she forced her tongue in between Dana's fanny lips and searched out her hidden button, she waited for her lover to groan as she made contact. Now that she had located the tiny button she teased her by flicking her tongue continuously over her clit. After a few seconds she stopped the flicking and closed her lips over her clit and taking her slowly but sensually to another earth shattering orgasm. Em pushed her tongue into Dana's fanny and searched for her lovers cum, she located it quite easily as the love juice began oozing from her, Em took her fill and then looked up at her lover and said

"Let's get dressed and go shopping", Dana said,

"Shopping after that, what do you want to buy?", Em answered by smiling and saying

"We will need some toys if we are going to continue to see each other" Dana said

"Why can't you and I live in this brand new house, we could be really happy here?"

Em agreed in principle, she knew where the sex shop was located and walked in as casual as you like, she studied the wall where the vibrating toys were displayed she knew what she fancied and she also knew what Dana would like. She made her purchases and took them back to the house. Dana was sat in one of Billy's dressing gown's, Em walked over and stood in front of her new lover

"Do you want to see what I have bought, I have bought you something really special", Em placed the bag by the side of Dana, who opened the top of the bag and looked inside. Seeing long brown boxes her curiosity got the better of her and she reached into the bag and took out one of the brown boxes. She opened the box and gasped out loud and looked up at her new lover, inside the box lay a long red rubber cock that was as thick as a babies arm.

The implement had a lot of straps attached to it, she turned the rubber cock this way and that way and examined it closely. The strap on cock was then placed on the couch by her side, she reached into the bag and took out another box, this time when she opened it she clapped her hands, she then took a vibrator out of the box that was maybe ten inches long and really very thick. The knob was big and bulbous and there were thick veins all the way down the shaft, she turned the control button to on and felt the head as it buzzed, she held the knob against her cheek and smiled broadly and said
"I really like this one", Em said

"Open the other box, it's for you" the blond woman took out the box and held it in her lap. She looked up at her lover who was smiling down at her, she opened the box and lay inside was a long black strap on cock with nobles all the way up the shaft. The knob again was big and bulbous with a thick rim around it. Left in the bag were three smaller bags which contained different flavoured lubricants.

"When can we try them out?" asked the blond woman. Em began removing her clothes and said   "get your clothes off and we can start right now" Dana stood up and opened the dressing gown to reveal her naked body and said

"I'm ready right now" Em picked up the black strap on and fitted it around her waist, she picked up a plastic bottle of lubricant. They both watched as Em lubricated the long thick cock. Em kept her hand moving along the thick shaft and looked at her new lover and said

"On your hands and knees then lover, I am going to give you a good fucking", Dana looked at the thick cock and dropped to her knees. She took up her position and waited for her latest lover to mount her, as Em pushed the thick knob into her lovers fanny, the blond woman groaned out loud and looked back at the woman that was stretched her insides. When the thick cock was fully embedded Dana faced the front and Em began to move her hips back and forward. Dana had her head hanging down, but she had begun to move her hips back and forth in time with her lovers forward thrusts, within seconds they were in perfect time, Dana came time and time again until she had had enough. Em stopped fucking her and knelt there with the thick cock still deep inside her lover. Dana turned and looked at Em and said

"That was just like being fucked by Billy, it was as if he was still in this room, still fucking me" Em pulled the cock slowly out of Dana bringing forth a deep moan and a shiver. The blond woman turned and looked at the thick cum covered cock, and said

"Fuck me that was good, now it is your turn" Dana unclipped the rubber cock and laid it down on the floor, she picked up the red cock and strapped it around her hips, she reached for the lubricant and covered the cock from one end to the other. Em was lay on the couch looking at the red cock and she opened her legs wide.

She lifted her bum and placed a cushion underneath her bum in readiness. She then bent her left leg and held it against the back of the couch, she bent the other leg and held it up with her right hand, her fanny was now at the mercy to the world.

Dana knelt between her lover's legs and positioned the red knob at her lover's entrance and pushed forwards. Em groaned out loud as the big knob made its way into her hidden depths, she closed her eyes and pictured Billy Ridge fucking her.

She moved her hips in time with the big red cock and was totally lost. If this was to be her future then so be it, she could live with that, lay on her back here in Billy's house she could feel his presence even now while she was being fucked by a rubber cock.

She just knew that he was watching her enjoying getting fucked, she could see his face as clear as day, his face was imprinted onto the insides of her eyelids.

ABOUT THE AUTHOR

Brian is a new author, he is a long-term dialysis patient of over 20 years and uses his 4 weekly sessions of treatment to write his many different genres of books, these include fiction novels, adult novels, a biography [A Badsey Boy] and many beautifully illustrated children's books.

Born in the mid 50s, Brian is a disabled man with a lifelong passion for angling, when his illness forced his retirement, he discovered his creative imagination, which shows in his love of writing.

Made in the USA
Columbia, SC
09 August 2020